THE MAXWELL SERIES

Dare to Dream

S.B. ALEXANDER

Dare to Dream
Book Two: The Maxwell Series
Copyright © 2015 by S. B. Alexander. All rights reserved
First Edition: July 2015

E-book ISBN-13: 978-0-9887762-8-9
Print ISBN-13: 978-0-9887762-9-6

Visit www.sbalexander.com
www.facebook.com/sbalexander.authorpage

Editor: Red Adept Publishing, www.redadeptpublishing.com
Cover Design by Streetlight Graphics, www.streetlightgraphics.com

This is a work of fiction. Names, characters, places and incidents either are the product of the author's imagination or are used fictitiously, and any resemblance to locales, events, business establishments, or actual persons-living or dead-is entirely coincidental.

Adult Content Warning: The content contained is the book includes adult language, violence, and sexual content. This book is intended for adult audiences 18 years of age and older.

Dedication

To all my readers and fans, thank you for taking this journey with me.

Chapter 1

Kade

KELTON, HUNT, AND I SAT in the bleachers in Gary's Gym, waiting for Kross's boxing match to begin. My gut twisted into a big knot as though someone had pried open my stomach, stuck in their hand, and squeezed like a motherfucker. Lacey had flown to California for the weekend with her old man. Something about her trip had me on edge. The apprehension was almost as strong as the feeling that had rolled through me when I'd come home to the blue-and-red flashing lights of a cop car and an ambulance parked in the driveway and two medics wheeling away my younger sister's dead body. I gripped my phone hard as I tried to conjure up images of life rather than death.

Lacey.

She was the only one who could take me to a place where the world was perfect, where nothing else mattered. A place where there was no pain, no hate, no nightmares—just her and me and the sanctity of our world. I pictured her naked with my fingers tangled in her long wavy brown hair, her legs wrapped around me, our bodies pressed together in a heated passion, getting lost in each other. Yeah, that image usually erased the bad. God, I loved that girl. I needed her. She was sunshine. She was my future.

People started to fill the gym, a spacious facility in Boston that hosted amateur night on Fridays. The place reminded me of a high school gym with bleachers, hoops, and mats stacked neatly in a corner. Even the air had a hint of sweat.

"You alive?" My brother Kelton nudged me in the ribs. "Is your dick hard thinking of Lacey? She's only been gone a day, man. That's one of the reasons why I won't do love. I hate seeing the pain on your ugly mug when you're away from her."

One day was far too long. Even when I couldn't see her on weekends for one reason or another, it drove me crazy. She was like a drug for me. The image of her naked body fell away, and with it the high I usually got when I thought of her.

Lacey hadn't been back to California since she buried her sister and her mom, and I was worried about how she was going to react when she visited their gravesite. I was afraid her PTSD would relapse. Her symptoms had diminished over the last six months, thanks to her psychiatrist. But more importantly, the cops still hadn't found the perp who murdered her family.

I eyed Kelton, who sat on my left. "Fuck off, man."

He was shaking his shaggy black head of hair back and forth, and I wanted to slap the disgusting expression off his face. He was the cockiest of the triplets with a strong infallibility complex. I worried constantly that he'd be the first of us to die. Fear never resonated in him. At times I envied him. He approached situations with strength and purpose—something I tried to do, except with a little more caution.

I checked my phone again, waiting for Lacey to return my calls. I'd gotten a text from her when she landed early this morning, but that was it.

"She'll call, dude," Hunt said from my right. "She's probably catching up on sleep after her red-eye."

I rubbed my temple with my free hand. A headache was beginning to make an ugly appearance.

"Your headaches back?" Hunt asked in a voice so low I barely heard him.

I checked on Kelton to make sure he hadn't heard the question. Thankfully, he was fiddling with his phone. I didn't want any of my brothers or my father to know my migraines were back. They'd worry, and then I'd be in the hospital getting my brain scanned again.

"Later." I narrowed my eyes as I zeroed in on the scar over his left eye. The one he'd gotten sparring with Kross. Maybe he wanted another one to match.

Kelton cocked his head toward Hunt and me. "What are you two talking about?"

"Hunt is making predictions. He thinks you're going to break your vow of not falling in love." I was quick on the draw.

"I'll be in the pits of hell before I say those three words," Kelton said with a serious expression. "And even then I'll be telling the devil I love him before some chick."

"Man, I'd pay big money to see that." Hunt chuckled, his deep voice breaking through the soft hum of voices around us.

"Is your heart still broken from Lizzie leaving?" I couldn't resist. At thirteen years old, the boy had pouted for weeks that one summer in Texas when Lizzie Reardon moved away.

"Blow me. Both of you." He shifted his gaze forward as he growled.

Hunt and I cracked up. It felt good to release some of my anxiety.

"Laugh it up, big bro. And when that sexy girl of yours drives a stake through your heart, I'll—"

I slapped the back of his head. "Don't use Lacey and 'stake' in the same sentence." Could we break up? Sure. Would we? Hell, no.

"What the fuck are they doing here?" Kelton snarled.

I followed his line of sight to the bleachers on the other side of the ring and saw Sullivan and Seever. My body immediately tensed again. I couldn't catch a fucking break. I almost jumped off the top row of the bleachers, stalked across the gym, plucked Greg Sullivan down from his high horse, and rammed my fist into his face to end the feud we had going on. But I had two problems. One, Hunt had a tight grip on my arm, holding me back, and two, if I did end it, that meant someone would get hurt or die. I couldn't handle any more death, not even my enemy's.

"Easy, man. In due time," Hunt said then released his hold.

Sullivan nodded at me as he sat down. The harsh gym lights made his dark hair look even greasier than normal. Next to him, his psychologically unstable cousin, Aaron Seever, narrowed his green eyes as he rested his back against the empty row behind him. What *were* they doing here?

"I'm beginning to believe that fucker is all talk," Kelton mumbled.

"How soon you forget." I bit the inside of my mouth. "Just because he hasn't followed through on his revenge against us doesn't mean he's given up." Sullivan's MO was to threaten then walk away, only to surprise us months later. When he thought we'd gotten complacent, he'd hit us with the element of surprise. I had to give it to him. It did work the first time when he and his buddies put Kody in the hospital. However, Kody was ready the second time around when Sullivan had shown up after one of the football games back in September. He and Sullivan fought then, and even though Kody ended up in the emergency room with a broken nose, that was all that had broken. Plus, he wasn't ambushed. My brother had help from Tyler Langley, the quarterback of our high school team.

Whatever he was scheming, we were all on full alert. Where ever we went, we always checked our surroundings. Before we got in our vehicles, we checked the area. When we got out, we checked the area. We always kept our senses open, just like our old man taught us. We also sparred a lot with Kross, which helped keep all of us in shape.

"It's not Sullivan we should be worried about," Hunt said as he rested booted feet on the empty row in front of him. "Seever is the crazy one."

He was right. Seever got off on getting into people's heads and fucking with them. It still pissed me off how he tried to worm his way into Lacey's head, hoping he would scare her enough so she wouldn't try out for the baseball team. There'd been some bad feelings about the idea of a girl on the team, and he'd had his girl, Tammy Reese, break into Lacey's locker and steal her gear right before one of the tryouts then stick it back when Lacey reported the incident to Coach Dean so Lacey would come off as crazy. My girl pushed through all her demons and made the team despite Aaron's threats and games. Still, baseball season was ramping up, and I was holding my breath to see what Aaron had up his sleeve.

"Let's just get this over with and put them in the hospital," Kelton said. "I'm tired of waiting to see if Sullivan will follow through on his revenge."

The triplets, Hunt, and I had a pact. We wouldn't initiate the first punch. But we would damn sure protect ourselves if the moment presented itself.

"We put them in the hospital. Then what? The vicious cycle continues. Do you want to go back to the academy with only three months till graduation?" I leaned back against the wall. I sure didn't want to go back to jail, but every fiber in me wanted to wipe that smug grin off Sullivan's face.

"Fuck no." Kelton rested against the wall. "But by the time I got done with him he wouldn't be able to rat us out again."

"Kel, use that Mensa brain of yours before you let your ego get in the way." I ground my teeth together.

Our conversation died when the doors creaked open and all heads turned to watch a beautiful blond girl, who appeared to be eighteen or nineteen, sway in, her ass wiggling in skinny jeans, her hair flowing down her back, and her heeled ankle boots clicking against the hardwood floor. Behind her, a middle-aged man with black hair and graying sideburns strutted in with two large muscled men who appeared they'd taken a year's supply of steroids in one shot. Both were bald, same build, although one had a scar that traveled from his temple to his right ear.

Kelton said, "Well, damn me to hell."

Hunt said, "I can't believe Pitt is here."

I smirked at Kelton's remark. The blonde had long legs, perfect breasts, and a smile that would render any guy speechless. Not that I was one of those men. No way. I had my girl. But I wasn't blind.

Everyone seemed to be staring at the girl as she sashayed over to the opposite side of the gym and sat directly in front of Sullivan and Seever. Pitt and the steroid twins settled next to her.

"Maybe he owns this gym." I braced my elbows on my knees while still holding onto my phone.

Pitt owned several businesses in Boston. I knew he'd built a gym for the Big Brothers Big Sisters organization. Maybe this was the place. Or maybe he liked boxing. Whatever the case, it wasn't any of my business. What I had to do was reel in my horny brother. Normally, I wouldn't get involved, but he wasn't getting anywhere near that blonde. Not when the media speculated that all the businesses Pitt owned were just cover-ups for his ties to the Russian mafia.

I angled my head to find Kelton's blue eyes. They were filled with lust. "Stay away from her," I said firmly. "Or you may be declaring your dying love to the devil sooner rather than later."

"I can eye fuck her if I want. The devil would be proud of me. Besides, she seems to be doing the same to me."

I shot a quick glance over that way as Hunt cracked up. Sure enough, blondie was leering at Kelton. Then she waved, and my idiot brother waved back. Pitt leaned into her and said something. Then he glared our way. I wanted to bang my head against the wall, but not before I knocked that lusty grin off Kelton's face. We were either going to end up in jail for fighting with Sullivan or we were going to end up dead in some alley.

That knot in my stomach had tightened as my brain pounded against my skull. It was going to be a long night.

Chapter 2

Lacey

COLORFUL ARTWORK HUNG ON THE walls around me as I sat in a chair in a tattoo parlor in California. I had this crazy idea to get the tattoo I'd always wanted. At first, I'd hesitated when Dad asked me if I wanted to fly to California for the weekend with him. He had some business to take care of at his label, Eko Records. It wasn't that I didn't want to see my brother, Rob, or spend time with Dad. If I went, I would miss baseball practice. The season started up mid-March, which was just around the corner. I would also miss Kross's first boxing match. I really wanted to see him crush his opponent. Most of all, I was reluctant to spend time away from Kade. We'd spent weekends apart before, but he seemed on edge when we said goodbye. When I asked what was wrong, he said nothing. Maybe since baseball season was starting up, he was worried that Aaron Seever would follow through on his threats that he'd made to me during tryouts last fall. His words had carved a home in my brain: "If you do make the team, I'll make it so you never pitch again."

I've had months to stew on his threat. A threat I thought he would've followed through on long before now. Aside from Aaron's snide remarks at recent practice outings, I also had to deal with his hateful glares whenever we passed each other in the school halls. But I pushed him and his words out of my mind. I'd come to the conclusion that if he took me down, I would take him down with me. Even if that meant that neither of us could play baseball.

I flinched at the steady pain the tattoo machine was delivering to my system.

"Lacey, you need to be still," Dave said as he hovered the tattoo gun over my lower left hip and lifted his blue gaze to mine.

"Sorry." Biting down on my lip, I shoved Aaron and my irritation aside and glanced at Rob.

He sat in a chair beside me, holding my hand. He squeezed lightly. "How's Kade?" His wavy brown hair toppled over his forehead.

"Probably freaking out right about now. He's been calling." At least I thought it was Kade who was causing my phone to vibrate in my back pocket.

"So if you don't mind me asking, why a polar bear?" Dave asked, as he concentrated on inking the image of the creature onto my skin.

When I'd entered the tattoo shop, a polar bear design plastered on the wall behind the counter had jumped out at me. "Special meaning." My cheeks flushed as I fingered the charm on my necklace Kade had given me for my birthday. He'd told me polar bears represented intelligence and strength, two traits he saw in me. I wanted to be that person, and the tattoo was a good reminder.

"Very cool," Dave said as the needle scored my skin. "I'm almost finished. Is there anything else you want on the bear?"

While Dave had been preparing his equipment earlier, I thought long and hard on the design. "Can you put a *K* on one paw and an *M* on the other?" I'd chosen a small polar bear in a sitting position with his hind legs extended.

Rob choked, and his green eyes swirled with uncertainty. With the furrow between his brows and his lips mashed into a thin line, I could have been looking at our dad.

"Are you sure about that?" Rob asked in a strangled voice. "I mean, those are Kade's initials. What happens when you two go your separate ways? This is permanent, Lacey."

I hadn't pondered my future with Kade. I was trying to get through high school. I was trying to get into ASU. At that moment, I couldn't imagine my future without Kade. I couldn't imagine not kissing him. I couldn't imagine not feeling those strong arms of his wrapped around me, making me feel loved and safe.

"It's my decision." I shrugged. "If we don't stay together, he's helped me with my PTSD. Granted I'm not healed, but the bear and Kade are my reminder of how my life began again."

"I can't stop you, but—"

"I get it." I sighed. "I know you're watching out for me. This is what I want."

Kade had been there for me during my blackouts, my panic attacks, and all the shit I'd doled out. As a result, my nightmares had diminished, and life had become bearable again. I'd only had one panic attack since the last one during tryouts. The lights had gone out in one of the snowstorms, and I'd freaked. Luckily, I was with Kade. Besides, I didn't owe him anything. This tattoo wasn't for him, but for me. It was a symbol of my healing, and I wanted to be reminded every day how I was moving forward and not backward or stagnant like I had been since I'd found my mom and sister dead on the kitchen floor. I continued to gnaw on my lower lip so I wouldn't move again, even though my pulse increased. It always did when I thought about them.

The hum of the tattoo gun stopped, and Dave went over to a table on the back wall where he kept his equipment. I released the hold I had my lip and tasted a little bit of blood as I focused on his work of art. I absolutely loved the polar bear and would love it even more when he inked in the initials.

Rob smoothed back his hair. "Don't show it to Dad."

I'd prepared Dad on the plane ride over. He was cool with a tattoo. He just didn't want me to cover my body in ink. I didn't know if Dad would have the same reaction as Rob about Kade's initials. I'd take his scolding if it came to that. After all, I was eighteen and could make my own decisions. I gave Rob a weak smile.

Dave came back, checking the tattoo gun he was holding. "You two done? Are we doing this?"

"Yes," I said firmly.

Silence filled the small room as Dave regarded Rob before he continued. I caught a glimpse out of my peripheral vision of Rob nodding. Not that Dave needed my brother's approval. But they were good friends, and I suspected Dave didn't want to strain his friendship with Rob.

As Dave began the final steps, I closed my eyes and thought of Kade. What would he think of my tattoo? Would he like it? Would he say the same thing Rob had said?

"So, when we're done here, can you take me to the cemetery?" I asked Rob. One of the main reasons I had agreed to fly out for the weekend was to visit Mom's and Julie's graves. I hadn't been to their gravesites since the funeral over a year ago.

"First we need to stop by the police station. We're meeting Dad there," Rob said hesitantly.

My eyes flew open.

The sound of the tattoo gun died.

A familiar buzzing in my head started. I jerked my head to the side. "Is Dad in trouble? Did something happen?" I was ready to leap out of the chair.

"No." His eyebrows knitted. "Dad's fine."

My muscles loosened a tiny bit.

Rob popped out of his chair then shoved his hands in his jeans pockets. "Detective Fisher called earlier. He heard you and Dad were in town and wants to…" He seemed to be searching for words. "He wants to chat with you, me, and Dad." Rob began pacing.

Excitement bloomed. Dad had been checking in with the LAPD over the last six months. Each time, Detective Fisher had nothing to report except that he was working diligently to investigate a handful of leads. While I was eager to run over to the police station, Rob looked like he'd rather run in the opposite direction.

"Why are you nervous?" I asked. The more I thought about it, the more nervous I became, too. I was afraid to recall details of that night. I didn't want to plummet into a deep depression or panic or black out. I was on the mend with my PTSD, and a relapse didn't sound like fun. Maybe Rob had similar reasons to be nervous.

"Let Dave finish. I'll be outside." Rob stalked out. The bells on the entrance door chimed as he did.

After Dave was done, he applied a small amount of anti-bacterial ointment to the tattoo then covered the bear with a bandage. "Leave it on overnight. Then wash with a mild soap, using your hands. Nothing abrasive." He removed his latex gloves and threw them in the trash.

I inhaled the musty air then released it in the hopes the little Pac-Men in my stomach would stop chomping on my insides. I wasn't certain if the police had a break in the case. I prayed like hell they'd have great news. Maybe then I could heal a little bit more.

Chapter 3

Kade

WE'D BEEN SITTING FOR WHAT seemed like hours, waiting for the fight to begin. I bounced my knee up and down as I tried to call Lacey again. No answer. If she couldn't talk, why hadn't she at least texted me? Was she okay?

Kelton fidgeted and kept eyeing the blond girl, who in return kept staring at him, smiling every now and then—really not a good sign. I envisioned plucking my brother's dead body from the Charles River. Not that Pitt was paying much attention. He'd been focused on his phone, but his bodyguards were very alert, continually scanning the room as though a threat lurked.

"Wes confirmed that's Pitt's daughter," Hunt said, while reading a text on his phone. "Her name is Chloe."

Wes's job at the Guardian, Pitt's bodyguard and bouncer service, came in handy at times like these.

"Didn't want the name, man," Kelton said. "Too personal."

Hunt shook his head. "You really are screwed up."

Three men entered the gym with clipboards in their hands then took their seats at a table to the right of the ring. No sooner had they sat down than the referee, a husky dude, sauntered in and climbed into the ring.

Hunt pocketed his phone. "It's about time."

I agreed. Another minute of doing nothing was another minute closer to me flying off the bleachers and finding something or someone to drive my fists into to take the edge off.

Finally, the fighters and their trainers came in. My brother, Kross, with his black hair cut high and tight, his blue eyes focused, and his upper body toned to perfection, looked ready to kill his opponent. He hopped into the ring, rolling his muscled shoulders back and forth. His trainer, Jay Crandall, a man known in the industry for producing prizefighters, slipped a towel into his back pocket before joining Kross. He pinched his hooked nose as his mouth began to move. I couldn't make out what he was saying, but Kross bobbed his head.

I sized up his opponent, who seemed like an even match with Kross. The dude was at least six feet, well toned and with arms as big as Kross's. Since this was Kross's debut match, it was a big deal for him. He'd been training hard.

As the trainers gave their fighters last-minute advice, my brother Kody ran in with a water bottle. I'd been wondering where he was.

"Kody interested in boxing?" Hunt sounded shocked.

I shrugged. I didn't know why Kody wanted to help Kross. I hadn't hung out with my brothers as much since dating Lacey. I knew Kody had been spending more time writing songs and playing the guitar. When I'd asked him about boxing, he'd said he might take up the sport. Others had always dubbed Kody the weakest of the triplets. My gut told me he wanted to get rid of that stigma.

"Ladies and gents," the referee said, "are you ready for the first fight of the night?"

The crowd applauded.

"Weighing in at just over two hundred pounds in his first amateur fight, let's give it up for Kross Maxwell."

People clapped, others whistled. Kross banged his gloved hands together, acknowledging the crowd.

"Fighting in the other corner and weighing in at two hundred and three pounds is Reggie Stockman."

The majority of the room whistled and shouted.

I guessed they liked this dude who had an expression that said he was here to kill. "Why does that name sound familiar?" I glanced sidelong at Hunt.

"He's one of the assholes who helped put Kody in the hospital the first time. You don't remember?" He leaned forward on his forearms.

Fuck me. Now the puzzle pieces fell into place. That was why Seever and Sullivan were here. That was why Kody was helping Kross. Kody wanted revenge, not only against Sullivan, but against those who had helped beat Kody to the point where he couldn't walk.

I didn't know whether to be excited Kross would have a chance to knock this guy's lights out or nervous for Kross, since Reggie glared at my brother.

"Kross is going to knock him out in the first round," Kelton announced.

With the fire blazing in Reggie's eyes, I had my doubts. I crossed my fingers that Kross would find his zone. Inwardly, I grinned. Before Lacey left, she'd coached him on how to get into the zone. She'd told him, "Focus on one point. Think of winning. Think of knocking out your opponent. And whatever you do, don't look at the people in the crowd." That was my girl—intelligent, beautiful, feisty, and strong. All qualities I loved.

Reggie and Kross met in the middle.

"Nothing below the waist. Keep it clean, and have a good fight," the referee said. "Now, shake."

Kross and Reggie touched gloves before stepping back into their corners. The bell dinged. Kross stormed forward, confident and determined, and threw the first punch. Reggie ducked then returned a jab to Kross's face. Back and forth they went, punching, jabbing, and moving around each other. Thwacks and grunts from the fighters and shouts from the crowd echoed through the room in turns as the two went at each other.

Amateur boxing usually consisted of three rounds, each three minutes long. The fighters were judged for every clean blow they delivered.

A guy in the crowd said, "Knock him out already, Reggie! What are you waiting for?"

It had already been the normal three minutes for the round.

Then Sullivan stood up. "Knock the fucker's lights out, Reggie!"

Kross threw an uppercut. Reggie fell backward. His body thudded on the mat. The crowd shot to their feet, some applauding for Kross and others begging Reggie to get up.

The referee started counting. *Son-of-a-bitch. Kelton called the fight.* On each count, the ref held up a finger. When the count reached nine, Reggie lifted his head, shaking it back and forth. He slowly got to his feet. By then the ref had stopped counting.

I didn't know all the rules of amateur boxing. I knew they were slightly different than those in the professional arena, but a knockout was a knockout. My heart raced as we waited for the judges to render their verdict. After a tense minute, Kross was declared the winner. A chorus of boos ensued, matched with whistles for Kross. Hunt and I high-fived.

"Told you," Kelton said as he and I bumped fists. "That's my kin." Then he flipped Sullivan the bird. At least, I thought the gesture was directed at Sullivan, although Pitt angled his head as he drew in his eyebrows. Sullivan returned the gesture as Aaron said something to his cousin. Then Sullivan lowered his hand.

Well, kill me now. That vision I had earlier of my dead body in some alley or Kelton's in the Charles River flashed again like a neon sign. The only one who seemed to be off scot-free was Hunt. His safety was shored up since his brother worked for Pitt.

I swung out my arm. "Sit. You have Pitt looking at us right now. For all he knows, you were telling him to fuck off."

His blue eyes burned a hole through me. "You know, bro? I could give a shit about Pitt. And I'm tired of you reeling me in. I'm tired of you trying to do good all the time. I'm tired of Sullivan and Seever. If you don't do something, I will." Then he ran a hand through his hair and climbed down the bleachers and out the door.

Whoa! What changed his mood all of a sudden? People in front of us glanced over their shoulders. I snarled when all I wanted to do was tell them to mind their own business. I was the level-headed brother. The one who tried to do the right thing most of the time. The one who was the adult, or at least tried to be when my own temper didn't get in the way. The one who had taken care of my brothers since my sister's death. The brother who was there for them when they acted out their aggressions. The brother who went to jail for them. The brother who loved them so much it hurt.

I'd given up my teen years to take care of my family. All of us were walking a tightrope. We had been for years now. We were reaching for good when all we got was bad. Our family balloon was about to burst, and it scared the fucking daylights out of me. I wasn't going to get any answers now, especially with Sullivan and Seever following Kelton out the door. I wasn't sure if Sullivan and Seever were leaving since the match was over or if their intentions were to ambush my brother. I wasn't taking any chances.

Hunt and I searched for Kelton inside and outside the gym. I called his phone and then texted. No response. Standing on the street, I racked my brain, thinking of all the reasons why Kelton would snap like that. I expected moodiness from Kody, not Kelton. My blood boiled as I thought about the night I'd gotten the call from the police about an accident involving Kody. My heart stopped that night.

Hunt slapped me on the arm. "Snap out of it. Kelton can take care of himself."

He was right—if it was a fair fight. Sullivan didn't do anything fair. Sullivan's idea of a fight consisted of a group of assholes ganging up on someone, beating them until they couldn't walk or breathe.

"Let's check the garage. Maybe he went back to the truck," I said.

A cold wind blew. The area was quiet for a Friday night, which was surprising since we were close to Boston University. I half expected more people roaming the streets with all the restaurants and bars in the neighborhood. Maybe since the threat of snow hung in the air people were hibernating.

I tucked my hands in my jacket as we crossed the street behind a passing car. Once we were in the garage, Hunt pressed the elevator button, and it immediately opened. We jumped in and rode the car up to the fourth floor. I bounced on my feet, watching the floors tick by ever so slowly.

The doors slid open, and Kelton's voice echoed through the garage. "You boys hit like girls," Kelton spat. "Come on. Is that all you got?"

Hunt and I dashed out and to our right. As we got closer, I grabbed ahold of Hunt's arm behind a row of cars.

On the other side of the pillars, we could see Sullivan punching Kelton while Seever held my brother's arms pinned behind his back. Each time Sullivan's fist connected with Kelton's jaw, my brother laughed, the sound menacing. Then he spit out blood at Sullivan's feet.

Quickly, I scanned the area. No one around except us. I motioned for Hunt to go right. Then I went left. We both circled around and came into view at the same time. As I watched Sullivan punch the shit out of my brother, I clenched my hands into fists and locked my jaw. Doing the right thing flew right out of the window. We were going to end this once and for all.

Seever's eyes grew wide when he saw me. Sullivan smirked as though to say welcome to the party. Oh, it was going to be a hell of a party. When I got done with the asshole this time, I would definitely belong in jail.

"So, boys. Or should I say cowards. You can't fight fair?" I stalked up to them while Hunt sauntered down from the opposite end. "Why don't you let Kelton go, Seever, and let my brother fight Sullivan? Or aren't your balls big enough, Sullivan, to fight someone who's not tied down?"

Seever frantically darted his head in all directions, more than likely wondering if Kross would jump out from between the cars. Seever would mouth off to any one of us. When it came to Kross, though, the dude shut down. Kross was probably showering and debriefing with his coach. Although it would've been satisfying to see Seever and Kross go at it. But the first rule of fighting was never lose focus on the enemy. That small mistake gave Kelton the advantage.

In a blur, my brother head-butted Seever right in the face.

"Fuck," Seever bit out as blood oozed from his nose.

Without missing a beat, Kelton pinned Seever against the white Mercedes. Poor car. As they went at it, Hunt crossed his bulky arms over his chest.

Sullivan started to back away. The only out he had would be in between cars, and that would slow him down. Either Hunt or I would get to him before he had a chance to get away, and I salivated like a hungry animal to get at my prey.

"Going somewhere?" Hunt lunged and grabbed Sullivan's arms then twisted them behind his back as he laughed.

Sullivan wiggled and fought, but Hunt was a big-ass, scary dude. He played linebacker for Kensington High last year. I was glad we were friends. I'd hate to be on the other end of his fist.

I ambled up to Sullivan. "So now the tables are turned."

Grunts sounded behind me as Kelton and Seever battled it out. I flicked my head at Hunt, and he let Sullivan go. I wasn't about to beat the shit out of him while he was tied down, and I wasn't about to throw the first punch either. If he was going to have his lawyer daddy press charges, I wanted to be able to claim self-defense.

With a guttural sound, Sullivan charged at me, fists in the air. The guy might be three inches shorter than me, but he was in good shape and had strength behind his punch. He delivered a left hook to my jaw, and I suddenly felt alive for the first time tonight.

He plastered a cocky smirk on his face. I let loose, ramming my fist into his face then his gut. The feeling was euphoric as I released the pent-up frustration that had been building since he'd returned to town last fall. Maybe I understood now why Kross liked boxing.

"Is that all you got, Maxwell? You punch like a pussy." Sullivan's voice was sardonic as he returned a blow, catching the corner of my mouth.

As the metallic taste of blood coated my tongue, two things happened at once. Sullivan pulled a knife from his jacket, and the sound of someone chambering a round on a Glock, a sound I knew all too well, reverberated through the garage. I glanced past Sullivan to Hunt, who'd backed away to watch the fight. He shrugged with a lopsided grin. He knew the men behind me with their guns drawn. They couldn't have been cops either. The law would have identified themselves immediately.

I didn't want to turn. Not with the knife Sullivan was holding, even though his posture was ramrod straight as if he'd been flash frozen. Hunt wandered toward me. When he reached Sullivan, Hunt shoved him toward a parked car. Sullivan stumbled, and the knife clanged to the ground.

"It's just Pitt and his men," Hunt said. "Turn around slowly."

Wiping the blood from my lip, I pivoted to find the steroid twin with the scar had a gun pointed at Kelton and Seever. The Charles River was looking like a good resting place for my brother. The other steroid twin had his gun pointed in my direction. I wasn't leaving my brother here. So running was out of the question, and attacking Pitt or his men without a weapon was suicidal.

"Hunter, good to see you." Jeremy Pitt hung to our left near a dented van with his hands in his dark pants. His daughter, Chloe, was next to him staring at Kelton and Seever.

Fuck me. We were out here in the first place because of her.

"Have you made your decision yet? Your brother Wes speaks highly of you," Pitt said in a gritty tone, as though he'd been smoking cigars since he was ten.

"What's he talking about?" I asked Hunt without taking my eyes off the guns or my brother.

"Not now," Hunt whispered out of the corner of his mouth. "Pitt, tell your men to lower their weapons. You have no reason to point them at us," he said matter-of-factly.

I could always count on Hunt for not taking shit from anyone, even from a man who supposedly had ties to the Russian mafia.

"Oh, I do. You see, these two morons"—Pitt wagged a finger at Kelton and Seever— "have managed to spew blood all over my Mercedes. And my daughter doesn't like the sight of blood. Also, I can see a dent from here. Which means someone is going to pay." He gave me a death glare.

Sure, Kelton, Seever, and the Mercedes were spattered in blood, but why the hell was he eyeing me?

"Mr. Sullivan," Pitt said. "Are you that stupid?"

All eyes went to Sullivan, who was on my right, halfway bent over, reaching for his knife.

"Stupid is too kind of a word." Kelton licked the blood from his mouth.

Then all hell broke loose. Seever elbowed Kelton. My brother stuffed his fist into Seever's gut, slamming him against the Mercedes. By the time Kelton was done with him, we were all going to be tied and beaten.

As Pitt tucked his daughter behind him, Sullivan picked up his knife. Hunt reacted quickly, knocking it from him. When the knife hit the ground, Pitt's daughter flinched.

With one gun trained on me, I held my breath, afraid to move until the scar-head twin slid closer to Seever and Kelton. He aimed the gun inches from my brother's head.

Death flashed before my eyes. The rage lingering inside me exploded. I was hotfooting it toward Kelton when a gun went off. I dove in between the Mercedes and a truck, hoping and praying that the pain searing through my right shoulder was not from a bullet, but rather from the impact of my body slamming onto the concrete. I pushed to my feet quickly, checking myself for any signs of blood. I sighed heavily over the ringing in my ears when my hands came up clean.

What the fuck happened? Where was Kelton? My heart was in my throat.

I cautiously moved out from between the two vehicles. After several scans of the garage, all I saw was Seever squatting down in front of two cars a few paces away from me. He was trying to help someone while Hunt and Pitt watched. At that moment, I almost puked. I couldn't live with it if one of my brothers died.

I rushed up, praying like a priest that the body on the ground wasn't Kelton. I lowered my gaze, and my heart stopped then started again. Sullivan lay on the ground with his eyes open and blood seeping through his left jeans leg. As much as I hated him and wanted to settle our score, I was glad he was alive.

"Where's Kelton?" I asked Hunt, blowing out a breath, trying to slow my pulse.

"Pitt's man dragged Kelton with him to flag down the ambulance."

Immobilized, I glared at Pitt then past him to his other moronic bodyguard, who was shielding Pitt's daughter. I didn't know if the gun had gone off accidently or if one of the two bodyguards fired on purpose. Sullivan had been stupid enough to reach for his knife. Regardless, I had to get out of here before I killed someone with my bare hands.

"Bloody bastard," Sullivan said through clenched teeth. "Your employees are idiots." He winced at Pitt as Seever removed his belt then wrapped it around his cousin's leg to slow the bleeding.

I had to agree with him.

"You're the idiot, Mr. Sullivan," Pitt said. "That's what you get for trying to get my men to do your dirty work." Pitt scoffed. "I despise anyone who wants to hurt a woman. You didn't think I would find out that you"—Pitt tossed his head at Aaron—"and your cousin want to hurt Lacey Robinson?"

Hunt and I exchanged a what-the-fuck look. I wasn't sure why I was surprised that Pitt knew about Sullivan's plan. I'd been keeping my ear to the ground after I heard that Sullivan and Aaron had been seen with two of Pitt's men at a restaurant we frequented in Ashford. They were scheming to ruin Lacey so she wouldn't be able to play baseball.

I couldn't see Aaron's face. I didn't have to. His hands froze on his belt.

"You mean you shot me over that?" Sullivan said *that* as if Lacey were the scum of the earth.

My muscles were vibrating with the need to crush his bleeding leg. "Dickhead. If Lacey so much as gets a broken nail, I'll beat both your asses until you'll need a wheelchair as a permanent part of your body."

Pitt grinned as though he was a proud father.

"What the fuck is your problem?" I seethed at Pitt.

"No problem." He set his sights on Sullivan. "You just happen to be in the wrong place at the wrong time. Karma's a bitch. Now, while I have your attention"—he looked from Sullivan to Seever—"if I catch wind that either of you hurt Kade's girl, I'll be sure to send your parents the details about where they can find your bodies."

Sullivan's eyes got as big as golf balls.

"I don't need your help," I said, sneering at Pitt.

Hunt elbowed me. I ignored him.

"You may not, Maxwell, but I need yours."

I let out a nervous laugh. "In hell," I mumbled as I plucked my phone from my jeans pocket. "I'm going to find my brother," I said to Hunt. If the goon had dragged Kelton out with him, I had to make sure Kelton was okay.

What could Pitt possibly need my help with? It didn't matter. Aside from the need to lay eyes on Kelton, I needed to hear Lacey's voice.

Right about now, I'd even be happy to hear her voicemail message. She had a way of calming me.

I bagged the elevator and took the stairs. The adrenaline was pumping through my veins faster than the speed of light. If I didn't keep moving, I'd collapse. What a fucked-up night. We were supposed to be rooting for Kross and having a good time. Instead, we ended up fighting to stay alive.

Once I made it onto the street, the line connected and her sultry voice filtered into my ears.

"Hey," she said in a soft but low tone.

I relaxed my shoulders, closed my eyes, and let out a huge breath. When I opened them, Kelton was standing at the corner, battered and bruised, seemingly okay since he was arguing with one of the steroid twins. Across the street, Kross and Kody were just exiting the gym. I tipped my head at Kelton, and they both hurried to his side.

Sirens wailed in the distance.

I looked up at the dark sky. Everything was right in the world. Even if I suddenly felt like I'd lived forty years since the boxing match.

Chapter 4

Lacey

MY LIFE HAD SETTLED SOMEWHAT since Dad and I moved to Ashford, Massachusetts, about eight months ago. At first, the pressure of a new school and a new place heightened my panic attacks and blackouts. Somehow, though, when I started dating Kade, my PTSD symptoms lessened. Plus, my sessions with Dr. Davis were helping. I still had nightmares, but they weren't as frequent. I still panicked but have had only three blackouts since the move. As I learned my triggers, I tried to push past the pesky demons in my head. Despite that, sitting in an interrogation room of the LAPD waiting on Detective Fisher stirred up the bad memories of the dead bodies, all the blood, and my mom's lifeless brown eyes.

I shivered as my phone rang, breaking the silence. It was Kade. "Hey."

"Why haven't you returned my calls?" he asked. His tone held a mixture of emotions. I couldn't quite figure out if he was frustrated, angry, or sad.

"I can't talk right now," I said as Dad, who sat to my right, raised an eyebrow. I figured he could hear Kade, he was talking so loud. "I'm in a police station, and—"

"What? Why? Are you okay?" There was no mistaking the panic in his voice now.

Detective Fisher, a large man, walked in with a folder in his hands. Rob, who sat to my left, kicked me under the table.

"Baby, I'm fine. I promise. I need to go. I'll call you later. Okay?"

"If you don't, I'm flying to California tonight." The phone went dead.

I didn't doubt him. He always backed up his words with action. One of the qualities I loved about him. Also one I didn't. If he ever said he was going to kill Greg Sullivan, then he would, and that frightened me. Not that I liked Greg. The guy was an asswipe. Between my family and the Maxwells, death had been a staple in our lives. I didn't need to see anyone else die and neither did Kade, not even his enemy.

"I'm sorry to keep you waiting," Detective Fisher said as he sat down at the opposite end of the table from me and placed the folder on the table. "Thank you for coming in."

I'd met the detective briefly when he was trying to ask me questions the night I'd found Mom and Julie. He hadn't changed that much. He still had a big belly and a bald head. He seemed like a nice enough man. Since it was always my dad who spoke to him, I wasn't sure how hard he'd been trying to crack our case.

"I won't go into all the details. We're working on a strong lead, and I would like to ask you a few questions."

I straightened my spine and clasped my hands together on the table, excited that I might finally get closure. When we'd first moved to Massachusetts from California, I didn't dwell too much on who killed Mom and Julie. The police didn't think the killer had any interest in finding us, and I had been too absorbed in my own hell to even think straight, although the question had been simmering.

The detective played with the folder as though it held the answers to the one question we all had. "Shortly after the murders, we suspected that the home invasion was part of a string of robberies in a neighborhood not far from yours." He pinned his dark eyes on Dad. "But a week ago we arrested the group responsible."

I had been about to jump across the table and hug the man until he said that "but." That freaking word severed an artery. I hated that word. Absolutely despised it.

Dad placed his warm hand over mine. Rob gnawed on his lip.

The detective scratched his head. "Their alibies check out. They weren't anywhere near your neighborhood that night."

I slumped in my chair.

Detective Fisher considered me before he set his attention on Dad. "Was anything taken that night?"

Dad let go of me. "How many times do I have to tell you? No."

Rob fidgeted, and his jaw flexed.

"Mr. Robinson, we have reason to believe whoever invaded your home was after something specific. I know you want to put all this behind you. Frankly, so do we. So, I'll ask you as many times as I think is necessary." His tone was even.

"And what makes you believe that?" Rob asked.

I wasn't aware that anything had been taken from our house that night, except two precious lives. Dad had mentioned several times that he went through his valuables and Mom's and didn't find anything missing.

"We have a reliable confidential informant who has given us some information. Right now we're checking into it, so I can't divulge much." He scrubbed fat fingers over his bald head. "It would be nice to know from you what they were looking for. Frankly, if they didn't get what they wanted, there's a possibility they'll be back."

The tension in the small room was climbing. Detective Fisher stared down Dad, who in turn wore a pinched expression.

"It's been over a year since the murders," I said. "Maybe they did get what they wanted." My nerves were ready to burst out of my skin. I chewed on a fingernail. What if the detective was right? What if they were hunting for something specific and didn't find it? Dad, Rob, and I had always assumed that the home invasion was random. Now that my head was clearer, I suddenly remembered Mom had once told me she kept family heirlooms in a safe place. Maybe something in her collection was of interest. I knew Dad had all those treasures somewhere.

Dad gently pulled my hand from my mouth. "Maybe you should wait outside."

The police station could burst into flames, and I still wasn't leaving. I lowered my hands to my lap. "I'm not going to freak." This would be one time when I would welcome a panic attack if it meant I got to hear some news, even if it was scary.

Detective Fisher's eyes turned soft. "Lacey, while I tend to agree with you, sometimes criminals do things that don't make sense. Sometimes they lay low until they think we've forgotten about them. And as long as we're still beating the streets asking questions, they probably won't surface." He rubbed his unshaven face. "Do any of you know the name Dennis Weeks?"

"No," Dad said flatly.

I shook my head.

"What about you, Rob? You manage your father's club. Ever hear that name around there?"

Rob eyed Dad. "Can't say I have."

With my brother's nervousness and curt responses, I was beginning to get the feeling he knew something. Then I dismissed the thought. He would tell the police if he knew anything. He wanted justice just as strongly as Dad and I did.

Detective Fisher opened the folder, pulled out a picture, and slid it across the table. "Maybe this will jog your memories."

Dad studied it briefly. Rob hunched over the table, quickly checked the photo, then sat back in his chair. I picked up the picture. A mug shot of a Caucasian guy with red hair, gold- rimmed glasses, and a peace-sign earring in his left ear held up a numbered sign in front of him. He had pockmarks on his face, and if he hadn't had red hair, he probably could have passed for Tommy Lee Jones's brother. I'd remember a guy who looked like the actor.

"Is he in jail?" I asked.

"Weeks did some time, but no. He's not behind bars anymore," the detective said. "Does he look familiar to any of you?"

I pushed the picture back to the detective. "I've never seen him before."

Dad and Rob said the same.

"So is this Weeks guy your suspect?" Dad asked.

"Not sure." Detective Fisher unfolded his bulk to stand. "That's all I have for now. If you can think of anything, please give me a call. We'll be in touch." He stretched to his full height. "Thank you for coming in."

A feeling of hopelessness clung to the pit of my stomach. I was beginning to think we would never find the person responsible, and we had to. I had to understand at least why someone would kill my family. More importantly, I wanted someone to pay for their sins.

Rob jumped to his feet. Dad was quick to stand too. They made their way out as if they needed air. It still puzzled me why Rob was so nervous.

"Should we be worried about these people coming back into our lives?" I knew Detective Fisher couldn't say for sure, but I had to ask.

"Like you said. They probably got what they wanted. Although if I knew what that was, it might blow this case wide open." He pulled a business card from his shirt pocket. "If you need to talk or if you think of something, I want you to call me."

I slipped his card into the back pocket of my jeans. "I will." I started for the hallway then turned. "Thank you."

He angled his bald head. "For what?"

"For sticking with this case for so long. I know it's your job, but you seem emotionally involved for some reason." That softness returned to his eyes again, and it spoke volumes.

He smiled, showing a crooked eyetooth. "Sooner or later we'll get them."

I left the police station with my mind twisted in a heap of worry and a little bit of excitement. While Detective Fisher hadn't given us great news, he did have a lead.

Once Rob and I were in his car and on our way, I asked, "Why were you so nervous in there?" Rob had a way of closing down when something was bothering him. Sometimes getting him to talk was like pulling a chew toy from a dog.

He sucked in his bottom lip as he braked for a red light. "I hate talking about this. I just want our lives to be normal. I just want to stop hurting. I just want the fucker who killed our family to rot in hell." His voice shook.

My mouth fell open. Rob had said more in a few seconds than he had since Mom and Julie's funeral. Like Dad, he always avoided the touchy-feely topics.

The light changed to green. As we inched our way through the LA traffic to the next stoplight, I asked, "What do you think the person was after?"

He gave the car some gas. "Lacey, if we knew the answer, it still wouldn't bring back Julie or Mom." His voice was calmer. "Dad and I have been through all the valuables we own. Nothing was taken."

"I get that. But what were they looking for?" That was the million-dollar question.

He shrugged. "I'm sorry. I wish I had the answers."

I wished he did too. I wished for a lot of things. Like time travel back to the past, which was impossible. I made a mental note to go through some of Mom's things when I got back to Ashford.

Chapter 5

Kade

As Hunt and I sat in the reception area of the Guardian office, I sifted through the events of Friday night. The cops had been right behind the ambulance. We had to hang around so we could give our statements. At first, I was a little apprehensive, given I had a record. But I quickly learned that Pitt had the Boston Police Department in the palm of his hand. I didn't hear what he said to the cops. Whatever it was, they let Hunt, Kelton, and me go without so much as a question. I didn't know whether to thank Pitt or punch him. I'd been leaning toward thanking him for scaring the piss out of Sullivan and Seever. I didn't. Too many things were unresolved, and until I knew for sure that both dickheads would back off, I didn't want to celebrate just yet.

The second thing I learned was that Pitt hadn't been at the amateur fight to watch anyone. He was there to talk to me. He wanted to make me a proposition. After the cops left, he told me—didn't ask—that Hunt and I would meet him at the Guardian office today. I knew why he wanted to talk to Hunt. He'd offered him a job and was still waiting on Hunt's answer. What the fuck did he want with me? I hoped he didn't think I was indebted to him now for shooting Sullivan. I'd contemplated not showing, but between my curiosity and knowing Hunt was requested to be here as well, I had to come.

I pinched the bridge of my nose. The headache I'd had yesterday had never left me. I woke up with my head pounding harder than ever before as if someone were wielding a hammer against my skull over and over. The bright lights above only served to increase the pain. I'd popped two aspirin prior to leaving the house, except they weren't working. Stretching out my legs, I settled into the soft leather couch of the waiting room. I might as well try and relax before we met with Pitt.

"So, how come you never told me about the job offer?" I asked, eyeing the pretty receptionist, who appeared bored as she flipped through a magazine at her desk.

"I'm not taking the job," Hunt snapped. "What does it matter?"

"Fuck, man. We're tight. Aren't we?" We told each other everything. I knew his secrets like he knew mine.

He rolled his shoulders. Clearly, he didn't want to be here, and neither did I.

"Why did you elbow me last night when I was mouthing off to Pitt?"

"I was trying to get you to can it. Let Pitt put the fear of God in Sullivan and Seever. Maybe they'll back off. Otherwise the battle will never end."

"I don't want Pitt to think I owe him now."

He let out a grizzly laugh. "A little late for that, dude. We're here, aren't we? Besides, he probably wants to offer you a job. You're getting ready to graduate. So, maybe he wants both of us."

Hunt had graduated last year, and his dad had given him a year to figure out what he wanted to do with his life. All Hunt really knew was football. He'd played linebacker for Kensington High and was damn good at it. He'd been instrumental in a lot of key plays, which led Kensington to the playoffs his senior year. Kensington could've used his skills last fall.

"Bodyguard and bouncer didn't make my career list." Hell if I was going to work for someone who could be tied to the mafia.

"Did you talk with Lacey?"

"Yep." I'd talked to her twice after the incident in the garage. "I didn't tell her anything about last night, though." I didn't want to stress her out over the phone.

He chuckled as he sat back down. "She's going to know it when she sees you."

"I'll deal with it then." She wouldn't be able to miss my split lip or bruised jaw. She was due home tomorrow night, and they wouldn't heal that quickly. "She did tell me the cops might have a lead in the murder case."

"And is it a hot lead?" Hunt asked, sitting up straighter.

"Not sure. I'll find out more when she gets home." She didn't want to get into too much detail, and she gave me the impression the cops didn't elaborate, which didn't surprise me. Even so, I was just as anxious as she was to find out who the guilty party was. Maybe then it would bring her closure.

A phone rang, and the receptionist answered. "Yes, Mr. Pitt. Sure will." She hung up and said, "You boys can go in now. Last door on your right." She pointed with a red-painted nail down a hallway to her right.

Hunt and I snickered. She called us boys. Hunt hated to be called a boy.

As we headed to Pitt's office, Hunt stopped at her desk. "Honey, I may be young enough to be a boy, but I promise you I'm all man."

The brunette, who had her hair twisted up on her head, blushed a hundred shades of red.

I chuckled as we both swaggered down to Pitt's office as if our shit didn't stink. We crossed the threshold into a massive corner office of mahogany wood and chrome furniture. A bar banked the left wall, and a plush seating area sat to the right. Adjacent to a low-back couch was a door carved into the wall, probably leading to a bathroom, and the oblong solid chrome desk was positioned in front of a window overlooking the Boston skyline.

"Come, fellas. Sit." Pitt waved at two wingback chairs in front of his desk.

As my feet dug into the thick carpeting, I caught a whiff of cigar smoke. When we reached the chairs, I sat. Hunt didn't. He used his chair as a shield.

Pitt scrutinized him. "You don't like me, Hunt, do you?" He reclined back in his leather chair. Any farther, and he just might fall into the floor-to-ceiling windows behind him.

"No, I don't. And if I'm here because you want to convince me to work for you, then you're wasting your time." Hunt gripped the back of the chair so tightly that his knuckles turned pale.

Pitt popped forward and clasped his hands together as though in prayer, almost knocking over the ashtray with a cigar in it. "I'm doing a favor for your brother."

Hunt sneered. "Don't."

"Your brother wants you to get a job. And I'm willing to hire you. Your size fits the mold. You'd make a good bouncer at one of the under-twenty-one clubs here in Boston."

Hunt's nostrils were flaring, hard and fast. "So you think because I'm six foot four and could lift your scrawny ass over my head and throw you through those windows that my future is to be a bouncer? I don't need a job."

Ballsy. Pitt was far from scrawny, and I'd agree that Hunt could crush Pitt in fight. But still, ballsy.

Hunt looked at me. "Man, I'll wait for you in the lobby." He pivoted on his heel and got halfway to the door before Pitt spoke.

"Not even if I pay you a hundred dollars an hour and offer Kade here a job alongside you? You two are joined at the hip, right?"

Oh, fuck no. I jumped to my feet. I wasn't working for Pitt to keep rowdy teenagers under control. I'd seen what my old man's friend, Buster, had to go through at the teenybopper club, the Cave, back in Ashford.

"Is that why I'm here? So you can bribe my friend with me?" I curled my fingers into a fist.

Pitt casually stretched to his full height and circled his desk to the liquor-laden bar. He plucked ice cubes from a container and plopped them into a glass before pouring amber liquid into it. "How's your mom, Kade?" Pitt asked as though he were an old family friend.

Hunt went ramrod straight, and I lost my breath.

Fuck me. The last person to bring up my mom ended up in the hospital with a broken arm.

Pitt brought the glass to his mouth, eyeing me with those empty black eyes.

"What's your game?" I asked. "Are we here for you to shove personal shit in our faces? Mention my mother again, and I won't hesitate to break every bone in your body."

His eyes went wide. "I like you, Kade," he said with that gritty voice I hated. "At first I didn't think you would be up for the job, but after last night and now with you making idle threats, I know you would." He sipped his whiskey.

"I told you I'm not working for you." I felt around in my pocket for my pocketknife.

He smirked as though he knew I had a knife and he was daring me to pull it out. The idea did sound enticing, especially since his idiot guards weren't around. Still, Pitt seemed like a guy who could handle himself, considering his bulked-up arms. Or more than likely he would have the steroid twins or the police here before I could act.

"Let's go," Hunt said to me. "We're done here."

I stalked closer to the door when every ounce of energy in me wanted to follow through on Hunt's threat to throw Pitt through the wall of windows.

"Not even if it has to do with your girlfriend's life?"

The blood rushed out of me, freezing me in place. I swallowed, and it felt like razor-sharp tacks were piercing my throat. Hunt had a look of horror on his face. I probably did too. What the fuck was Pitt talking about?

Ice cubes clinked in the glass. I spun on my heel and practically dove for Pitt with my fists up, ready to beat his head in.

With lightning speed, Hunt caught my arm. "Not worth it, man."

"Listen to your friend." Pitt set his glass down. "Now, do I have your attention?" His smug grin morphed into an intense glare.

Dick.

Hunt let go of me as Pitt sauntered over to the windows. "My daughter needs a tutor." The Rolex on his right wrist shimmered as the light caught it.

A disrespectful laugh fell from my mouth. "Are you fucking with me?" My nails dug into my palms. He was threatening Lacey's life so I would tutor his daughter? This guy couldn't be serious.

"Kade, how much do you know about the death of Lacey's family?" Pitt's cockiness vanished, and his voice took on an all-business tone.

For the moment, his question masked the hatred I had for him. Maybe it was the seriousness on his face. "Nothing." I knew as much as Lacey did. Something told me Pitt knew more than the cops. A light bulb went off. He could use his relationship with the BPD to help find out more about that LAPD lead.

"Mm," he muttered, rubbing his sharp jaw. "Word on the street is her father is in bed with the Lorenzino family out of LA."

Who the fuck was he talking about? Hunt and I returned to the wingback chairs. I could tell Pitt's mind was working from the way his eyes shifted every second, and my mind was going a mile a minute, too, trying to connect Mr. Robinson to the mob.

"How well do you know the Robinson family?" Pitt didn't take his eyes off me.

I'd met her brother briefly at Christmas. I hardly knew her father. He was always working at his club, Rumors, in Cambridge. So, not at all really, except that I knew Lacey inside and out, and she never mentioned any family by that name.

"Just spit out what you're trying to say."

"The Lorenzino family is associated with the mob in LA. If my sources are correct, James Robinson has something they want. Do you know what that is?" His dark eyes drilled a hole right through me.

A growl erupted from my chest. "How the fuck would I know? Aren't you tied to the mob? Don't mob bosses all know each other?"

He let out a sinister laugh. "Oh, yes. The more I get to know you, the more I like you, Kade. Regardless, I own businesses and support charities. If you call that the mob, then I suggest you check the definition. Better yet, why don't you ask James Robinson about it?"

I just may. Suddenly, another realization dawned. When Lacey was in the hospital after she blacked out during baseball tryouts in September, her father showed up with cuts and bruises all over his face, cuts that needed stitches. He'd said he had to break up a fight at his club. Was that true? Or had he pissed off the mob?

"You look like you know something." Pitt's voice cut through my trip down memory lane.

"How is Lacey in danger?" I locked my jaw as my brain knocked against my skull. That bad feeling I'd had yesterday came back like a tornado.

"The Lorenzino family will go to great lengths to get what they want when the time is right. Which means your girl could be used as a pawn or worse, if you get my drift." He lifted a thick eyebrow. "Anyway, I've invited you here to offer my protective services in exchange for you tutoring my daughter."

No way in hell was I tutoring his daughter. Not that I couldn't. Hell, I had a high IQ. I could've tested out of my senior year. But my old man wanted to see me graduate, and my brothers and I always talked about graduating together. Besides, Hunt and my brothers could help protect Lacey.

"A few minutes ago you were offering me a job as a babysitter at some club. Now you want me to babysit your daughter?" No damn way was I getting near that chick. If I tutored her, then Kelton would be sniffing around, and I didn't want her near Kelton. "It doesn't matter, I can protect my girl. I don't need your muscle. I saw how careless they were last night."

Hunt swore. "We protect our own."

I let out a quiet breath. I was confident Hunt would have my back, but hearing him say it out loud to Pitt made me stand up a little taller.

"It was an accident caused by your brother," Pitt said. "If he hadn't fallen into my guy, then the gun wouldn't have gone off. What are you complaining about? Didn't we do you a favor shooting your enemy? I'd say you should thank me. After all, I literally scared the living piss out of them. Or at least that Seever boy." He harrumphed.

Hunt laughed. "Seever did piss his pants."

I didn't give a shit about Sullivan or Seever, and I despised the fact that Pitt knew more about me and Lacey than I cared to imagine. I wasn't sure why I was surprised. If he was connected to the Russian mob, he probably knew how to get information on anyone. "Do you know who killed the Robinsons?" Something wasn't adding up. Why not just pay me to tutor his daughter?

He studied me for the longest time. I stared right back.

"He's not going to tell you," Hunt said. "If he did, that would make him guilty or some shit like that for not going to the cops. Nah, the mob takes care of their own problems."

Pitt flicked his head at Hunt while keeping his eyes on me. "Listen to your friend."

I heaved to my feet from the fancy leather chair. "We're done here." Hunt was right. Pitt wasn't going to say a word. "I can handle my own shit. I don't need you or your thugs to get anywhere near Lacey."

"Are you going to protect her twenty-four, seven? Is her father going to let you sleep at the house? And what about when you're not together? I can take that worry away from you." He sounded desperate.

I threw my hands on his desk and got in his face. "Why should I trust you?"

"You shouldn't. Although if I'm willing to trust you with someone precious to me, do you think I'd blow smoke up your ass? Don't you think I've done my research on you, Kade Maxwell? I know you're fiercely protective of your brothers and your family. I know you are an excellent shot with a gun. Honestly, I wouldn't trust anyone other than myself or my wife when it came to my daughter. But you… I know my gut is right. I know you wouldn't touch her, harm her, or let anyone get near her. I also know you have a way of getting people to listen to you." He sat back in his chair.

I didn't want to know what he meant by his last statement. Or how any of what he said related to tutoring. My head was throbbing to the point where my vision was blurring. I blinked twice before the panoramic view of the Boston skyline became crystal clear. Snow was falling, blanketing the rooftops of the buildings around us. I needed to get out of there and release some tension and think. I tapped Hunt on the arm as I started for the door.

"You'll be back," Pitt called after us.

Like hell I will.

Two and half hours later I was standing in the reception area of Whitaker Manor. After Pitt brought up my mom, I had to see her. Not that I thought he would do something to her, I just hadn't seen her in two weeks. And seeing her always helped me put life in perspective and settle my nerves.

Robin, the receptionist, looked up from her computer. "Kade, your father mentioned you would be visiting." She tucked a strand of her red hair behind her ear. "You just missed him."

"I know." I'd called him on my way to let him know I'd be here. He was heading back to the apartment he rented close by to take a shower. He spent most weekends up here with my mom. I signed in before Robin buzzed me through the door.

Once inside, I wound my way to the nurses' station. Lynn, the gray-haired nurse on duty, stopped writing in a chart as I approached. "Kade, good to see you."

"Can I go in?" I dipped my head at my mom's room on the right directly across from Lynn.

"Yes. Your father told her you would be here. She's been quiet all day though." Sorrow shone in her dark eyes.

My mom had days where she chatted about nothing in particular, and sometimes she didn't talk at all. It was hit and miss with her. After my sister died four years ago, she fell into a deep depression and even tried to commit suicide. My heart ached every day for her. I wanted more than anything in this world for her to heal, to have her home with us, to sit in the kitchen and watch her. She loved to bake. Kody was our baker in the house now. He'd always helped her when she was baking cookies or cakes.

I ambled over to her doorway then hesitated. A vase of lilies graced the wooden dresser on the right wall, the perfumed fragrance filling the room. As I inhaled, I angled my head to find my mom sitting in her fabric armchair on the other side of her bed near the window. She was dressed in a violet silk robe that fell to her feet. Her black hair flowed around her while her long lashes framed her deep ocean-blue eyes. She lifted her chin and beamed at me.

Tears burned my eyes. "Hey, Mom." I went over to her and bent down to kiss her on the forehead.

"Kade." Her eyes lit up. She caught my cheeks between her soft palms. "I've missed you."

I was about to lose my shit, and I tried not to cry in front of her. My father said to show happiness. Our positive energy would help to elevate her mood. I should've told the triplets to meet me here. She always came alive with them. They had a way of acting like hams and not dwelling on the sadness of the situation.

I dragged an ottoman from in front of the window over to her and sat down. I grabbed her hands. "How are you? Have you been watching any movies?" She loved old movies like *Gone with the Wind*.

She smiled. "I watched *Cleopatra* today, the one with Liz Taylor in it. Your dad fell asleep."

Over the years, several people had said my mom resembled Liz Taylor.

She lost her smile. "Then..." She glanced out the window. Her eyes lost that spark.

I rubbed the backs of her hands and looked out the window with her. When she got quiet, we weren't supposed to press her. So, we sat there. Manicured shrubs and trees poked out of the snow-covered landscape.

"The angels were out last night," she said. "Isn't it pretty?"

The snow sparkled as if tiny diamonds littered the ground, which was what she used to tell me when I was a little boy. She'd also told us boys that snow was an angel's blanket. Water filled my eyes. "Diamonds are a girl's best friend," I said softly. "The angels sprinkled a lot of them last night, too."

She turned her head slowly, her teary eyes locking with mine. "Karen is with the angels. I saw her. She's happy now."

Don't lose it, man. Be strong for your mother. It was so fucking hard. I swallowed and smiled as best I could, lifting her hands to my lips. "She certainly is, Mom. She's among the beautiful angels." After a soft kiss, I lowered her hands to her lap but didn't let go.

She dozed until my old man came in an hour later.

"Good?" he asked in a low tone, shifting his gaze between my mom and me.

Despite his weather-worn skin from all his missions in Afghanistan and the streaks of gray in his brown hair, he and I greatly resembled each other—more than he and the triplets. Sometimes it was like I was looking at my older self.

I carefully let go. She moved a little but didn't wake. Then my father and I left, closing the door softly.

"Mom seems good one minute, then the next she shuts down. Is today an off day?" I asked. Dad had told me a couple of weeks ago that she was responding better to her new medication.

"The snow sometimes sends her into a deeper depression. I'm not sure why."

I guessed because she associated angels with Karen.

"You look tired, son. Is everything okay?"

No. I was a minute away from bawling and throwing myself at my father so he could hold me like a baby and tell me we would be a family again, to tell me my mom would come home again. "Yes."

"Go home and get some rest. And inform the triplets I want them here tomorrow," he said in a gentle but firm tone.

I had a long haul home and suddenly felt drained from the fight last night, Pitt's conversation earlier this morning, and seeing my mom. Not to mention, I was missing Lacey terribly. But something told me I probably wouldn't be able to sleep.

Chapter 6

Kade

I RUBBED MY EYES, TRYING TO clear the blurriness. I'd gotten up early and was sitting at my desk in my room, surfing the internet for anything on the Lorenzino family. I replayed the conversation Hunt and I had had with Pitt over and over in my head. Was Lacey in danger? What did Mr. Robinson have that the Lorenzino family wanted? Were the deaths of Lacey's sister and mom a result of a deal gone bad? Did Pitt know who killed them? Then there was this nagging voice in my head that Pitt was involved somehow. Maybe it was the way his eyes pierced through me when he asked me if I knew what the Lorenzino family wanted.

The more I thought about his offer, the more I was leaning toward accepting it. He had a good relationship with the law, which might help to find out what the LAPD knew. I would have more protection on Lacey, not that I couldn't handle that on my own. But I had to table my pride. Her life could be on the line, and if I took the job, I could leave my brothers to concentrate on school and staying out of danger.

I scrubbed a hand over my face. First and foremost, I needed Lacey with me. I needed her in my arms so I would know she wasn't in any danger.

I stretched then cracked my knuckles, staring at the computer screen at the pictures I'd found of Lorenzino. Harrison Lorenzino was a gray-haired man with a gray beard to match. LA news dubbed him a knight in shining armor since he'd recently donated fifty thousand dollars to a children's hospital in LA.

I was about to do more surfing when I checked the time. I bolted out of my chair. I was supposed to tell the triplets to head up to see our mom, and I had to get a shower and get ready to head to the airport to pick up Lacey.

I stalked out of my room. On Sundays, the triplets were either lounging in our theater room or in the garage working out. I found them in the theater room in the basement. We all loved it down there. No windows, two comfortable leather couches positioned in the form of an *L*, a fifty-inch TV, a fridge, and thick carpeting. It was a perfect place to watch movies, and a cozy place to curl up with Lacey.

"Where've you been?" Kross asked in between bites of popcorn.

It was eleven a.m. So there was still time for them to drive up to the Berkshires. I dropped down on the coffee table, blocking their view of *The Italian Job*. A slew of popcorn flew at me. "Dad wants you guys to go up and see Mom today."

"Was that why you came home late last night?" Kody asked as he snagged the remote. The sound from the TV vanished.

"After I left Pitt's office I needed to think. She needs to see you guys."

Kelton sat up straight. "Is she okay?"

I held up my hand. "She is. But she could use some cheering up. You know how she gets in the snow." I massaged the back of my neck.

Kody smoothed a hand over his hair. Kelton lowered his gaze. Sadness swam in Kross's eyes as he set down his popcorn. "We'll get dressed and get on the road," he said. He rose then sat back down. "Everything else okay, bro? You want to talk about your meeting with Pitt?"

Kody and Kelton fixated on me.

Hell, no. I didn't want them involved, especially after seeing Kelton. His face was all fucked up with bruises, a split lip, and the beginnings of two black eyes. Kross looked better than Kelton, and his opponent had delivered several punches to Kross's face. Then images of Kody beaten to a pulp by Sullivan and his buddies surfaced. His eyes had been swollen shut. His nose and jaw had been broken. I'd barely recognized him.

Still, if I didn't bring them up to speed, then I would be violating our one rule—band of brothers, which meant we told each other everything.

I launched into the details of the conversation with Pitt, from how he wanted Hunt to work for him to the deal he'd offered me and everything in between, including the Lorenzino family. I also shared with them what Lacey had mentioned about the lead in the case. Usually Lacey didn't like others knowing her personal shit. I knew I didn't like people knowing mine. Since we were dating and she knew my brothers well, she shared things with them.

"So, let me get this straight. Pitt wants to put men on Lacey for protection in exchange for you tutoring that beautiful goddess." Kelton sucked in his bottom lip as he groaned.

One of my hesitations about telling him had been the girl. "That's all you took from everything I just said? This is about Lacey's life." I flared my nostrils. A pain began in the back of my neck. "I told you. Stay the fuck away from Chloe. Now, I haven't decided yet if I'm working for Pitt. I'm not even sure if what he told me is true. So until I get my head around this, I don't want you guys to breathe a word of this to Lacey. I don't want to scare her, not with her PTSD and with baseball starting." It was bad enough Seever's threats to hurt Lacey lingered.

"Let's say all this is true," Kody said. "And you do work for Pitt. Are they going to follow her? Are they going to go to school with her? In my opinion, they may only serve to scare her even more. And her panic attacks may be epic if she thinks someone is following her. Have you thought about that?"

I hadn't thought through any of those scenarios yet. I was still trying to get my head around my conversation with Pitt. But Kody was right.

"If we protect her, she may be none the wiser," Kross added.

"And how will that go over?" Kelton asked. "She's not stupid. She's going to figure out we're up to something if we're on her ass constantly."

They all had good arguments. Maybe telling her would keep her safer. At least then she would be more aware, more alert. I filed that idea away for now. Her plate was full. She needed her head clear to concentrate on baseball. Her chance for a baseball scholarship at ASU was extremely important to her, and her PTSD concerned me the most. I wanted to shoulder the worry on this topic with Pitt until I knew more details. I wasn't about to scare her when I didn't even know what the hell was going on.

"I don't have it all figured out yet." I rubbed my neck again. "Anyway, all I need you guys to do is keep your eyes open. We have school. She shouldn't be in any danger there. It's the nighttime."

"Look, bro. She knows how to handle a gun, and she's good. Just make sure she has her weapon handy and not locked up. Plus, Mary will be with her at night when her old man works," Kross said.

I wouldn't be able to sleep, and I wasn't taking chances in the event someone broke in and repeated what they'd done at her California home. She might not be able to get to her gun in time.

"What does her old man have that this mob family wants?" Kody asked.

All three of them braced their arms on their thighs.

"No fucking clue." I shrugged. "I'll be staying with Lacey for the next couple of days. I'm going to try and find out. Mary is out of town, and her old man is staying in LA for a few more days." I glanced at my watch. "Why don't you guys get going?" I still had to take a shower. "I'll see you at school in the morning."

"Hopefully you won't be such a dick after you get laid," Kelton said as I headed to the door.

Kross and Kody burst out laughing

I threw up my middle finger as I walked out.

The ride to the airport was brutal for a Sunday. Traffic through the tunnel was stop and go. Hinder's "Lips of an Angel" played on the radio. As I drove, I called Hunt. I wanted to bounce the idea of me working for Pitt off him.

My nerves were tight. I had to get it together before I saw Lacey. If she suspected anything, she'd fire questions at me, and I wanted one night where I didn't have to think, just feel.

The line connected through my Bluetooth, and Hunt's voice replaced the music of the radio. "What's up?"

"I'm leaning toward taking the job with Pitt. Before you say a word, hear me out." I took a breath. "If what Pitt says is true, then Lacey will be protected. He also has a connection with the law. Maybe BPD can talk to the LAPD. Or somehow I can get Pitt to trust me so he'll tell me what he knows."

"So, you're going to tutor his daughter? And how are you going to explain that one to Lacey? Are you going to tell her why you're tutoring a mob princess? Or why Pitt called on you for the job when there's a whole fucking city of qualified professionals? Which bothers me. Why you? And the way he asked you if you knew what Lacey's old man had that the Lorenzino family wants. My gut is telling me Pitt is fishing for them. Or maybe he wants in on the deal."

Between all the valid points Hunt and my brothers were throwing at me, my head was about to explode. "I don't have all the answers. I'm considering it. I haven't said I would sign up for the job."

"We can protect Lacey. But whatever you decide, I have your back. In fact, I was also thinking of working for Pitt. I could do some snooping on my end if I did."

"You told Pitt to fuck off. How are you going to convince him? The man will see right through you."

"You let me figure that out. You're not going at this alone. Remember our motto. Thick or thin. Dead or alive. Friends until the end."

"Man, that's our motto if we decided to join the military. Not against the mob. At least I'm tutoring, not playing detective with an organization that could get me killed. Also, I can make demands if he wants information that badly or he wants a good tutor for his daughter."

"My mind is made up."

He did have his brother, Wes, if he got himself into a bind.

A door slammed in the background.

"Hunt, you better watch your ass." Hunt was more than a best friend. He was the older brother I never had, and I couldn't deal if something happened to him.

"One more thing," Hunt said with a smile in his voice. "Kiss Lacey for me."

The radio blared through after his parting words, leaving a grin on my face. I'd planned on doing more than that.

I wiped Pitt from my mind as I made my way through the tunnel and found a parking space at Logan Airport. I had to hoof it about a mile before I even got to the baggage claim area. The place was packed with people running and dragging suitcases and pushing strollers while others walked briskly out into the cold weather. Lacey was due to arrive at six. I was five minutes late.

I dodged a family of eight pulling their suitcases toward an exit. As I searched for a monitor, my phone went off.

The text read, *Just landed. Be down in five minutes.*

I planted myself in front of the escalator and scanned the crowd. With each minute that ticked by, my pulse sped up. I felt like I was thirteen again, waiting for Jill Learner to walk out of school. She'd been my first crush. My stomach had hurt whenever I was around Jill. Lacey made me feel that first crush again and again. *Crazy shit.*

I fidgeted. I was nervous and excited at the same time. On a slow blink, my breath caught when I latched on to her sultry green eyes. Time stopped, and so did my heart. She held onto the moving stairs, her brown hair in a mass of waves spilling over her shoulders. Her skin had a sun-kissed glow, no doubt from the California sunshine. As I followed the length of her curves, my dick hardened. She wore those over-the-knee fuck-me boots I so loved. All I could picture was her on a bed with nothing on except those boots. I was so screwed. No way was I going to make it out of this airport.

Chill, man. Be a gentleman.

That was my problem. I didn't want anything but rough. What with all the pent-up frustration over the last three days coupled with Pitt's enlightening conversation and all the shit with Sullivan, I wanted to strip her naked and bury myself in her.

A middle-aged guy behind her was staring at Lacey like he wanted to attack her. Seriously? She was jail bait to him. Then my antenna went up, and Pitt's words roared in my head. *They'll use Lacey as a pawn or worse.* I straightened, ready to pounce and beat his face red to match his hair. Then he turned to the lady behind him and planted a chaste kiss on her lips. Relief washed through me as I switched my attention back to the most beautiful girl I'd ever seen.

She waved, and her tongue darted out before she touched her lips. I almost fell to the floor. Gone was the need to kill. In its place was a need that grew inside me like wildfire. I was going to explode if she didn't get off that fucking escalator. A little old lady shuffled off first, taking her time. Damn, if she didn't move, I was going to pick up the fragile woman and carry her off the thing.

Finally, the people in front of Lacey exited. As she drew closer, my heart fluttered, beat hard, stopped, beat again. I would've run to her like a love-struck dude, but my jeans were so fucking tight it hurt to move. She dropped her bag near my feet then jumped into my arms, wrapping those toned thighs around me.

Fuck me. I buried my face in her hair, inhaling her tropical scent of orange and sunshine. With my hands on her butt, I anchored her to me.

She tugged on my hair, and I almost threw her against the nearest wall. She knew I loved it when she did that.

"We're in the middle of an airport, baby," I drawled in a husky tone. I was surprised I could even speak.

"And I want you, Kade," she breathed as she squeezed her thighs against my waist.

"Oh, fuck. Lace, you're going to have to recite some nursery rhymes or something. Otherwise, I'm not going to be able to walk out of here."

She giggled against my ear. "Humpty Dumpty sat on a wall..."

I laughed, the act freeing for the moment. Even a nursery rhyme sounded sexy coming out of her.

Chapter 7

Kade

SILENCE FILLED MY TRUCK AS Lacey and I drove back to her house. I was so thankful her old man hadn't come back with her. All I could think about was holding her in my arms all night, keeping her safe, our bodies intertwined—legs, arms, lips.

Lacey peered out the truck window into the nighttime snow. "What happened to your lip?"

I touched the bruised area. "Nothing. Just brothers fighting." I raised her hand to my mouth and kissed her palm. "I've missed the crap out of you. And, right now, all I can think about is you underneath me." I wasn't ready to tell her the real story. She'd freak, and then we'd argue. Both were a mood killer.

"Tell me more." She closed her eyes and leaned on the center console.

I shifted my gaze back and forth between the road and her. We were two blocks away from her house. I would've slammed on the brakes and taken her right there if the roads hadn't been slick from the recent snow and freezing temperatures.

"Well?" she said.

I lowered our hands to the console. She loved when I gave her a play-by-play of things I wanted to do to her. The woman took foreplay to a whole new level.

"Nope. Not tonight. You're just going to have to wait."

She stuck out her lower lip, batting her luscious green eyes.

"Can you tell me another nursery rhyme?" I begged.

With a seductive smile, she snaked her fingers between my legs. When she found what she wanted, she sucked in a sharp breath.

"Nursery rhyme," I said again. Not that I really needed to hear one now. I couldn't get over how erotic it was to hear her recite "Humpty Dumpty" in her sultry voice. She'd had to recite a couple of them to me before I left the airport.

"Oh, no. Tit for tat. You'll just have to crawl into the house."

"Careful, Lace." I rolled into her driveway. "I'll take you here in the truck." I threw the gears into park, almost growling.

She giggled, the sound warming my heart. "You wouldn't dare."

"You know what I'm capable of."

"And you know what I can do too." She tightened her grip on my groin.

Did I ever. The woman had a mean kick. The second time I'd ever seen her, she'd kneed me in the balls. It hurt like a motherfucker too. And with that thought, I didn't need any more nursery rhymes.

"Baby, if you want me to make love to you, I do need what you're holding." I ground my teeth together.

She snaked her icy hand underneath my shirt, a welcome relief on my heated skin. "Who says you're getting any?"

The corners of my mouth curled up slowly, very slowly. Then, without a word, I jumped out, circled around to her side, and opened the door.

"Not speaking?" She took my hand eagerly.

I yanked her to me, hard, blocking her from stepping off the running board. "You don't want my lips all over you?" My body was on fire for hers.

"I want all of you." She locked her hands around my neck.

That's my girl.

I wrapped my arms around her waist and helped her down. Without another word, we made our way to the front door. I was grateful the lights were on. If not, Lacey might've been traumatized. A dark house was one of her triggers—a major fucking trigger. The first time I ever brought her home, the house had been pitch black, and she freaked out to the point where she threw her body into the garage door until she passed out.

Tonight, once she was inside, she went over to a panel near the front door and punched in the security code for the alarm. I didn't move until the beeps sounded. When we were in the clear, I pinned her to the wall between the door and the window. She slipped her cold, delicate hands into the waist of my jeans. My heart thumped, and so did my dick. I crushed my mouth to hers.

"I need you, Lace. I need every inch of you." Edging back, I slowly swept my gaze up then down, stopping on her boots. Fuck, I wasn't going to last a second.

She bit her bottom lip as her green eyes darkened. Her cleavage peeked out from the scoop-neck sweater she wore. Her cheeks flushed red as she erotically dragged a hand down one side of her leg. Tilting her head, she caught in her hand a strand of hair that had slid forward.

"You're beautiful."

"Are you just going to stand there? Or are you going to do something about him?" Her long lashes fell, and she gazed pointedly at my crotch.

I closed the tiny distance between us, framing her face in my hands. "If you ever leave me again, I'll hunt you down."

"You've captured your prey, Maxwell. No sense in making threats when I'm a willing participant."

I kissed along her smooth cheek until I reached her ear. "You know I don't want you too willing. I like it when you fight back."

She bent her neck to one side. "Not tonight," she breathed. "I'm all yours. Any way you want me."

I nibbled on her earlobe. "Any way?"

"As long as it involves him," she said as she pressed her hips into me. "So tell me then."

"Tell you what, Lace? How I'm going to bury myself deep inside you? How you'll scream my name again and again? How I'll kiss and lick your entire body?"

She squirmed, fumbling for my belt.

I reached between us and steadied her hand. "Patience, baby." I wanted to savor every moment. I wasn't sure I could. But I had to try.

She deserved to be worshiped, and all I wanted was rough, wet, hot, steamy, hair-pulling sex.

"Shower," she said as if she'd read my mind. She squirmed away from me and darted upstairs.

I tore after her. I barely had one foot on the bottom step when my phone rang. *Fuck.* I checked the screen. *Kelton.* I was going to ignore his call before I remembered that the triplets had gone up to visit our mom. "Is Mom okay?" I asked into the phone, my voice breaking as my pulse sped up.

"We just wanted to make sure Lacey got in safely," Kelton said in a serious tone.

I wanted to tell him to fuck off until I heard Kody ask, in an even deeper tone, "Well? Did she?"

"Yep. Everything is good." Then Lacey called my name. My gaze drifted up, and I stumbled.

She was posed on the top landing like a model with her hands on her hips, wearing nothing but a ball-squeezing pink thong. She batted her long lashes. "You shouldn't keep your prey waiting." Her hand slowly moved over her abs up toward her breasts. When she touched one nipple, my dick pounded for freedom.

I pushed End on my phone then sprinted up the stairs and stopped two steps below her. Perfect height. I sucked in one nipple as she played with the other, moaning.

"The shower is ready," she said.

She could've told me the world was ending. I didn't want to move from that spot. I was about to rip off her thong when she backed away, pivoted, and tossed a sexy smile over her shoulder before wiggling her beautiful ass as she disappeared into the bathroom.

I shed my clothes as fast as I could. By the time I reached the bathroom, she was already in the shower. Steam swirled around, fogging the mirror and the glass-encased shower. I opened the door and climbed in. She stood under the spray with her head tilted back. I watched, relishing the sight of the water cascading down over her breasts. I followed each drop as it slid lower down her body over her abs to her hips, and my gaze shot up to her face then back down to the tattoo of a polar bear on her hip.

She grasped my hand as she moved out from under the water. "You don't like it? It's just a tattoo."

No, it wasn't. It was more than that—way fucking more.

"I can't wear jewelry playing baseball. So I decided I wanted my good luck charm on me at all times."

I'd given her a polar bear charm for her birthday. But neither the sentiment nor the tat was what had my heart in a frenzy. The letter *K* was inked on one paw and *M* on the other. I softly rubbed two fingers over the small, tasteful creature, careful not to hurt her. The area around it was red.

Then I lifted my gaze to find tears in her meadow-green eyes. "I fucking love it."

"It doesn't look like you do." She worried her bottom lip.

I gently brushed my lips over hers. "You're my unconscious beauty. You're my whole world, Lacey. I love the tattoo."

Need rocked my body so fucking hard. I shaped her hips, easing her back until her shoulders touched the tiled wall. Her eyelids slid shut when I pressed against her. All the self-control I'd had earlier vanished.

Tangling my fingers in hers, I raised her arms over her head. My heart pulsed uncontrollably. I kissed her chin and down her smooth neck then back up. I gave both sides equal attention, covering every part of her before I made my way down to her breasts then lower until I reached her tattoo.

She mewed little noises as her body writhed against me.

I smiled against her tat. I fucking loved seeing my initials on her smooth skin and in a place only I would see. I licked it gently. She arched her back, shoving her breasts higher.

"What do you want, Lace?" I whispered, snaking my hands around to the small of her back. "Is it this?" As I kissed my way back up her toned body, I drew her to me, hard to soft, sucking one breast then the other. She tasted like all kinds of sugar, refined and yet raw.

I'd barely released her nipple when she climbed up my body, twining her legs around my waist. I braced my legs as I anchored her against the wall.

"Please, Kade," she whimpered, digging her delicate fingers into my shoulders.

Rough or gentle? I was torn. I wanted to savor her tropical scent, the honeyed taste of her skin, the heated feeling coursing through my body. She gave me a rush like I got when I skydived—euphoria.

She bit on my ear. A rumble barreled up my chest. She dug her heels into my ass and yanked on my hair. Gentle went out the fucking window. I became a madman. Our slick bodies slid together as she bit my ear hard. I couldn't wait any longer. I had to be inside her. One of the best things about sex with Lacey was that I didn't have to wear a condom anymore. She was on the pill, and we were both clean. My old man made sure of that. He made all us boys get tested at least once a year.

"I love you," she said between moans.

Slowly, with her body pinned between me and the tiled wall, I entered her.

She mewled. She was tight and wet as she squeezed her legs harder against me.

"Holy fuck, baby." I stilled. *Breathe, man.* I couldn't lose it so fast.

"Kade." She rocked forward.

Christ, between the way her body fit perfectly with mine and the way she purred my name, my legs damn near gave out.

The hot water continued to beat down, the sound a whisper, the feeling subtle.

She traced the outline of my mouth with her tongue, biting, sucking, then nipping everywhere except where it was cut. I guided her body as we moved together, making certain I had her secured comfortably.

"Heaven," I whispered against her lips before plundering my tongue inside the cavern of her mouth, claiming what was mine.

Our rhythm picked up. She held on tightly to my shoulders, her nails scoring my skin. Then her body tensed.

I tugged gently on her hair. "Look at me, baby." I had to see her beautiful face as she went over the edge.

Holding me prisoner with her lustful gaze, she arched her back slightly. Then a soft moan escaped her as she quivered against me.

My heart rate ramped up, and so did my pace. Her nails dug deeper into me, sending me that much closer to the cliff. She gripped the sides of my waist with her thighs. A tightness grew low in me, and with one last thrust, I exploded.

Goddamn. I held onto her as the tremors wracked my body.

"Amazing," she finally said, planting kisses all over my face. "So freaking amazing."

"You are," I said, trying to catch my breath. I couldn't believe this woman was all mine.

"Kade?"

"Mm." I inhaled her female scent again, making sure it was imprinted on my brain.

"The water is freezing."

Funny, I hadn't even felt the water turn cold. My mind was still fogged, and my body still burned. I released her gently as she slid down, almost falling.

I steadied her with both hands. "Can you walk?" I wasn't sure *I* could.

"My legs." She hugged herself, teeth chattering. "I need warmth."

I didn't. As she went in search of a towel, I stood under the cold shower. The icy droplets felt wonderful. After a couple of minutes, I shut off the water and stepped out.

She had a towel wrapped around her and held one out for me.

"Bed," I said as I dried off. All the pent-up energy and adrenaline slowly dissipated, and my body was shutting down fast.

"I need to dry my hair. Give me a minute." She lifted up on her toes and lightly kissed me. "You can get the bed warm for me."

"Baby, the bed will be hot when you get in it." That much I was sure of.

Her plump lips split into a smile.

I dried off quickly and made my way across the hall and into her room. I switched on the bedside lamp. Posters of Lacey's two favorite major league players, Jacoby Ellsbury and Clayton Kershaw, hung over her bed. I pulled back the comforter and slipped in. Sleep threatened, but I wanted to wait for her and enjoy every waking minute I could with her. I'd never liked cuddling until Lacey. For me, the act was too intimate, and before I'd met Lacey, I didn't do intimate.

The hair dryer droned, lulling me toward sleep. No sooner had I relaxed than a cold naked body curled up against me.

"Hey." I rotated on my side so we could spoon. "You're shivering." I rubbed my hands all over her silky body.

"California was so warm."

"Tell me more about your visit with the cops." The other night she'd only told me about the lead then changed the subject. She had a habit of switching topics when she didn't want to talk about something.

"Do we have to talk about it now?" Her voice began to trail off.

If I pushed her, it would send off alarms, or worse, she might have a panic attack. I pulled her tighter to me. "We'll talk tomorrow. Get some rest." After the weekend I'd had, I needed sleep.

"Kade, do you like... my tattoo?" She was fading.

"I love it, baby." I smoothed a hand over her hair.

"You're... not freaked out by your initials inked on me, are you?"

"You know my brothers might be."

"They'll never see the initials on my hip." She wiggled her gorgeous ass into my groin.

I'd kill them if they did. Her breathing deepened, and her body melted into mine. I kissed her head. The beautiful creature in my arms was so strong on the outside and so delicate on the inside. She was my strength—my polar bear. I'd bleed for her. I'd break every bone in my body for her. Right there, right then, I vowed I'd give my soul to protect her, even if that meant working for the devil.

Chapter 8

Kade

I COULDN'T SLEEP. AFTER LYING AWAKE for three hours, I decided to get something to drink. My mind was twisting and turning with shit I didn't want to think about.

I hesitated before I climbed out of bed, making sure Lacey was sound asleep. She was curled up in a fetal position facing me, her eyes moving rapidly, her long brown hair fanned out above her over her pillow. Her breathing was even, and if I weren't mistaken, she was dreaming of something nice since her luscious lips curled upward.

I slowly got up, threw on my jeans, then padded down to the kitchen. The house was eerily quiet save for the fridge humming. Moonlight sprayed in from a window in the small breakfast area just off the kitchen, allowing me to move around without having to turn on the light. I searched the cabinets adjacent to the fridge and snagged a glass.

I had my hand on the faucet when a bang from the front of the house caused me to drop the glass in the sink. I grabbed a knife from the wooden block, spun around, and carefully made my way out of the kitchen. As I veered into the hall, icy cold air slapped me, practically knocking the wind out of me.

Straight ahead, tree branches swayed in the distance as the sound of leaves rustling filtered into the house. The front door was wide open, the back of it banging against the doorstop.

What the fuck?

We probably hadn't closed it all the way earlier. With the knife ready to strike, I shuffled forward. I didn't think it would be necessary to call the cops unless I found signs of an intruder.

I passed the staircase and peeked into the front living room on my way to the front door. After a quick scan, I quietly closed the door and locked it. My heart slammed against my ribs as I darted upstairs, hoping Lacey was still asleep. She wouldn't handle this well. God, not after the home invasion in California.

I poked my head into her room and relaxed. She was still sleeping soundly. After I checked the three rooms upstairs and every room downstairs, my pulse slowed even more. The garage was my last stop since the house didn't have a basement. Lacey's Mustang sat in the far bay. I quickly walked around then went back in. I had to remind myself to talk to Lacey and make sure she switched on the alarm when she was home, although I'd been the last one in and as soon as she'd deactivated the alarm I'd been all over her.

I returned the knife back to the block and rummaged through my mind, wandering around the first floor checking every room again. Maybe the door didn't latch, and the high winds had blown it open. I scolded myself for being so careless. I'd only had Lacey and sex on the brain. *Think with that Mensa brain of yours, Maxwell.*

Raking a hand through my hair, I realized I was standing in the middle of her old man's office. A nightlight glowed from somewhere in the room. Just about every room in the house had a nightlight of sorts for Lacey. Maybe I could find a connection between Robinson and Lorenzino and validate what Pitt had told me. Something to give me some form of assurance Pitt wasn't blowing smoke up my ass. Not that any of what he'd said would ease my mind.

Music awards hung on the walls. The top of the desk was covered with file folders.

I crossed the carpeted floor to sit in the leather chair behind the desk. I switched on the desk lamp and started opening drawers. The top right one was laden with pens and paperclips. A box of cigars was the only thing inside the second. The last drawer was empty. The remaining three drawers on the left held computer cables and power cords.

I directed my attention to the file folders. The first five contained what appeared to be contracts and letters, all bearing Eko Records' letterhead. I opened the next one and found a picture of Harrison Lorenzino. *Fuck me.* I was about to flip it over when a scream tore through the house. I bolted upright. The picture and the folders fell from my hands. Someone was in the house. I sprinted out of the room, up the stairs—taking them two at a time—and into Lacey's room, where I stopped dead in my tracks.

The ominous scene in front of me sent ice through my veins. I knew she had nightmares. This wasn't one. This was a full-on night terror. I only knew the difference because my mom had them.

A ray of moonlight spilled in through a crack in the curtains, shining on the very spot where Lacey was kneeling on the bed, cradling her pillow in her hands, rocking back and forth. "No! No! No!" she screamed. "Please wake up, Mom. Please. You can't die."

Tears poured out of her wide-open eyes as her hair stuck to her damp face. I slowly approached her and eased down on the bed.

She continued to rock and cry and shake and breathe heavily in a trance-like state. Then she started petting the pillow as though she was smoothing a hand over someone's hair, murmuring, "I love you," over and over again.

I held my breath. Memories of my mom flooded back. She used to wake up with night terrors right after my sister died. My father taught me not to wake her, but to gently place a hand on her or hug her if I could. Night terrors usually occurred shortly after one fell asleep. It didn't matter. Demons didn't follow the definition of a night terror. Hell, they made their appearance whenever they wanted to.

I maneuvered myself so that I was sitting in front of her with my legs extended on either side of her, careful not to jar her awake. I got closer and wrapped my arms around her. When I did, she stopped rocking. I rubbed her back and kissed her hair as she snuggled into me.

I repeated over and over in a hushed whisper, "I love the crap out of you, baby. I'm here for you."

I didn't know if she could hear me, and if she did if it would help. Shit, but my mantra was definitely helping to calm *my* nerves. I did love the crap out of her. I'd never loved anyone as strongly as I loved the broken woman in my arms. PTSD was a hard illness to overcome, and I would do anything to help her heal.

As I kept repeating the two lines in a soft tone, my eyes began to burn with tears.

Once her breathing evened out, I removed the pillow from between us and gently tugged her to my chest. I dozed off while I held her, waking again as sunlight replaced the moonlight.

She stirred awake. I didn't move. Actually, I didn't think I could. My legs were asleep. Her hand started moving over my morning erection. Shit. The more she lazily rubbed, the harder I grew.

"Mornin'," she said sleepily. "Why are your jeans on?" she asked as though it was a sin for me to be wearing them.

For fuck's sake, it *was* a sin in my book. I should be naked like her and rolling on top of her as we slowly woke up together.

"And why am I sitting in your lap?" She lifted her head and kissed my neck.

I growled angrily at the voice in my head. She mistook that as her cue to slip her hands inside my jeans.

Control, asshole. With all the willpower I could muster, I pulled away her hand, when all I wanted to do was feel her hand wrapped around me.

She protested with a soft whine, and that sexy tone only served to make my entire body pulse with the need to repeat our earlier shower scene—only in bed.

"Baby, do you remember anything from last night?" I dragged the backs of my fingers along her cheek.

"Should I?" She batted those long lashes, and I thought back to when she'd recited those nursery rhymes for me. "Are you okay?" She got on her knees, and I lost it.

I pushed her onto her back and leaned over her, nipping at her lips, her neck, then her breasts. She arched into me, letting out a soft moan.

Then my phone rang.

I kissed my way up to her lips, ignoring the irritating piece of technology. When it stopped, I said, "We should get ready for school." We still had a couple of hours, but I needed to straighten up the folders on the desk. I leveled up on one hand. "You had a night terror earlier." I brushed a thumb over her eyebrow.

"Do I want to know what I was doing?" Her eyes were downcast.

"Let's just say it was about your mom." I nipped at her nose so she would look at me. "Did something happen in California?"

According to Lacey, she'd had nightmares for the longest time after she buried her mom and sister. My guess was she'd also had night terrors. My old man had explained to me that nightmares occur during REM sleep and people usually wake up kicking and screaming. In the end, they remembered either the last of the nightmare or sometimes all of it. With night terrors, nine times out of ten, people hardly recalled them at all.

"Maybe visiting my mom's grave stirred up old memories."

No doubt. "Can we talk about what the cops said other than the lead?" I hated to jump into this conversation while she was naked and my body was begging to do so sexy things to her again, but I had to find out what she was afraid to tell me while we had some privacy.

She tensed beneath me. "The police believe that whoever killed Julie and Mom were after something and that they may not have gotten it."

Every muscle in my body tightened. Pitt's words filled my head: "James Robinson has something the Lorenzino family wants."

Looks like I'm going to be a tutor.

Chapter 9

Lacey

SILENCE FOLLOWED US TO SCHOOL that morning. I rode with Kade since I hated driving in the snow. I stared out the window, not paying attention to the passing landscape. I was searching deep within my mind to recall any part of my dream, but I was coming up empty. Kade had said it was about my mom, and I wanted to remember. My psychiatrist, Dr. Davis, had said that analyzing a dream sometimes helps you to cope with and control intrusive memories. Between the discussion at the police station and visiting the cemetery, my subconscious was probably working overtime.

Kade's rough fingers grazed my cheek, and I leaned into his touch. "I'd love to be in your head right now."

"Was I doing anything weird when I was having the bad dream?" I glanced at him. *Hopefully nothing embarrassing.*

His copper eyes filled with concern. "You were calling out your mom's name." He interlaced his fingers with mine. "It's okay. You weren't sleepwalking."

I'd been known to walk in my sleep. He brought my hand to his lips and kissed my fingers.

"Do you want to tell me why you're so tense?" Something seemed to be bothering him. I didn't know if it had anything to do with my dream. He always worried about me. He'd seen me black out.

He made a right into the lot of the sports complex and parked in his usual spot behind the school. A mixture of deciduous and evergreen trees dotted the landscape in front of us. Several trees were showing signs of spring with tiny buds on their branches.

"We didn't turn on the alarm last night. You usually do turn it on every night though, right?" He cut the engine.

"Of course, but last night I had a sexy guy distracting me," I teased, trying to lighten the mood.

One dimple emerged, then two, then his honey-brown hair toppled over his eyes. He met me halfway. Once his lips touched mine, delicious tingles shot down my belly, erasing any thoughts of bad dreams or alarms. Kade always did that for me. I loved being able to sleep with him without worrying about the time or rushing home. I had at least two more nights to snuggle with him.

"My dad might not be home until the weekend," I said against his lips.

He had meetings at Eko Records, and he wanted to check on Zeppelins, the club he owned in LA. I'd encouraged him to stay as long as he needed, but the conversation had turned into a full-blown argument. I understood his worry about me staying home alone, considering what Detective Fisher had told us, but I couldn't live with someone babysitting me all the time. I knew how to handle a gun. I knew self-defense, and I had a group of guys who would protect me at all costs. Kade and his brothers were fiercely protective to the point where they could suffocate a girl.

So, I'd come clean. I told Dad that Kade was staying with me while he was in California. After all, I was eighteen. Initially, he'd protested. After I explained to him that Kade would kill anyone who touched me and that we were responsible adults, he reluctantly gave in. He liked Kade, but I was his little girl.

Kade's kissing my ear jerked me back to the present. "Shower again tonight, then?" he asked.

A bang on the window made both of us jump. Kade pulled away and turned to the driver's side window. I peeked around Kade to find Kelton's not-so-handsome mug staring at us.

I gasped. "What the hell happened to his face?"

Black and purple bruises marred the area around his eyes and jaw. His nose even appeared broken.

"I told you. Brothers playing around."

"You beat him that bad?" My voice hitched. "What did you do? Take a baseball bat to his face?" There was no way Kade would inflict bruises like those on his brothers. I thought back to our phone conversation on Friday night when I was at the LAPD. He'd sounded out of sorts on the phone.

Kade growled before he said, "Why don't you say 'hi' to the triplets?" He tipped his head at Kross's Jeep. "I'll be out in a minute. I need to send a text to Hunt."

"You've been on that phone all morning."

"I'll be out before Kelton gets his hands on you."

I doubted that. Kelton was a guy who liked to hug, and not a simple hug—a grizzly bear hug. I shrugged, grabbed my backpack, and jumped out. Once outside, I zipped up my jacket as I rounded the back of the truck. Before I could even lift my head or protest about the freezing temperatures, I was tucked into strong arms.

"Hey, girl." Kelton squeezed me as though he was trying to get the last of the toothpaste out of the tube.

"I thought I taught you how to hug gently," I managed to say before he let me go. "What happened to you? You look like a raccoon." We wandered over to Kross's Jeep, parked on the other side of Kade.

Kross and Kody were leaning casually against the Jeep mumbling something. Kade got out of his truck, his eyes narrowed and his lips pursed.

Kelton grinned at me like the cat who caught the canary. "The girl I dated over the weekend was wild in bed."

I rolled my eyes. "I smell a lie." I hadn't said much about Kade's bruised jaw or fat lip. The brothers always helped Kross spar in the boxing ring they had in their garage. So when Kade had said it was brothers fighting, I brushed it off.

I cozied up to Kade against his truck. "What happened for you to beat Kelton like that?" Anger was beginning to bubble to the surface. "Dare I ask if you guys saw Greg over the weekend?" If they had, I didn't understand why they didn't just tell me. I was getting angrier that they kept evading my questions.

Kross and Kody choked or laughed, I couldn't tell which. Kade glared at them. I got the feeling I'd hit the nail on the head. I wasn't going to blow a gasket, yet. I wanted Kade to come clean. I knew his brothers wouldn't. They could be interrogated by the law or an enemy of our country and they wouldn't give up information, no matter how much pain was inflicted. Although trying one more time might spur Kade into action.

A gust of wind whipped my hair in all directions. I brushed it from my eyes and skimmed my gaze over Kross. "You're the one who has a legit excuse, and your face is practically clear." He had a small cut over one of his eyebrows.

"Darling, I'm the best." He crossed toned arms over his chest, his massive biceps bulging through the letter jacket he was wearing. "The dude didn't stand a chance against me. And neither do my siblings."

Cocky much? I diverted my gaze to Kody. In the past, he'd been the one who was always willing to talk.

He lifted his hands shoulder height. "I had my fill of fighting. I don't need another broken nose, especially not from my brothers."

Just for good measure, I pinned a look on Kelton. He combed a hand through his disheveled hair as his blue eyes stood out in stark contrast to the blackish bruises. I waited for him to say something, but the only sound was the wind.

"And all of you are full—"

Kade popped off the truck, pivoted, and blocked me from his brothers. When I opened my mouth, he planted his lips on mine, warm and soft, tasting like mint.

After he'd had his fill, I said, "Your kiss may make my panties wet, but it doesn't fog my brain. You're not telling me something. You know how I hate that, Kade. Let me decide what I can and can't handle." It had been a while since Kade and I had fought, and when we did it was usually about things he held back from me or didn't want to talk about until he was ready.

He eased back and shot a quick glance over his shoulders. I peered around him. His brothers were gone. I didn't blame them. Anytime Kade and I got into an argument, they scurried away like cockroaches.

"We're going to be late," he said. "We'll talk tonight."

I didn't like when anyone demanded I tell them something I wasn't ready to tell either. Regardless, I had the urge to stomp my foot and scream. "Tonight it is."

He went to grab my hand, and I shoved it into my coat pocket. He angled his head at me. I shrugged. We strolled down the path to the main building. Kids were trampling across the snow-covered lawn, heading into school. Puffy clouds skated across the sky. The way it had been snowing, I doubted Coach Dean was going to have baseball practice outdoors this week. We'd been using the indoor facility for the last three weeks. Coach had started practices mid-February.

Kade took long strides, his boots leaving large footprints in the thin layer of snow on the black pavement. I had to take an extra step to keep up with him.

The tension between us vanished when we made it to the back entrance of the school, where we saw Aaron. Then all my ire was transferred to him. He sauntered toward us with a swagger that said, "Fuck with me and you're dead." *We'll see about that*, I thought. I'd been stewing on what I would do if he messed with *me*.

As he approached, I did a double take. Purple bruises contrasted with his green eyes and dotted his jaw. He appeared worse than Kelton. He smiled broadly as though he was genuinely happy to see Kade and me. Again, I had to look twice. He never smiled at Kade, let alone me. I felt like I was in some alternate universe.

"Maxwell," Aaron said as he blocked us from the school's entrance. His blond hair stuck out of his blue ball cap.

Kade scowled.

"Hi, Robinson. We have practice inside today." His tone was kind, not snarky like it usually was.

I looked behind me just to be sure he was talking to me. I wasn't the only Robinson in the school.

"I'll be there," I said in a sarcastic tone. It was hard to be nice to him. He'd had his girl, Tammy Reese, break into my locker to steal my sports gear during tryouts last September. "Did Tammy do that to your face?" I raised my fingers to my face. I didn't think she had, but maybe my question would throw him off and he would come out and tell me who did.

Aaron asked in sugary tone, "Your arm ready for a great season?"

"I'm ready for anything." Again, I couldn't help but be scornful.

"Well, then. I guess you're in for a fun time." He was talking to me, but his eyes were on Kade.

The scowl never left Kade's face.

Whatever. Aaron Seever might be crazy. He also might be extremely smart. It didn't matter. I was onto him and ready for any psychological games he had in store. I was also ready to get into a boxing ring with Kade.

After the little encounter with Aaron, Kade went his way and I went mine. We only had one class together—psychology—and that was the last class of the day, although we would see each other at lunch. Maybe by then I would have calmed down, and it would give him time to process whatever he was keeping from me.

Most of the morning dragged. I tried to concentrate on my subjects, the teachers talking, even Becca, my best friend, jabbering about her weekend. But all I could think about was why Kade wouldn't tell me what had happened to him and Kelton. After seeing Aaron, I suspected Kelton and Aaron had gotten into it. I could be wrong though.

Since it was our free period, Becca and I headed to the library.

"Do you want to talk about what's bothering you?" Her dark eyebrows furrowed.

The final bell rang, and the students in the hall scattered.

"I will." I thought the separation from Kade would help me to calm down. Maybe talking about it with Becca would help. Maybe Kross had filled her in. "I'll meet you in the library. I need to use the restroom."

She went on ahead and disappeared around a corner. As she did, Coach Dean, the baseball coach, spotted me and headed my way. His bald head shined. Next to him was none other than the bane of my existence, Aaron. He had a sinister grin glued to his face as though he was up to something. Or maybe it was all the cuts and bruises that made him appear more evil.

I silently growled.

They both settled in front of me. I kept my focus on Aaron, tightening my hand around the strap of my backpack.

"Lacey, just the person I wanted to see," Coach said flatly. "I'd like a chat with you and Aaron in my office in fifteen minutes." Then he left Aaron and me alone.

Aaron's green eyes roamed up and down the entire length of my body. I yearned to punch him. My problem was that I already had one strike against me for fighting with Tammy Reese last fall. I'd also promised my dad I'd be good. More importantly, I had to be an angel. Otherwise, Coach would reprimand me or, worse, throw me off the team, and I couldn't get thrown off the team. The college scouts would be at our games, and I needed to be on the team for them to see me.

"You got a problem?" I removed my phone from my jeans and pretended to read a text. I was really hitting the record button. I decided that anytime I was alone with Aaron, I'd record what he said to me. I had no intentions of letting him scare me away. I slipped my phone back in my jeans.

"I see you made it back from California. What a shame." He dragged the back of his thumbnail just under his bottom lip as he sized me up again.

"How come you didn't lead with that statement when I was with Kade earlier?" I wanted to scrub my body with a pumice stone to rid my skin of all the oily sleaze he was giving me. "Afraid he would've added to your collection of bruises on your ugly mug?" Anger began to coil inside me like a rattlesnake getting ready to strike. I balled my hands into fists.

He scanned the empty hall in all directions then slid closer to me. He lost the creepy smirk. "A plane crash would've been best." He went to touch my hair.

I moved back, holding in a gasp. "It would be kind of hard for you to cause a plane crash, unlike a motorcycle crash. Isn't that how you got rid of Mandy Shear?" I didn't think he would tell me, but why not ask the tough questions even though all I wanted to do was run, panic, and puke?

"We need to see Coach." He started to swagger off like he was above everyone else.

I grasped his arm. "Who messed up your face?"

He half snorted, like an ass. "Your boyfriend hasn't told you?"

I felt my eyebrows coming together as I inclined my head, releasing his arm.

"Oh, this will be good. Have you asked Kade how he got his fat lip or Kelton how he got his bruises?"

Voices peppered the hall. A couple of kids were congregating near a bank of lockers not far from us.

"Get to the point." My hands were still balled at my side.

"Well, let me be the bearer of some fantastic news. Kade beat the shit out of my cousin. Kelton and I went at it. Then my cousin got shot by one of Pitt's thugs." He laughed, a sound that sliced through every one of my nerves. "Classic Maxwell brothers. Not sharing." He made a pouting face. "I also bet you asked what happened and they gave you some bullshit answer."

I pushed my tongue against my bottom teeth as I held my breath, debating whether to push this asshole out of my face or find Kelton and give him more bruises to match the ones he already had. Or hunt Kade down right now. A buzzing in my head started low.

"You're dating the wrong guy, sweetheart."

The word *sweetheart* unleashed my pent-up rage. I raised my balled-up fist. The buzzing in my head grew louder. Over the noise, two words resonated. *Baseball scholarship.* My hand stopped just before Aaron's face. He didn't flinch.

"Go ahead," he said. "I'd love to see you get benched your first game."

Baseball scholarship. Scouts.

I lowered my hand but moved closer to him so only a paper-thin space separated us. His breath smelled like onions. "You're not worth it. It's sad you get off taunting girls with your psycho horseshit. You're going to end up a lonely man." I realized at that moment that he had to have low self-esteem to be jealous of a girl. Or maybe he was screwing with me because his cousin and Kade had a longstanding feud. Kade had said at one time that Greg would do anything to get back at him. Whatever the case, Aaron needed to know he wasn't getting under my skin.

I stormed into the bathroom, went directly to the sink, and splashed water on my face. Why couldn't we just get along? The only good thing to come out of the conversation was he confirmed my suspicions about Kade lying to me, which wasn't even good. Unless Aaron was lying, which I didn't think he was. He had satisfaction written all over his face.

My heart hurt. I didn't understand why Kade would keep that from me. He knew the rumor mill at school. He also knew I would notice Kelton's bruises. Something wasn't adding up.

The door creaked open.

"Get out, Aaron," I sneered. "Do you want to get benched your first game for being a stalker?"

"Touch Aaron and I'll use my last strike with Principal Sanders," said a familiar voice. "It sure would be worth it to break your limbs so you can't play ball at all this season." Tammy sidled up to the sink next to me and posed in the mirror, smoothing a hand over her cheerleader uniform like she thought she was beautiful.

Well, she was. Her wide blue eyes stood against her silky reddish-brown hair that fell below her ears. But she lost all that prettiness when her snarky attitude got in her way.

I grabbed a couple of paper towels. "Mind your own business." I patted my face.

She pushed me away from the sink. "Aaron is my business."

"Then tell your boyfriend if he dishes out his psycho crap then he better be prepared to take what's coming."

I marched out because otherwise I wouldn't be playing any ball. The only strikes I wanted were on the ball field—not the kind given out by the principal.

I jogged all the way to the sports complex. Once inside, I sent Becca a text about my meeting with Coach. Then I stuffed my bad mood into a box, rolled back my shoulders, and ambled down to Coach's office. I'd read an article in a magazine on the plane about attitude. I couldn't remember all of it, but the one line that had stayed with me said that life is ten percent what happens to you and ninety percent how you react to it. Why not experiment to see if I could control myself? So, I checked my attitude at the door.

The buzzing in my head diminished as I entered. A boy I hadn't seen before was sitting in one of the two chairs in front of Coach's desk. He had curly blond hair and wore black-rimmed glasses. Aaron sat in the other chair.

"Come in, Lacey." Coach waved me in.

Immediately the new guy stood like a gentlemen while moron Aaron didn't move.

"Hi, I'm Shaun Spears. Take my chair," he said as he moved to stand to the side of Coach's desk.

"Thank you," I said before silently snarling at Aaron.

"Shaun enrolled today," Coach said. "He moved up from North Carolina and is interested in the remaining pitching position we have open. He'll be joining you at practice today. I won't be there, so Aaron," Coach said to our captain, "show him the ropes. Get him warmed up. Work with him on pitches. See what he has. I'll have time to put him through drills later in the week." Coach glanced at Shaun. "Lacey is our starting pitcher. She'll also help you. I want you both"— his head bobbed from Aaron to me—"to be civil. If Shaun is as good as his stats say, and with Lacey's arm, we have an even better shot at State." He clasped his hands on his desk. "Any questions?"

No one said a word.

"Good. Shaun, you can go. I need to speak to these two alone." Coach wagged his finger at Aaron and me.

Shaun smiled at me then left.

"I promised a colleague of mine at Swain Middle School that I'd supply two of my ballplayers to help him with ball practice at some point within the next few weeks. I wanted to give you a heads up that you two have been selected. I'll let you know when Mr. Camp is ready." He picked up a pen.

"Why us?" I crossed my arms over my chest. Not that I minded helping out, but I wasn't sure working with Aaron was the best idea.

"Helping and teaching others the game of baseball helps you to sharpen your skills. Volunteer work will help your college applications."

Aaron went to open his mouth.

Coach held up his hand. "That's all."

Aaron glowered at me and stomped out. I stared at Coach, trying to figure out what he was up to. He knew Aaron and I didn't get along. Not that we argued on the field, but the tension was super thick between us.

Coach also suspected that Aaron had been involved with Tammy when she stole my gear, and he knew Aaron had bullied Mandy.

Somehow Aaron and I had to find common ground so we didn't kill each other. Otherwise, the chemistry of the team would go to shit, and we wouldn't be a well-oiled machine. I wanted to win State, and I wanted to impress the ASU scouts. I couldn't have Aaron rattling my cage the entire season.

Chapter 10

Kade

THE NEWS OF SULLIVAN GETTING shot spread around school like wildfire, and the ass didn't even go to our school. By lunchtime, I knew I should've spilled the beans about the fight to Lacey before school. I was an idiot. I wasn't thinking straight. I was so worried she would panic. I knew she was starting to connect the dots, especially after we ran into Aaron. I was scratching my head as to why he hadn't bragged about the incident. He'd also sounded sweet. I chalked up his nice demeanor to his psychological games. Or was he really being nice because Pitt put the fear of God into him? He did piss his pants, after all.

I was sitting with Kelton in the busy cafeteria when I caught sight of Lacey walking toward me through the crowd. With her shoulders back, fury swimming in her eyes, and her nostrils flaring like a raging bull's, she looked like she wanted to knee me in the balls. She knew about Friday night. I didn't think it was Aaron who'd told her since I'd sent him a glare of warning. I wasn't sure if he'd gotten the message or whether he would keep his mouth shut if he had. I shrugged it off. I'd been in the doghouse before now anyway.

All of sudden my head hurt as I tried to anticipate what the fuck I was going to say. *The truth, asshole.* The bustling cafeteria certainly wasn't the place to have a conversation. No, first I had to make sure she wasn't going to make a scene. When she got mad, her emotions got the best of her to the point where she wouldn't listen. It was a normal reaction for anyone, but her rage was stage worthy. She'd flipped out in this very room when she'd thought I'd lied about my feelings for her. The cafeteria ladies had run for cover.

"Who pissed in her Wheaties?" Kelton chomped on a toothpick. "Uh oh, I bet she knows about Friday. You're going to have to come clean, bro." He lifted his legs to rest on the chair beside him.

I knew he was right. I was waging a war with myself about telling her about my meeting with Pitt. The fight was one thing, but my conversation with Pitt was a whole different ballgame. I had to verify what Pitt had told me. I didn't want to ruin Lacey's relationship with her father for no reason. I didn't want her panicking or blacking out. Her blackouts ripped my heart to shreds each time. Maybe I was trying to protect myself more than her. All I wanted was for my girl to be happy and healthy and live her dream instead of her nightmares. She wanted that scholarship to ASU as bad as I wanted a future with her. I had to keep her focused on her dream and keep her safe at the same time.

"I will when the time is right. Whatever she's mad about, I'll deal."

"It's your funeral. That girl will have your dick twisted forty different ways." He winced.

I was about to tell my brother to fuck off when Tyler Langley strode up to Lacey. I kicked out my legs and crossed my ankles, keeping watch on Tyler. The star quarterback of Kensington High wanted Lacey badly. Too badly in my book. I still wasn't over the fact that he'd been at her house when I'd shown up unexpectedly a few months back. The fact that I'd found Lacey with her blouse open just made matters all the worse, but she'd told me they were just friends. I trusted her. I sure as hell didn't trust him.

"It's kind of sad," Kelton said. "Tyler wants to eat your girl. You better pray she doesn't dump your ass for lying."

"Tyler knows I'd lose my shit on him if he ever touched her the wrong way," I muttered.

Kross came out of nowhere and slid into the seat next to me.

"Since you're both here," I said, "can one of you give Lacey a ride to and from practice and afterwards stay with her until I get back? I set up a meeting with Pitt this afternoon. I shouldn't be too late."

"Sorry, I can't," Kross said. "I have to meet Jay. He lined up another fight. So I need to work out."

I swung my gaze to Kelton.

"No way." Kelton shook his head. "I got a date tonight."

"Kel, I don't want her alone." I checked on Lacey. She was laughing. What the fuck was Tyler saying to make her laugh?

"Well, I don't want my balls to be alone." Kelton swiveled in his seat to face Kross and me.

Some girl snickered at the table one over from us.

"Postpone the love fest." My tone dropped. I hated to exert my big-brother authority. But we were talking about Lacey. If I lost her, my life was over. She gave me the strength to move forward, to see that life could have a purpose. "It's a couple of hours at most. Kody has guitar lessons. I'd ask Hunt, but he's meeting me at Pitt's office. You'll still make your date. Besides, after tonight, we'll have bodyguards on her."

"So, you're taking the tutoring job?" Kelton asked, dropping the attitude.

"If Pitt meets my demands, then yes." I hadn't figured out all my demands, except that I wanted Hunt to be one of her bodyguards. He'd told me on the phone this morning he was now working for Pitt.

"Probably a wise move," Kross said.

I prayed it was. I also prayed I'd relax a little and get my head clear enough to figure out the connection between Mr. Robinson and Lorenzino.

Lacey wasn't talking to Tyler anymore. Becca was standing with her and another dude who I'd never seen before, and I knew practically all the faces in this school.

"Who's the dude with Becca?" I asked. The guy wore black-rimmed glasses that were bigger than his face. And he clearly had a death wish, since his hand was resting in the small of Becca's back. She appeared to be oblivious to the guy's touch, but Kross sure wasn't.

He growled, and his body went rigid. "Whoever the fuck he is, the dickwad better get his hands off my girlfriend."

"Let's go." I wanted to talk to Lacey, and I needed to get some air. I hooked my backpack over my shoulder.

The three of us got up. Kelton hung back to talk to a table of girls.

Kross sneered at the guy next to Becca as we approached the threesome. We had about twenty more minutes before lunch ended. Kids were still coming in while others were leaving.

"Hey," Becca said, pressing her tiny hands on Kross's chest as she lifted up on her toes to kiss him.

He drew her to him, his gaze never wavering from the stranger as he let Becca peck him on the lips.

"This is Shaun. He's new here." Becca's cheeks flushed.

Kross snarled at Shaun.

"Don't worry, man. I'm not hitting on your girl." Then his hazel eyes landed on Lacey. "So, I'll meet you at the indoor facility today?"

She batted her lashes at me. Did that mean she wasn't mad anymore? Or was I making too much out of her earlier body language? Yeah, guilt always made me think the worst.

"Shaun plays baseball. You know Coach Dean has a spot for one more player." She grabbed my hand.

I grinned at my girl. "Can we talk outside?" What with the news about Sullivan getting shot and the tension between Lacey and me, it was time for me to at least tell her about Friday night.

We wound our way through the halls and out the main entrance. Just outside the glass doors was a cement bench. She shivered. I immediately removed my sweatshirt and gave it to her. She slipped it over her head.

"I did lie to you." I kept her hands in my lap so they'd stay warm.

"Why?" Her tone was even.

"Honestly, I'm an idiot. Sullivan and Seever ambushed Kelton. Then Sullivan got shot by one of Pitt's men who was at the fight with Pitt. It was an accident, and it scared the hell out of me. I thought Kelton got shot. I wanted to tell you when you got home. But I was selfish. All I wanted was you and a quiet night. Then when you saw Kelton this morning, that's when I panicked. I'm sorry. Will you forgive me?" I rested my forehead against hers as a weight lifted off my shoulders.

"I'm still mad at you, Maxwell. I gave you ample opportunity to tell me. I hate that you tried to shut me up in front of your brothers by kissing me. You shouldn't put your brothers in a spot where they have to lie either. None of that was cool." She mashed her lips into a thin line.

She was right on all levels. "I'll apologize to them as well." Hell, as brothers, we owed each other a lifetime of apologies. "Are we okay?" *Please say yes.*

She gave me a weak smile. "For now."

I briefly closed my eyes. I was okay with *for now*. Lacey stewed on things longer than most people I knew.

"So, when you walked into the cafeteria, you were seething. Then Tyler had you laughing. Care to share?" Since Lacey did let things bother her, to turn from mad to happy in an instant wasn't in her nature.

"I saw Aaron in the hall. He told me all about the fight. Since you weren't talking, I asked Tyler about it. He said something sarcastic about fights among boys being about who had the bigger penis." Her lips split into a dazzling smile.

My muscles had tensed when she'd mentioned Aaron, although I didn't know how to respond to Tyler's analogy except to kiss her. She didn't return the kiss. I knew she needed time, but that didn't stop my stomach from hurting at the rejection.

"How did that conversation go between you and Aaron?" I clenched my teeth.

"He's was an ass, but I can handle him," she said with conviction. "He knows I'm onto his psychological games. He's not going to ruin my season. If he does, then I'll ruin his."

At least for now I wasn't worried too much about Aaron. My brothers would be at practice anyway if Aaron got out of hand. Her determination to push toward her dream of a baseball scholarship always made me smile.

"I'm going to hang with Hunt while you're at practice. Kelton can give you a ride to practice and then home."

"Or I can get a ride from Renee or Shaun."

Renee would be fine. Lacey had been hanging with her since they'd both made the team. But Shaun. *Like hell.* In light of everything Pitt had told me, there was no fucking way Lacey was getting in a car with a total stranger alone. I'd almost be happier with Aaron giving her a ride home. Almost. I wasn't going to make a big deal about it. Kelton would bring her home.

"What do you think they want? I mean, the ones who killed your mom and Julie?"

"Where did that come from?" Her delicate brows were pinched together.

"It's been on my mind since you told me."

She lifted a shoulder. "I don't know. I asked Rob, and he doesn't know either. At first, when Detective Fisher asked him about this guy, Dennis Weeks, and showed us a picture of him, Rob said he'd never seen or even heard of the guy. But I got the impression he did by the way he hesitated, looking at my dad before he answered. It was like he was asking my dad for permission to answer. Like they both knew something. I asked Rob why he was so nervous, but he said he's just on edge. He wants to put all this behind him just like I do." Tears clouded her eyes. "Tonight I'm going to look. My dad keeps a box of his and my mom's treasures. I'm not sure I know what to search for, but I have to try." She blinked and shivered.

"The bell is about to ring." I heaved to my feet, pulling her up with me. "Can I help?" Maybe we could figure this out together. Maybe I'd have some new information after I saw Pitt.

"I'd like that." She peered up at me, relief coloring her gorgeous face.

"So fights among boys are all about penises, huh?" I held the door open for her.

She laughed, and my heart lit up like fireworks. I wanted nothing more than to see her happy. I didn't know what was going to happen in the near future, or if the cops would ever catch the fuckers who'd ruined Lacey's world. But I was extremely certain of one thing. I was going to marry this beautiful girl someday.

Chapter 11

Kade

THE SCHOOL DAY COULDN'T END fast enough. I was relieved Lacey and I were able to talk at lunch but was anxious to get to Boston, meet with Pitt, and get back to Ashford. Plus, I'd been thinking about the guy she'd mentioned, Dennis Weeks. We hadn't had much time to dig deeper into who Dennis was before the bell rang.

I was inhaling the fresh air as I hurried to my truck when I heard someone call my name. I turned and found Tyler jogging toward me. I thought I should thank him for making Lacey laugh.

"Kade, wait up." He shoved his hands into the pockets of his hooded Kensington sweatshirt. "So, what went down on Friday night? Are the rumors true? Sullivan got shot?"

I hated gossip. "Yeah. But I got to run, man."

He shifted his stance. "When are you going to end that feud with Sullivan? Are you going to keep putting Lacey through hell? What if she was with you? What if he decides to hurt her to get to you? Have you thought about that?"

I laughed hauntingly. Sullivan was the least of my worries. I got in Tyler's face. "Stay out of my business, Langley."

His hands came up to push me away. He succeeded too. The dude's six-foot-one height matched mine, and he was all muscle. He reminded me a lot of Hunt but with a broad chest and blond hair. The only difference was Tyler had what Lacey called ocean-blue eyes. I hadn't paid much attention to the color of anyone's eyes until I looked into Lacey's. How could I not notice those deep, mesmerizing green eyes framed by the longest fucking lashes I'd ever seen? They made my heart race and my stomach flip.

"You're going to fuck up your relationship with Lacey." His tone held a bucketload of jealousy and animosity. "And I don't want to see her get hurt."

I opened the door to my truck before I ended up sending my fist into his face. "I can take care of my girl," I shot over my shoulder. Lacey and I still had a lot to learn about each other. Hell, a relationship with a girl was new for me. My fucking up along the way was going to happen. No one was perfect. One thing I knew for sure. I'd fight with every ounce of strength I had to make sure I didn't hurt her.

"Kade, she's one of my best friends. I'd kill anyone if they hurt her, including you."

I halted midstride. He had huge balls. I stormed back to him. "Friends or not, you want more with Lacey, and I don't trust you."

"You should, because you're going to need me." His tone was cocky.

"Okay, I'll bite. Why is that?"

"I'm the only one who's going to keep you two from splitting up."

I tilted my head one way then the other. "Come again?"

"That rainy night in September right before the last baseball tryout when you found me at her house? You got so fucking pissed seeing me there and then seeing her with her blouse open. After you left, I was the one who held her while she cried her eyes out. I was the one who rubbed her back, telling her you were a good guy. I love her enough to make sure she gets what she wants. Sadly, for me, she wants you. I'm not an asshole who runs from my friends. Whatever the fuck is going on, get your shit together. Because if you don't... Well, you can finish that sentence." He studied me as his eyebrows knitted. No doubt eyeing my fists. "When you decide that you don't want to beat my face in, we can talk." The fucker walked away as rage filled every part of my body.

I stewed on what Tyler had said on my drive to Boston. I tried to push his words—*I love her*—out of my head. I couldn't. I'd never been the jealous type. Then again, I'd never been in love before. I knew lying to her was one way to push her away from me.

"Fuck," I screamed as loud as I could, the word practically echoing inside the confines of my truck. "Get your shit together, Maxwell."

By the time I reached Pitt's office, my head was pounding like someone had increased the bass on a stereo to its highest setting. The same receptionist as before gave me the all clear to proceed to Pitt's office. Hunt was already seated in one of the wingback chairs. Pitt wasn't around.

"You look like shit, man. Rough day?" Hunt asked in a concerned tone.

"You could say that." I took a seat in the remaining chair. "Where's Pitt?" I wanted to get back to Lacey. I wanted to make up for lying. I wanted us to put our heads together to search her house. Sometimes when people are too close to things, they miss what was in front of them all along. Most of all, I wanted to find the killer.

"He had to step out for something. Are you sure you want to do this?"

"Tutoring? No. Finding the killer? Yes." I rubbed my temples.

Pitt's voice filtered in from the hall before he entered and circled his desk. "Gentlemen. Can't say I'm surprised you're both here."

I growled.

"Save the *I-told-you-so* crap," Hunt said.

"Easy, bro," a familiar voice said. "Where are your manners? Mom and Dad taught you better than that."

Hunt rolled his eyes as Wes, Hunt's brother, sauntered in. Tall, husky, and meaner than Hunt, Wes grinned, his front teeth overlapping each other. He was dressed all in black with a gun on his hip.

"Now that we're all here." Pitt smoothed a hand over his tie as he eased into his leather chair.

Wes went to stand at the front corner of Pitt's desk.

"Wes is in charge of all the security and bodyguards. He'll have two men on Lacey at all times. Kade, you'll be tutoring Chloe one day a week up until her finals. You'll meet her here in the conference room." He was all business now.

"Whoa! Slow down." I straightened. "I told you on the phone, I have some demands before I sign my kidneys over to you."

"Of course." Pitt opened his palms and bowed his head.

"Don't patronize me." My jaw tightened.

"You mean Chloe really needs a tutor?" Hunt asked. "And with all the tutors in Boston, you chose Kade? Or are you using him to get closer to Robinson?"

I flicked a thumb at Hunt. "He has a point. Tell me what you know about the connection between Lorenzino and Robinson. We're going to be working together, and you're entrusting me with your daughter. I deserve to know at least that much."

Pitt pursed his lips.

"Tell him, boss," Wes said. "You know how stubborn Robinson is. He's not going to tell Kade. Shit, he hasn't even told his daughter yet. We need to keep planning."

Hunt and I shared a confused look. Nausea was eating my stomach lining at the direction the conversation was taking.

Pitt covered his chin with his hand as he studied me. "I don't know the connection. I don't know what Lorenzino wants. Robinson doesn't even know. At least that's my assumption. But in my organization, we protect our own."

Dryness scratched my throat. "Meaning what? That you're related to Robinson?" I didn't see the resemblance.

"My wife, Gloria, is," Pitt said. "Her parents adopted James."

My head jerked back. *Fuck me.* Hunt gaped.

To say I was shocked would be an understatement, but I was still confused as ever. "Why were you so cryptic when we met the other day? Why not just come out and tell me then? Why smoke-screen all this with tutoring your daughter?"

"I was feeling you out, and Robinson doesn't want help," Pitt said. "He's trying to handle this whole situation on his own. I get that. A man wants to be able to take care of his family. You certainly understand that, Kade. I don't have a caring bone in my body for Robinson. I *do*, however, when it comes to my family. If Lorenzino finds out the connection, my family could be in danger, too. I need to know what Lorenzino is after." Then he shifted his dark eyes to Hunt. "And Chloe does need a tutor."

"So you think I can convince Robinson to align with you? No offense, man, but I don't exactly want anything to do with the mob either."

"Sometimes, Kade, choices are made for us, especially since we can't choose our families. And family is everything. Isn't it?" Pitt steepled his hands, his face tightening.

Family was everything. I massaged the back of my neck. "And why do you think he's going to listen to me?"

"As I said to you in our meeting the other day, you have a way of getting people to listen to you. You'll figure it out. In the meantime, Chloe is finishing up her first year at Harvard. She's having trouble with one of her basic math courses. And you let us take care of shadowing Lacey." Pitt crossed one leg over the other.

I took in some stale air laced with cigar smoke. "Let's back up for a second. If Mr. Robinson hasn't told Lacey any of this, how much can I share with her?" I couldn't lie to her again. I wasn't even certain I could withhold this information from her. If she found out I knew, I'd be pushing her into Tyler's arms, and this was more than a fight about who had the bigger dick. I couldn't step into her relationship with her father.

Wes pressed his fingers into the desk. "Kade, talk to her father, if not Lacey. I don't care which." His voice was stern. "Mob trouble is not something we want to entertain on the streets of Boston or in small town America. The faster you get him to come clean, the easier we can all work as a team to do our jobs protecting Lacey. We don't know when Lorenzino will strike. We suspect he's been watching and waiting."

"Do you know who the killer is?" Hunt asked.

I was glad Hunt was here. I was still stuck on Robinson being related to Pitt.

Wes and Pitt shook their heads at the same time.

"Lacey did mention that the LAPD asked her about a guy named Dennis Weeks. Does that name ring a bell?" I wiped my palms on my jeans. I was in the middle of a shit storm, and so was Lacey. Suddenly, my gut twisted into a fucking huge knot. My family could be in danger, too.

"I'll check into it, but no," Wes said.

I didn't know whether to believe them or not, although Pitt hadn't lied yet, and I trusted Wes.

"People use aliases all the time," Pitt said. "I have a meeting to get to. We're not going to solve this today. Tell me your demands, Kade."

In light of everything he'd just said, I had to ensure my family's safety, too. I pinned a look on Wes then Pitt. I rose slowly, pressed my palms on the chrome desk, and bent forward. "You have some nerve." I drilled my gaze into Pitt. "Bringing me into your circle puts my family in jeopardy."

"Unlikely. Yet not out of the realm of possibility. May I remind you that you are dating Lacey? So, you're already part of the circle." Pitt's tone was calm.

Silence filled the room. He might be right about the unlikely part, but the mob could do anything to get what they wanted.

"I'm going to be one of the bodyguards on Lacey," Hunt said, taking hold of my arm.

When he said *Lacey*, I backed away and combed a hand through my hair. "Are you sure tutoring your daughter is wise given everything you told us? I mean, if they're watching Lacey and me."

Pitt adjusted his tie. "I've thought about that. She'll have a bodyguard and you."

His words from our first meeting came to mind: "I know you're fiercely protective. I wouldn't trust anyone other than myself or my wife when it came to my daughter."

"Then I suggest the Ashford Library." I knew the conference room in Pitt's building would be more secure. But in the event something went wrong, even with bodyguards tailing her, I had to be in close proximity to her, and if I needed help, I'd have my brothers, Buster, and my old man if we were closer to home. Not that I was prepared to tell my father any of this yet.

Chapter 12

Lacey

AFTER TWO HOURS OF BASEBALL practice, I collected my gear, and Kelton and I headed out to his truck. Practice had been a non-issue. Aaron was civil. Shaun pitched great, executing every pitch with a smooth delivery. I agreed with Coach. We had a great shot at winning State. Not only did we have Shaun and myself, we had two other decent pitchers, not to mention all our great batters and fielders.

Once in the truck, I sent Kade a text letting him know I was headed home. I was super stoked he'd come clean about the whole fight thing. His confession certainly made the rest of the school day bearable. I was anxious to get home and do some snooping around to see if I could find anything in Mom's or Dad's things.

I stared out the window, mapping out where I would start my search. I eliminated Dad's office since there weren't many places in it to store valuables. In our old house I thought my mom had placed their treasures in a box in her bedroom. I couldn't be sure, though.

The country road we were on was pitch black except for the truck's headlights. Kelton flicked on the high beams. Snow fluttered to the ground as the wind blew through the trees lining both sides of the road.

I glanced his way. The dashboard lights glowed, highlighting Kelton's five o'clock shadow. "You and Aaron were civil to each other at practice. I don't see how you guys turn your anger on and off on a whim." I hadn't had a chance to talk to Kelton. On our way over to the practice facility, I'd gotten a ride with Renee.

"There's a lot we turn on and off on a whim, if you get my drift." He chuckled as he flipped off his ball cap and threw it in the backseat.

I rolled my eyes. "Why is it always sex with you?"

"Girl, seriously. Do you have to ask that?" He pushed long fingers through his matted hair.

"Why don't you find a steady girl? That way you can have sex all the time."

"What makes you think I don't have sex all the time? I don't need a steady girl for that. I like sampling the different varieties. It's kind of like wine tasting." He shifted his glance to me every now and then.

I sighed. "You really should try love."

"Fuck love. And don't start preaching on how love makes having sex better either. The way I see it, love is pain. I want pleasure. Enough said."

He maneuvered through the back roads and then the streets of Ashford. As soon as we drove up to my house, I gasped.

"What is it?" he asked, looking from the house to the street.

"The house. Something's wrong." My hands began to tremble. My breathing grew shallow as I gripped the door handle. "Lights. Where are the lights? They're on a timer." I shook my head steadily. "No, this can't be happening." That familiar buzzing in my head shot to an all-time high. I had to cover my ears. "Turn the lights on. Please, turn the lights on." Blackness colored my vision.

"Lacey. Lacey, I'm here, girl. What do you need?" Kelton's voice rose.

I rammed my shoulder into the door. "I have to get out of here."

I barely heard Kelton telling me to breathe as cold air breezed through the truck.

I pushed the door again, and it opened. I fell into strong arms. I squeezed my eyes shut. Memories bombarded me.

Her brown eyes stared straight up at the ceiling. I fell to my knees into something warm, something that soaked into my clothes. "Mom! Mom, wake up. Wake up." I smoothed a hand over her hair. "Mom! Please! Wake up!" I dropped my head to her chest. "Why won't you wake up?" Tears poured from my eyes.

I crawled over to Julie on my hands and knees. "Jules?" I tapped her cheek. "Jules? Julie. You have to wake up." I sobbed, choking.

I rocked back and forth. I heaved once then twice before losing the contents of my stomach. The room spun as coldness set in. Then a black abyss consumed me.

Chapter 13

Kade

AFTER THE MEETING WITH PITT, Hunt and I had joined Wes in his office to discuss the details and logistics of bodyguards and tutoring.

During the day, two of Wes's men would be following Lacey, even if she was with me. I requested that the two men who had been with Pitt in the garage not be assigned to Lacey's detail. I certainly didn't get a warm and fuzzy feeling with them. Wes took note but didn't promise anything. I also asked Hunt for a third time if he was okay with taking the nightshift. I knew I didn't have to. Nevertheless, the guy was going above and beyond for me.

"Friends until the end," he'd said. "She's just as fragile and important to me as she is to you, man. I got this."

I almost cried when he said that. I hugged him so damn tightly I thought I must have crushed his lungs.

As I got in my truck, I got a text from Lacey. Kelton was taking her home. I couldn't wait to see her. I was excited and nervous to have a little more information about the situation and James Robinson. I wasn't sure yet how I would get him to talk. I didn't know Mr. Robinson well, but I had figured out that he didn't share a great deal. At Christmastime when I asked him about his mom and dad, he'd changed the subject back to antique cars. Lacey had mentioned that he never talked about his family. Gloria Pitt was married to a mob guy. Were her parents involved in the mob too? Either way, he loved his daughter, and he had to have a valid reason he hadn't told her.

The downside of all this was that I had to tutor Chloe one day a week until her finals began. My time was better spent working alongside Hunt and being attached to Lacey at the hip. Wes was supposed to let me know which day worked best for Chloe's schedule. I was debating whether to tell Lacey about Chloe. I could tell her I'd found a job tutoring. If I did, it would open up a host of questions that all tied back to her father. Even telling her about the bodyguards would have the same outcome. Although as perceptive as Lacey was, she'd probably figure out someone was tailing her, which increased the importance and the urgency of Mr. Robinson accepting Pitt's help and telling Lacey about his adoptive family and anything he knew about Lorenzino. The last thing I wanted to do was screw up any relationship between Lacey and her father.

As I exited off the freeway into Ashford, I tabled the question of what I should tell Lacey and thought of ways to convince Mr. Robinson to take Pitt's help. He and I hadn't bonded. He always worked at Rumors at night. We were in a dire situation that called for a swift and quick resolution. Wes said Mr. Robinson was stubborn. In my book, he was prideful, and pride wasn't something one could change for a person. I understood a man wanted to provide for his family with little help from strangers or people he didn't care for. On the heels of pride was trust. After what Mr. Robinson had been through, I had a feeling he didn't trust easily. I knew Lacey didn't. Without knowing James's relationship with his sister, I figured there was more to his story with her. If he'd had a tight bond with her, then he would've accepted help, especially when it came to Lacey's safety, and Lacey would have mentioned she had an aunt in Boston.

An incoming call through my Bluetooth connection interrupted the radio. It was Kelton. I pressed the phone button.

"I'm almost there," I said, slowing down.

"Bro, I can't wake her up. The house is pitch black. The front door is open. What do I do?" He fired each sentence off rapidly, tremors lacing his voice.

The blood froze in my veins. "Kel, calm down." I came to a screeching halt at a stop sign and was thrust hard against my seatbelt. "The lights aren't on at her house?"

"I called the cops." He sounded out of breath. "It looks like someone broke in."

My body went numb. I felt as if someone had taken wire cutters and clipped my brainstem, severing my ability to function.

"Kade, are you there? Kade!"

Headlights came up behind me. Then a horn blew.

I checked the road to my left before giving the truck some gas as I made a right. Kelton was freaking out. I couldn't freak too.

"I'm here. What happened?"

"We pulled into her driveway. The lights weren't on, and she panicked, shaking her head, banging her shoulder against the inside of the passenger door. When I ran around to get her out, she fell into my arms. Then she started petting my head, tapping on my face. Bro, just get here."

"Where is she?" My heart rate was all over the place.

"She's still out and lying down in the backseat of my truck. Cops are checking out the house. How far out are you?"

Too far. "Five minutes."

He sighed as the phone went dead.

After bends, curves, turns, and stop signs, I turned onto Lacey's road. Sweat coated my skin. My pulse thrashed in my ears. Red-and-blue lights flashed in the distance, and all of a sudden I was transported back to the day I'd gotten home from school to find a medic zipping up a thick black bag before lifting the body onto the stretcher.

I gulped in air, shaking the past from my mind. A cop car blocked Lacey's driveway. I parked my truck alongside the house next door and jumped out. I had to be strong. I had to be confident. I had to reel in all my emotions. I couldn't let Lacey see me in turmoil. She'd always said that one of the things she loved about me was my confidence. When she'd first told me that, I was taken aback. Last September she'd seen me in a rage when I'd gotten a call from Kelton that Kody was in the hospital again because of Sullivan. I didn't have an ounce of confidence then, and I didn't now.

Push past the fear. She needs your strength.

I flew past the cop car and straight to Kelton's truck. The spotlight from the cop car shone on the yard and Kelton.

He was pacing back and forth. "Man, thank God, you're here." His face was paler than I'd seen it in a long time, though it might have been the lighting. He hugged me. "I didn't know what to do." Then he eased back. "Wayland's dad is on duty tonight. He wanted to call an ambulance, but I explained her situation. He checked on her before he went in with his partner. Then I told him her father is in California and you would be here. She's still out."

I was grateful we knew one of the cops. Mr. Wayland's son was our team's catcher. Otherwise, we could be here all night answering questions, and I wanted to get Lacey to my house where she'd wake up in a place of light and warmth. "She may be out for a long time." It was always hard to tell how long her blackouts would last. "The first time I saw her have one, it started in her driveway, and she was out for almost two hours."

I peered into his truck. Lacey was lying across the backseat, sleeping soundly as though nothing had happened. I wanted to open the door, carry her into the house, get her comfortable, hold her, and not let go, like I'd done the first time. Her old man had instructed me to let her come out of it naturally. "Kel, she'll be okay. Her major trigger is a dark house." I always held my breath whenever I brought her home at night from a date.

"Easy for you when you've seen one of her blackouts before."

"You have too. Remember on the ball field during tryouts?"

"Yeah, man. But this was different. On the ball field she just fell flat forward. This one she was acting out, petting me, calling for her mom."

I gently grasped his shoulders. "This is why I worry my fucking head off. Seeing her in a state of panic shreds me into a million pieces. I don't want to baby her. I want to protect her from shit like this."

"Whatever you need, Kade. Whatever the fuck you need. I'll do it. I can't see her like that. Not that I wouldn't help." He walked away then came back, blinking rapidly. "Sorry."

"I get it." I couldn't remember the last time I'd seen water in Kelton's eyes.

Voices peppered the air. Mr. Wayland made his way toward us. The other cop went around to the side of the garage.

"Hey, Kade," Mr. Wayland said. Like his son, the man was stocky. "The house is clear of any intruders, although it's been trashed. The big items like the TV and the other electronics are intact. My partner is checking the electrical panel. I'd suggest not staying here tonight."

I hadn't planned on it. I didn't know if Lacey would panic more if she saw that the inside was trashed. I did want to go in and poke around.

"You know, my brother developed panic attacks in Iraq," Mr. Wayland said. "I know how debilitating they can be."

His partner stalked up. "They cut the main electrical line into the house."

Kelton mumbled a cuss word.

"Any other break-ins around the neighborhood?" I asked.

"Not here. We've had a couple though on the other side of town in the last month," Mr. Wayland said. "Does Lacey have a place to stay tonight?"

"She'll be staying at my house. I need to call her father."

"We'll have a car here for the night. I'd suggest you return in the morning."

I opened the front passenger door of Kelton's truck, and Lacey's phone was on the floor. I peeked over the seat. Her chest rose and fell slowly as a soft noise escaped her nose. Then I gently closed the door and punched in her passcode to unlock the screen. I'd seen her enter it numerous times. I scrolled through her contacts until I found her father's name and tapped on the screen. It rang twice.

"Hey, Sweet Pea," he said.

"This is Kade, sir."

"What's wrong?" Unease wove through his tone.

"Lacey's fine. But she had a major blackout. Your house was broken into tonight before she got home."

"Fuck," he said under his breath. "Will this ever end? I'm on the first flight I can get."

"She'll be staying at my house. I'll text you my number. Call me when you have your flight details."

"Kade, please keep her safe."

"Don't worry, Mr. Robinson. Just get home. Oh, and we need to have a man-to-man talk first thing."

Chapter 14

Lacey

MY EYES FLUTTERED OPEN, AND Kade's cedar scent seeped into my nose. I pressed a hand to his stomach as I slowly peered up at him. The dim light of his bedroom licked his worn-out but handsome features.

One corner of his mouth curled, and a dimple emerged. "Hey, there."

"Oh, my God. I blacked out." I pushed to get up. Embarrassment heated my cheeks.

He held me firmly to him. "I'm in this with you. You have to get used to that, baby."

"Kelton. Is he okay? Everything happened so fast. He drove up to the house, and I went into panic mode instantly. The last thing I remember was the fear in Kelton's voice as I scrambled to get out of his truck." Kelton had witnessed one of my blackouts on the pitcher's mound. Even so, my episodes were never the same twice. Dr. Davis had explained that different memories could elicit different reactions depending on the triggers. I was concerned about Kelton and embarrassed with myself. I'd been doing great. Blackouts weren't easy for me—or for whoever was with me, particularly when they didn't know what to do. I made a mental note to thank Kelton.

"He's fine. I'm just glad he was with you. Your house was broken into." He loosened his arm. "They cut the power line. That's why it was dark."

I gulped. "Was anything taken? Did you call the police? Did they catch the person?"

"Slow down, baby. We didn't go in. Mark Wayland's dad was on duty. He and his partner checked out the house." He stroked my arm. "No one was inside, but the house has been ransacked. He stationed a cop outside your house for the evening. We'll survey the damage tomorrow. Oh, and I talked to your dad. He's catching the first flight out."

A knock sounded on the door before it opened. Mr. Maxwell sauntered in, all six feet of him. He reminded me so much of Kade—honey-brown hair and the same copper eyes, but not as broad in the shoulders. "How are you feeling?"

I sat up. "I'm a little tense." Okay, I was tense times ten.

Kade rubbed my back.

"Has Dr. Davis counseled you on breathing exercises?"

"He has." That was my problem last night. I didn't get a chance to think or breathe. As soon as Kelton had driven up to the house, the darkness triggered my panic attack so quickly I didn't have time to stop the spiraling motion.

"If you need anything, you let me know," he said softly. "Son, take the couch in the theater room tonight." He tipped his head at the door. "Let Lacey rest."

Kade got up, kissed me softly on the lips, and said, "I'll be downstairs. We'll get through this. Okay?" He lingered a minute, hovering over me.

He didn't want to leave. I didn't want him to either, but he seemed to need rest more than I did. Kade carried the weight of the world on his shoulders, and at that moment, I was a huge weight drawing the energy out of him. I couldn't keep relying on his strength to pull me out of the darkness. I had to somehow push those pesky demons down into the deeper depths of my psyche.

"I'm good. I'll see you in the morning." I kissed him back as I forced a smile.

When Kade and Mr. Maxwell left, I called Dad.

"Sweet Pea, how are you? I'm just getting on the red-eye. I'll be there as soon as I can." Worry threaded through his every word.

"I'm at Kade's. I'm not hurt. Kelton was there with me when I blacked out." I hoped I sounded confident and strong. He was another person who carried the weight of an army of men on his shoulders. "Do you think the break-in has anything to do with what Detective Fisher told us?"

"I don't know. The doors are about to close. We'll talk when I get home. I love you."

"Ditto."

The line went dead.

I didn't have Detective Fisher's card with me. Otherwise I'd call him and let him know about the break-in. I knew he couldn't do anything from three thousand miles away, but I wanted to pick his brain about the lead he was working on and keep my mind focused on the future—not thinking of a dark house and blackouts.

I curled up and thought about what Dad could possibly have that was so valuable. I kept coming up with nothing. My dad made money from his nightclubs and record label. Maybe he owed a client, and they were looking for money. Or maybe one of his clients knew Dad kept valuables and wanted to hold those over Dad's head until he paid.

After a restless night, I woke up in a heap of sweat with my clothes sticking to me. When I'd finally dozed off, I had one of my recurring dreams. Anytime something bothered me, I found I dreamed Kade and I were sitting on the ball field in a thunderstorm. Neither of us spoke. The dream had been repeating over and over for the past several months without change until last night when words fell from Kade's lips. Words that were on a constant loop in my head when I awoke: "Storms will roll in, the sky will grow darker, the clouds will release their tears, but through the thunder, the lightning, the rain, the sleet, and the snow, the world will right itself." I didn't understand what it meant, although I'd take that scene over any nightmare.

I wrote Kade a note letting him know I was headed to my house to change. I didn't have any clean clothes, and I didn't want to shower at Kade's then slip back into sweaty underwear. I snatched his keys then slipped out around six a.m., careful not to wake anyone. Kade said there was a cop at my house. So this was my chance to find out how I'd react without Kade. I couldn't have him babying me every time I was faced with a challenge. Besides, he needed rest.

As I drove home, twilight waned and dawn set in. The streets of Ashford were dead. Rolling into my driveway, I concentrated on my breathing. With every intake of air, the sky grew lighter and my pulse slowed. A police car was parked in front of one of the garage doors. The cop got out of his car. I grabbed my bag and hopped out of the truck.

"Ma'am, do you live here?" a baby-faced man asked.

"Yes, sir."

We went through the normal identification process. Once he was satisfied, he said, "I'm Officer Yancey. I'll go in with you. But the power is still off."

Oh, damn. I'd forgotten. Kade had mentioned someone had cut the power line. No shower. I'd get my clothes then head back to Kade's.

My phone rang. I retrieved it from the front of my backpack. "Hey, I'm just getting clean clothes. I didn't want to wake you."

"You should've waited for me," Kade said in a sleepy voice. "I'll get dressed and—"

"No, I won't be long. The officer is here with me. I'll be fine. Seriously, it's not dark." The sky was turning a brighter blue.

The sound of an engine disrupted the morning quiet of the neighborhood. Officer Yancey and I turned. A black SUV rolled past my house. I didn't recognize it. I lived on a street with a cul-de-sac, and none of the houses surrounding mine owned a black SUV. My pulse sped up.

"Lace, are you still there?" Kade's voice rose. "Is everything okay?"

"Yeah. I'm good. I promise. I'll be back within the hour." Then I hung up before he protested. If I knew Kade, he'd be here within five minutes, even though we lived about twenty minutes apart.

The black SUV came back and stopped at the edge of the driveway. A faint buzzing started in my head. Suddenly, I wasn't sure I wanted to go into the house. I eyed Officer Yancey. He had his hand poised to retrieve his gun at a moment's notice.

The driver rolled down his window. "Yancey, everything okay?" a black man asked. "Wayland wanted me to check on things."

Wayland? Then I remembered Kade telling me the officer on duty last night was Mark Wayland's dad. I sighed.

"We're cool," Yancey said, then he turned to me. "One of our detectives."

My lungs expanded.

"Radio if you need anything," the man said before driving away.

I started for the house then hesitated, not sure I was ready to see the damage. I knew I wouldn't find any dead bodies. I could do this. It was just a messy house.

Officer Yancey was being patient behind me. He touched my arm lightly. "Why don't you let me sweep it real quick."

Not a bad idea. As the officer went in ahead of me, I waited outside for a minute before I peeked in. The couch in the front living room was sliced, its stuffing poking out. I hedged back. *It's just stuffing.* Yeah, but the creep had a knife. *He's not in the house.* Slowly, I stepped over the threshold and gave the front living room a once-over. The furniture was completely torn to pieces. Shuffling deeper into the room, I found the corner bookcase was knocked over, the contents of the shelves scattered on the floor.

The swishing sound of Officer Yancey's gait kept me in the present. I quickly checked the rooms downstairs. The house was freezing, and so was I. The TV and the electronics on the entertainment center were untouched, although the DVDs and books that had been on the shelves covered the floor. The kitchen had fared better than the other two rooms.

"It's all clear," Yancey's voice boomed from above.

A shiver crept up my spine as I picked my way down the hall. The sunroom was undisturbed, but there wasn't much in there except wicker furniture. In Dad's office the couch cushions were sliced in half. File folders, pens, a calculator, the house phone, and the music awards he cherished littered the brown carpet. Suddenly, I was transported back to the LAPD and Detective Fisher's words: "Whoever invaded your home was after something specific."

I was standing in the office doorway when heavy footfalls scuffed the hall floor.

"Are you okay, Ms. Robinson?" Yancey asked. "The upstairs wasn't touched. They might've heard your vehicle last night and taken off."

My body felt numb as my mind worked to figure out what my dad had that those creeps wanted. It could be that some random person had broken in. But if that were the case, then the TVs and other electronics would've been stolen.

"Do you have any idea what they wanted?" Yancey asked.

"No clue." I diverted my gaze out the French doors beyond the desk. The snow was melting, giving way to the brown of the wooded lot. "Maybe they found it. Maybe that's why the upstairs isn't trashed." A ray of hope coursed through me.

Yancey's radio crackled, and a voice blared through it.

"I'll be out front," he said before he answered the radio call.

I wandered through the sea of office items, my gaze scanning the floor. I started snapping pictures with my phone to send to Detective Fisher so he could see the mess. I squatted down at a pile of folders. Eko Records' contracts were scattered about with pictures of bands Dad had signed. I picked up each one as though I was playing a game of Go Fish, though I knew I wouldn't find a matching hand. Then I came across one folder with a lone picture of a handsome man with gray hair and a gray beard. I studied it. Why did he look oddly familiar?

Chapter 15

Kade

KNOWING LACEY HAD SLEPT IN my room last night while I slept on the couch sucked. She did need rest, and I knew sleeping with her we wouldn't get any. When we'd finally gotten back from her house, I'd told my father about the break-in. I was thankful he was home in case Lacey needed to talk with a doctor, even though she always came out of her blackouts like she had awakened from a restful sleep. On the other hand, my brother had been rattled when we got back to the house. So, I'd asked my father if he could check on Kelton. Man, I understood what he was going through. I didn't care how many times I'd seen Lacey black out or panic, a pain always gripped my chest so tight I couldn't breathe.

My phone rang early that morning. Hunt called to tell me Lacey was on her way to her house. I'd filled him in last night after I'd spoken to her father. Knowing Hunt and Pitt's men were tailing Lacey, I did feel a sense of calm wash over me.

I sent a text to Wes asking him when I'd be tutoring Chloe. His reply said Friday this week. I had three days to figure out how to tell Lacey.

I was drying off after my shower, thinking how to begin the conversation with Lacey's father, when my own father called my name. "Kade, are you in here?" he asked.

"I'll be out in sec." I finished toweling off and wrapped the terrycloth around my waist before walking into my room.

"Hey, son." He was staring at a picture of Karen on my dresser. "How's Lacey this morning?"

"Good. She went home to get some clothes." I pulled on jeans then slipped on a Mötley Crüe T-shirt.

"Is that wise, letting her go alone? Will she panic?" He studied me. *Like I could stop her.* "I don't think so. It's daylight. And there's a cop there with her."

"Other than last night, what else is bothering you? I noticed you weren't yourself when you were visiting your mother."

I combed a hand through my wet hair. "Do you think people listen to me?" My father and I had a great relationship. I always valued his advice, and on family issues, he always valued mine. Maybe that was why I always felt older than eighteen.

He studied me as I rested a shoulder against the doorjamb of my bedroom. "Does this have anything to do with Lacey or why Kelton's face looks like he collided with a wall?" He tucked his hands into his tailored suit pants.

"Kelton was ambushed by Seever and Sullivan. Hunt and I intervened, but not soon enough. You know Kelton will get his punches in when he's being attacked. Besides, Seever deserved it."

He gave me one of his fatherly looks that said *no one deserves to be beaten.* Then his features softened. "Son, people will listen to what they want to hear. However, in order for someone to *hear* you, you have to know what appeals to them. And you seem to have a knack for finding that one thread that hits a nerve in a person, whether it's conscious or unconscious."

I went to sit on my bed. "The LAPD speculate that Mr. Robinson has something of value that someone wants. The problem is Mr. Robinson, his son, and Lacey don't know what or who that is. I want to help. I just don't know how. And after last night, I'm terrified for Lacey."

"Hunt's brother works for the Guardian. Ask him to put some men on Lacey. Her father works nights, right? So, in the meantime, she can stay here. Or what about their former housekeeper, Mary? Is she still living with them?"

"She's away at the moment."

"I'll talk to Mr. Robinson and clear it with him for Lacey to spend her nights here. But, son, if a person doesn't know what people are after, it's hard to resolve the situation. I'm sure the LAPD is doing everything they can on the case." The bed dipped as he eased down next to me.

"What if I knew something about her family that she doesn't, and her father does? Do I let him tell her or do I? She hates when I keep things from her. But you've always taught us that we shouldn't come in between family."

"Is it life or death if you don't tell her?"

I had bodyguards on her now. She wouldn't die if I didn't tell her about her father and his connection to the Pitt family. I didn't know Mr. Robinson's connection to Lorenzino. "I can't be sure. I don't think so."

"Do you trust the person who told you? As I've always said, make sure your facts are straight before you share information. I've seen soldiers get hurt and some die when we didn't get our intel validated. I'm not saying you're at war with Lacey. Feelings are fragile, and with her PTSD, I want you to tread carefully." He unfolded himself.

He was trying to tell me something without scaring me, and I knew what it was. I'd done my research when I found out Lacey had PTSD. She wasn't suicidal. When I first met her, she did have a tendency to outbursts of anger. She didn't trust easily, partly as a result of her former cheating boyfriend. Knowing all that, I was a pinhead for lying to her. Still, I didn't know how to get around treading carefully without triggering any symptoms. I realized in that moment that I could empathize with her old man. He was probably waging his own internal war about what to tell his daughter, which neither Pitt nor Wes understood.

"On another note. Your mom expressed interest in coming home. I'm thinking maybe for just one night might be a good idea. I want to see how she responds."

My heart nearly exploded with excitement. Having my mom home with us as a family again was a dream of mine.

"That's great news." I smiled like a little boy who'd just gotten his first Tonka truck. I hadn't felt this happy in a long time. Then I lost my smile. "When I was with her, she wasn't herself."

"I know. A change of scenery might help. I was thinking that she could come to Kelton and Kross's first baseball game. You know how she loved watching you boys play ball." He relaxed his shoulders. Then he patted me on the back. "I hope to have your mom home permanently one day."

"I hope so, too. Do you think Mom will like Lacey?" Another one of my wishes I prayed for. I wanted Mom to see the beauty in Lacey.

"You're in love with her, aren't you?" He smiled, reminding me of my brothers.

My father and I never talked about women or love. Not after he'd explained the birds and the bees to all us boys. His only involvement in our dating relationships was to ensure we went to our annual appointments to get tested.

"I am."

He had one of those expressions that said *it's puppy love.*

"It's not just first love either." I'd dated several women. Not one of them gave me the rush or the tingles or made my insides turn upside down in a good way like Lacey did. "I can't imagine my future without her."

His grin grew wider as though he was remembering when he'd fallen in love with Mom. "She's a good girl, son. She's good for you, and I'm happy that you found someone." His smile vanished. "Protect her. Don't suffocate her. I also know how possessive all you boys are. That's not a bad thing in the least. Just make sure you know when to back off, and when not to. She's a strong girl on the outside, but she is extremely fragile on the inside."

"She won't let me suffocate her." Lacey could put me in my place in a heartbeat. Hell, she had a time or two already. "Oh, one more thing, Dad. I'll talk to Mr. Robinson about Lacey staying with us while he works nights. If he has any questions, I'll tell him to call you."

"Very well. I love you, son. I need to run. I may be late tonight." He left me with his wisdom.

I barely had a minute to process our conversation before Lacey shuffled in, rosy cheeked and red nosed, with mussed hair and a dazed look in her eyes. She cozied up to me. I wrapped my arms around her, rested my chin on her head, and closed my eyes. My world was complete, even if only for a moment.

Mr. Robinson was due to arrive at Logan around eight a.m. If rush hour traffic was flowing smoothly, then he should be at the house around ten thirty. Lacey was anxious to be home when her father got there, which put a wrinkle in my plan to talk to Mr. Robinson alone. While she showered, I asked Kross if he would meet me there. Somehow he could distract Lacey so I could get a minute alone with her old man, and if things got out of control between Mr. Robinson and me, I would have Kross available to intervene.

Silence carried us most of the way to her house. She worried her bottom lip.

"A penny for your thoughts."

"I found a picture this morning in my dad's office. It's been bugging me." She lifted her phone from her lap, tapped the screen, and showed me a picture of Lorenzino.

Given what she'd been through last night, I was stunned that her mind was firing well enough to spot a picture that was crucial to the problem we were facing.

"I sent this to Detective Fisher. I'm waiting for him to reply or call me. It was odd that this picture was in a folder among all the other folders that had Eko Records contracts in them. The folder with this picture in it didn't. What if my dad owes someone money? And they'll do anything to get it? He could've angered the wrong people. This guy may be someone's manager."

I hadn't thought about that. Harrison Lorenzino could own a band or two and had a contract deal go bad. "It's possible." In today's world though, people didn't keep cash hidden in mattresses. If Mr. Robinson owed money, then I would've suspected a ransom deal or some other kind of intimidation, not someone tearing up a house to find money.

By the time we got to her house, the power company technician was packing up his truck. The cop on duty was talking to him. Kross parked behind me.

"Ma'am," the cop said to Lacey. "Power should be on. Make sure you get the lock on that front door fixed. When your father gets home, have him contact us if you find anything missing."

"Thank you for all your help, Officer Yancey," she said.

The cop and the technician left the three of us standing in her driveway. We trekked down the path and into the house.

"I vote for bars on the windows and thirty locks on the front door," I teased.

"Are you trying to keep me barricaded so you can have your way with me?" Lacey asked playfully.

"Okay, you two. I know you both have sex on the brain, but don't forget how cold it probably is inside. Kade would have shrinkage going on," Kross said in a light tone.

Lacey burst out laughing. Kross slapped me on the back. He wasn't kidding. The house was freezing. I was glad he'd made her laugh though.

Lacey disappeared down the hall.

Kross looked around the place and said, "What the fuck."

Officer Wayland had said the house was trashed. Lacey's expression when she'd returned earlier had given me the impression the damage had shocked her too. But I hadn't asked. I was enjoying the feel of her soft body against my hard chest. I was also enjoying a cathartic moment I thought we both could use. Even so, seeing the hurricane that had whipped through the house rendered me speechless.

"Should we start cleaning up?" Kross asked as he wandered into the family room.

"We should wait for Mr. Robinson." If my calculations were correct, he should arrive anytime.

Lacey came back. "Heat should kick on. So you can both stop worrying about shrinkage." She rolled her eyes.

A car door slammed shut. *Showtime.* My nerves perked up, my hands became clammy, and my mind was still flipping through how this conversation was going to go, if I could get a minute alone with him. Although in light of Lacey having a picture of Lorenzino on her phone, I knew she was dying to ask her father who the man was. Maybe starting with Lorenzino would spark a domino effect that would lead Mr. Robinson to share what he knew about Lorenzino and, hopefully, his adoptive family.

The door from the garage creaked open and was followed by Mr. Robinson's voice, pitched as though he were speaking on the phone. "I got to run. I'll call you later. Yes, son. I'm home." He pocketed his phone as he entered the room. He barely had time to throw his keys on the counter next to the fridge before Lacey hurtled into his arms. "God, I've been so worried about you," he said. They hugged each other for a moment. He regarded Kross and me. Dark circles fanned out beneath his eyes, and a heavy growth of facial hair covered his jaw. "Thank you for taking care of her."

Kross and I ponied up to the kitchen island. I nodded.

"You kids should get to school. I'll take things from here," he said.

"We thought we could help clean up," I said. "I brought muscle with me." I flipped my thumb at my brother.

Lacey's phone rang. "Hi, Detective Fisher," she said excitedly, bouncing down the hall out of sight.

The blood drained from me. Mr. Robinson grimaced.

Kross whispered. "What's going on?"

I hadn't had a chance to tell him about Lacey's detective work. I shrugged as I widened my eyes at Mr. Robinson. I probably didn't have enough time to say what I had to say before she finished her call. Mr. Robinson was rooted to a spot in front of the kitchen sink, listening intently to Lacey. I was curious too.

"Do you know who that guy is?" she asked. "Hmm. He just walked in. Yes, the house was broken into last night. I will. Talk to you soon."

Her boots scuffed along the floor as she made her way back into the kitchen with a picture in her hand. She blew air out through her nose, seemingly annoyed. "Detective Fisher told me to talk to you. If you don't tell me who this man is, then he will." She skirted the island to stand near her father, holding up the picture in front of him. "The only thing he told me was that he was connected to the mob in LA. Fisher said you and he talked last night. Does the man in the picture have anything to do with the murders and the break-in?"

Straight and to the point. That's my girl. I gripped the icy cold granite of the island counter.

"His name is Harrison Lorenzino, head of a mob family in LA," Mr. Robinson said. "I don't know if he has anything to do with what happened to Julie and your mom. I do know he thinks I have something of value of his." His shoulders slumped, no doubt the weight of that one piece of information peeling a layer of stress away from him.

Lacey glowered.

"And what is that?" I asked. Pitt was right again.

"A red ledger book," Mr. Robinson replied. He pivoted, finding a glass and filling it with water.

"And why would you have a red ledger book that belongs to a mob guy?" Lacey mashed her glossy lips together.

"Because I suspect he's my father, and he thinks my mother gave me the book."

I was in the middle of a soap opera. I needed a storyboard to map all this shit out. The man was connected to two mob families. No wonder he looked like shit.

Chapter 16

Lacey

"I DON'T UNDERSTAND," I SAID, STARING at my dad like I didn't even know him all of a sudden. My eyebrows had to be deep into my hairline or maybe on the back of my head. "You always said your mom and dad were dead." He never liked to talk about his parents, and if someone asked him, he'd change the subject.

I recalled when Julie had pressured Dad on the subject about two years ago. We had been riding to church one day when it was unusually rainy for southern California, and Julie asked him how his parents had died. It was an innocent question, but to Dad the question was like the Bubonic Plague—to be avoided at all costs. I'd been sitting behind Mom, so I had a clear view of Dad while he drove. His knuckles grew white on the steering wheel.

He'd taken a breath then speaking. "You will never ask me about my parents again. They're dead." The word *dead* was spoken with hurt and disgust, and I couldn't tell why he felt such a mix of emotions over his parents. Later on, when Mom and I were alone, I asked her why Dad had gotten so angry. She told me Dad had a rough childhood and when he was ready he'd talk. He never did. I wasn't surprised either. Dad clammed up tight when something bothered him.

Several things in our lives were hard to deal with. I knew that better than anyone, especially when we were talking about two precious lives. I stared at my dad as the picture in my hand floated to the floor. "Are you going to answer me?" My voice trembled. The buzzing in my head began. I inched toward the island just as Kade came around with a barstool and helped me onto it.

Kross carried another barstool over to Dad. "Sit, Mr. Robinson."

Dad straddled the seat and scrubbed his hands over his face, drawing them down slowly. "Two months before your mom and sister were killed, I got a package in the mail from my adoptive sister, Gloria. In it was a letter and a book of nursery rhymes."

Oh, my God. "Sister? When were you adopted?"

Dad scratched his head. "The short story for now. I was adopted when I was a baby. I never knew my biological parents. My adoptive mom had only known my birth mother briefly from church, but they became fast friends. My birth mother vanished soon after I was born. They searched for her but never found her."

"Are your adoptive parents alive?" I pressed my hands into my legs.

"According to Gloria's letter to me, no. And she also mentioned that my birth mother isn't either. She'd tracked down Gloria just before she died of cancer and asked that she give me the letter and the book of nursery rhymes." He snatched his wallet from his jeans pocket, removed a folded-up piece of paper, opened it, and read.

Dear James, I struggled with my decision to give you up for adoption. In my mind, I had no choice. I had to make sure no one would ever find out that you came into this world and that I was your mother. I wasn't a good person. I had a hard life. I wasn't proud of some of the things I'd done or the choices I'd made. I prayed every day that the decision I made was the right one. I wanted you to have a good life, one where children thrived on good and not evil. I didn't write this letter to ask for your forgiveness. I wrote it to say that I love you. The book of nursery rhymes is something I cherished as a child. I loved reading "Here We Go Round the Mulberry Bush" at night while I was pregnant with you. Maybe one day you can read them to your children. You'll always be in my heart. With all my love.

Dad sighed, and water pooled in his eyes.

A pain clamped down on my heart at the thought that he never knew his biological mom, and now she was dead. I placed a hand on his shoulder. "I'm sorry, Dad. I would've loved to have met your mom, and your adoptive parents."

"I wished I would've known my mom." He folded the letter. "You wouldn't have wanted to know my adoptive parents. They've been dead to me for a long time." He pinched his lips with his fingers.

Kade gently laid his strong hands on my shoulders and began tracing circles. I reveled in his strength, something I needed at the moment. Kross relaxed casually against the counter, his face blank.

The soft buzzing in my head began to drone. "So your mom gave you a letter and a book. I'm still confused," I said. "Is the nursery rhyme book the ledger?"

"The book is all nursery rhymes, and it's not red," Dad said. "Now, your mom encouraged me to find out more about my parents. She kept telling me that I had to come to terms with my past. Since my adoptive parents didn't have much to go on regarding my mother, I hired a detective. He uncovered that my mother had been a mistress to a man who was head of a mob family. A month after we learned of it, your mom and sister were dead."

I sucked in a sharp breath as acid swished around in my stomach.

"Afterwards, I canceled the search on my biological family. I focused on moving here and getting our lives back to normal. I didn't think to connect my search for my mom with what happened to our family. If you recall, we thought it was a random break-in."

"And the mob boss your mom slept with was Lorenzino?" Kade asked.

Dad gave Kade a nod.

"Did he kill Mom and Julie?" I tucked my trembling hands between my thighs as I pictured Mom's and Julie's dead bodies. I wanted to bury myself in a dirt hole like a gopher and not come out until all this was over with.

Kade bent down, his lips at my ear. "Breathe, baby. I'm here."

I kept inhaling and exhaling softly, helping the buzzing in my head to quiet down.

"Possibly." Dad unfolded his bulk to get himself another glass of water.

"So you've talked to this man?" Kross slid down away from Dad. "Did he give you any clues as to where he thinks this ledger might be? Granted, if he knew, I'm sure you wouldn't be in this predicament, but if he's your father, maybe you can appeal to him. Get him to tell you more about your mom."

The Maxwells were all about family. Their bond was based on love, protection, and having each other's back. My dad didn't have any of that with Lorenzino. If Lorenzino was the killer, the man didn't have a heart.

Dad downed the clear liquid. "I've talked to him, only because he called me a couple of weeks ago and asked if I'd found the book. It was the first time I'd ever spoken to him. He told me he'd mistakenly left the ledger at my mom's apartment. Then she disappeared off the face of the earth. I told him that it's hard to produce something you don't have. His response was that the woman was cunning." Deep lines creased his forehead, and sadness swam in his green eyes.

"Is Rob in danger?" Everyone kept thinking about me, but my brother was the one in LA, where that man lived. "Does he know all of this, too?"

"Rob can handle himself," Dad said with surety. "And he knows as much as I do. I had to keep him in the loop."

Thank God. I wished Dad had told me when he'd found out all this information. I knew he walked on eggshells around me with my PTSD, school, and baseball, and while I appreciated his protective nature, to learn all the information at once was a little daunting.

"So, that's it?" Kade asked. "The man can't be okay with *I don't have it*, especially if it's something he's still searching for? No offense, Mr. Robinson. In my opinion, the man isn't going to stop until he gets the ledger. And why now?"

"Before we ended the call, he said, 'I've given you enough time to mourn. Find that book. We'll be in touch.' Then he hung up."

I hopped off the stool, picked up the picture, and placed it on the counter. "When I saw this picture, my first thought was that he looks familiar. Now that I'm looking at him again, I see the resemblance. It's the nose. He has the same nose as you."

"It doesn't matter if he's my father or not. I don't want anything to do with him. I don't even want to know if he is my biological father." Dad set his glass on the granite surface.

I didn't want anything to do with Lorenzino either.

"So you shared all this with Detective Fisher?" Kade sat down on my barstool then drew me to him to stand between his legs at angle where he could still see Dad.

"When Lacey, Rob, and I were at the LAPD, I didn't want to say anything for fear of Lacey's safety. However, after you called," Dad said to Kade, "I called the detective before I got on the plane and explained everything. We need all the help we can get. He's still working on the lead regarding Dennis Weeks. He knows Lorenzino won't talk. Despite that, he'll follow through. As far as the break-in, the detective speculates Lorenzino probably knew we were in LA, so he had one of his men check out the house. He'll keep us up-to-date. We need to be alert."

"Is Mary coming back?" I asked. I was worried she'd be in danger, too. She'd been on a mini vacation with her new boyfriend, Mr. Wiley.

"Mary will be staying in LA. Her mom had to have emergency hip replacement surgery," Dad said.

"I asked my father this morning, and Lacey can stay with us," Kade said. "Since you work at the club at night." Kade hooked a finger around one of mine.

It wasn't a bad idea. The notion of staying alone in my house after the break-in wasn't high on my list right now. Granted, I had to get over my fears, especially my fear of darkness, but taking the plunge and sleeping in the house alone—I wasn't prepared to do that.

Dad narrowed his tired, red eyes.

"Mr. Robinson, we're adults. But I get it. Separate beds is not an issue. I slept on the couch last night," Kade said. "And my best friend's brother, Wes, manages the Guardian. I've asked him if he could have a couple of men shadow Lacey."

"You asked Pitt for help?" I asked. Kade didn't like the man.

"His men are trained to protect," Kade said.

"I know how to use a gun. And I have you guys." I stuck out my chin. If the rumors that Pitt was the mob were true, then I didn't want Kade to get caught up with him.

"Kade's right. Let the men who are trained in this do their job. We have our own jobs and lives. I'd like to get some rest, clean up this mess, and talk to the local police to make them aware. And you kids have school."

"The school day's half over. Why don't we help clean up?" Kade suggested. "Kross, can you run and get us lunch? Baby, can you go with Kross? I'd like a few minutes alone with your dad."

I swung my gaze between them, not certain what Kade could want to talk to Dad about, unless it was the sleeping arrangements. "Are you going to ask him for my hand in marriage?" I asked in a somewhat playful tone, trying to lighten the mood and hoping to think of something other than the mess we were in.

"Say what?" Dad's face reddened.

Kross chuckled.

"Maybe." Kade slid on one of his famous sexy grins.

"Go easy on him, Dad." I hugged him. "I love you. We'll get through this." We had to. I didn't want to live not knowing who the killer was or that he'd never pay for what he'd done. Somehow, I had to dig deep for strength to keep my PTSD at bay. More importantly, I had to do everything I could to help. Right now, fresh air sounded good. "Come on, Kross."

Kross slapped Kade on the shoulder. "Good luck, bro. I'll be sure to place lots of flowers on your grave."

"Oh, Dad." I said. "Where's that nursery rhyme book? I'd love to see it." Dad had always read nursery rhymes to me when I was a little girl.

Kade lifted his eyebrows.

I rolled my eyes. The guy had loved *Humpty Dumpty* when I recited it to him in the airport. I was beginning to think I'd opened up a can of worms.

Chapter 17

Kade

WHEN LACEY AND KROSS LEFT to get lunch, Mr. Robinson and I shared a very long quiet moment with the hum of the fridge compressor. He had one arm crossed over his chest and the other resting on top of it while he stroked his unshaven jaw. It would be funny if he were thinking about his answer to my marriage proposal.

I strolled into the breakfast nook, pulled out a chair, and straddled the back of it. I stretched out my arms over the back and picked at a fingernail. I was the one who wanted to talk, but I just didn't know where to begin. It would be *easier* to ask for her hand in marriage.

"Have you thought about seeing Lacey walk down the aisle?" I briefly closed my eyes. I could picture how beautiful she'd be in a snug-fitting dress with a slit up one side.

He cleared his throat as he joined me. "That's what you wanted to talk to me about? And here I thought you two were kidding."

I had to break the ice somehow.

"You love her that much?" he asked.

I met his green gaze. "Yeah. But we're not ready for that step just yet." Lacey and I hadn't even talked about the future. It unnerved me a little. The thought of being apart from her was unsettling. I wasn't planning on college. I was hoping to stick around my house and spend more time visiting my mom and giving my father a hand with taking care of the house and our property.

"Are you planning to go to college?" He studied me intently.

I wasn't here to discuss my future per se, and I didn't have much time before Kross and Lacey returned. But I also didn't want to brush him off. We'd really never had a chance to get to know one another. "At this time, no."

"When Lacey goes to ASU, how will that work for you and your relationship with her?"

"I haven't thought that through. Rest assured that I would never think of stopping Lacey from pursuing her dream. I promise you that."

"Then what's on your mind?" he asked in a fatherly tone.

"Jeremy Pitt. I know your adoptive sister is Pitt's wife, and no, Lacey doesn't know. You know she's going to ask you more about your adoptive family. I'd like to ask that you tell her as soon as you can."

"You know Pitt how?" His nostrils flared.

I explained the relationship between Hunt and me and Wes. Then I said, "Wes works for Pitt. Pitt is worried Lorenzino will find out who your adoptive family is and that it could put his family in jeopardy. Pitt wanted me to encourage you to take his help. He said you wouldn't listen to them."

"I never blamed my sister for my father's abusive nature. But it's still hard for me to connect with her, even though he's passed away. But what's Pitt going to do for me?"

"Work as a team. Tell him what you told us." I cracked my knuckles.

"If I do, he could make waves and piss off Lorenzino. I can't take that chance. And if I tell him I could be related to a mob family, possibly a rival of his, where does that leave Lacey and me? How will he react?"

Fuck. I hadn't thought of that angle. Then again, I'd had a better shot at winning the lottery than concluding he'd be related to two mob families. I rubbed my neck. A headache was just waiting to bloom.

"The devil you know or the one you don't," I said. "The way I see it, you have a better shot at your adoptive family siding with you than a family you never knew. I don't know Pitt that well, although the couple of times I've spoken to him, he seemed like an understanding businessman. Apart from his arrogance, he's a man who believes family is sacred, even adoptive families."

I was way too young to be counseling grown men. I should be getting laid, throwing parties, hanging out with Hunt and my brothers, and taking Lacey on dates. Instead, I was sitting with a man who was just as broken as his daughter, giving advice. Maybe I was headed for a career like my father's.

He released a heavy breath. "I'm not sure the devil I know is any better than the one I don't. And I don't want my daughter to know some of the things I've done. Like my birth mother, I wasn't a good person. And how can I tell Lacey I'm related to two mob families?"

Not my problem. I cleared my throat. "With all due respect, you're putting me in the middle. This is not my story to tell. I've screwed up a couple of times with Lacey by not telling her something or lying to her. I promised her just yesterday I wouldn't do it again. I want to respect your wishes, but she comes first with me."

He pressed his fingertips to his forehead.

"Look at it this way," I said. "She could be the conduit to help build that relationship with your sister. You know when you tell her that she'll want to meet her and her cousin. This could be a win-win for both of you." I could envision more win-win situations, like Lacey hanging with Chloe at Pitt's place. I'd bet he had a Fort Knox set-up. I scrapped the thought. She had baseball, and the game schedule was brutal with three or four games per week once the season started.

He lifted his head. "I need to think."

Friday was my day with Chloe. I hated to give him a deadline. I understood the man was wiped out. Today was Tuesday, and I should factor in a cushion. "Please talk to her by Thursday."

"What's the urgency? There's something you're not telling me, son."

Now I was the one to press my fingers to my temples. "Pitt's daughter needs a tutor, and I'm the guy. Friday is my day with her. I would like to tell Lacey what I'm doing. If I do tell her about my new job, she'll have a thousand questions. And as I said, I can't lie to her."

"Tell her about your job. She doesn't need to know the girl is Pitt's daughter."

"Mr. Robinson." My voice dropped. "Lacey is going to be upset I've known about this for days now and haven't told her. I haven't lied to her, but I'm going down a road that is about to explode at the end. For you that may be okay. It's not for me." I had an urge to jump across the small distance between us and shake the cobwebs out of his brain.

His gaze roamed around the room. "I'll see what I can do."

I couldn't force him. "I prefer her to hear from you. But I'll tell her if you don't. Besides, she'll deal." Earlier, I was the one worried about telling her about Lorenzino. I was surprised at how well she handled the news. "She didn't go off the deep end when you told us about Lorenzino. She's delicately strong. I know that's a weird way to describe her. But if you peel back her outer layer, you'll find layers of compassion, understanding, and tenderness that allow her to see past the bad in people. While her PTSD has hurt her psyche, I believe as she works her way out of it, the illness is shaping her into a greater and stronger person. Lacey's my hero."

"I am?" Lacey asked.

Oh fuck. Where the hell did she come from? I didn't hear a door close or anything.

Mr. Robinson and I whipped our heads around to find Lacey standing like a zombie with an armful of brown paper bags and the aroma of grease permeating the air around her.

"How long have you been standing there?" The blood rushed out of me.

"Long enough to know I'm your hero."

A door slammed before Kross showed his ugly mug. "You left the door open, Lacey." He had more paper bags in his hands. "Um. Did I miss something?"

A tear slid down Lacey's cheek as her bottom lip quivered. I jumped out of the chair. Her father did too. He took the bags from her.

"No need to cry." I wiped a tear away with the pad of my thumb. "I hope those are happy tears." I could use some happy tears.

She blinked and gave me one of her heart-melting smiles.

I pinched her chin lightly as I guided it up, then I placed my lips over hers. "I meant it," I whispered. My pulse was on overdrive as I searched her face for clues as to how much she did hear.

"Let's eat," Kross said.

I flicked a quick glance at her father. He barely shook his head. I didn't know if he was signaling that she didn't hear our whole conversation or not. Lacey did wear her heart on her sleeve. So if she'd heard anything more than my last sentence, she'd be questioning and demanding answers. I tabled my panic as we dug into the hamburger and fries.

Kross devoured his pile of food. Mr. Robinson took a bite out of his hamburger and went down to his office.

"So, what else did you hear?" I nudged Lacey playfully with my shoulder. I was sweating bullets.

"'Lacey's my hero.'" She nudged me back.

"You said that, bro?" Kross stopped with a fry midway to his mouth.

I glared at him. "You got a problem with that?"

He shoved the fry in his mouth. "Nope. I know I was supposed to help clean up, but this is getting too mushy for my tastes. If you kids don't need me, I'm out of here." Kross wiped his face with a napkin.

"Go," I said. I'd mainly wanted his muscle in the event the shit hit the fan with Mr. Robinson.

The only shit that would blow up now would be if Mr. Robinson didn't meet the deadline.

Chapter 18

Kade

I LAY ON THE COUCH IN my theater room, staring at the ceiling. The past two days had been hectic. Lacey and I had helped her father straighten up. He had work at his nightclub. We had school. Lacey had baseball practice. I invited Wes and Hunt to my house. Everyone, including my brothers, my father, her father, Lacey, and me, listened as Wes detailed a plan of bodyguards and schedules. Wes showed us pictures of the three men, in addition to Hunt, who would be working Lacey's detail and of the two vehicles they'd use. Mr. Robinson had alerted the Ashford police to keep an eye out for any suspicious activity. At that point, we had our bases covered.

The outstanding issues were the red ledger and Lorenzino's actions to get it. Mr. Robinson had yet to explain to Lacey about his adoptive family, someone had to tell Pitt the connection between Lorenzino and Mr. Robinson, and I had to tell Lacey I was tutoring Chloe, her cousin. I was waiting to do the latter until Mr. Robinson did his part. Otherwise, Lacey would have a host of questions that would lead right back to her father.

Anxiety rolled through me, and I threw the covers off. The cold air of the theater room was a welcome relief. It was only four in the morning, and I couldn't sleep. Mr. Robinson had planned on speaking with Lacey last night, except her practice had gone beyond their scheduled time. The season was starting in a week, and Coach Dean was working the team overtime. By the time Lacey got home, Mr. Robinson had left for the club. Now I was under a time crunch. I was scheduled to tutor Chloe after school today.

A nightlight glowed below a family picture on the wall to the right of the TV. I stared at it as I thought about how easy our lives had been in Texas before Karen died. We were all happy in that picture. Karen was sitting on my father's lap, kissing him on the cheek. My father had his arm around my mom while my brothers and I stood behind them. I remembered that day like it was yesterday. Karen had been so excited to take pictures, and we boys were not happy that our mom wanted to drag us to some studio when we could be out playing sports.

Footsteps broke my concentration. I sat up to find Kelton walking in. His black hair was sticking out in all directions as he adjusted his sweatpants on his hips.

"Couldn't sleep?" I asked.

He plopped down on the other couch. "I see you're wide awake." He scrubbed a hand over his bare chest. "Why are you down here? Dad isn't home. You should be in your bed with that beautiful woman of yours."

I laughed weakly. "I told her old man we would sleep in separate beds." I hadn't told him we wouldn't have sex though.

"Always doing the honorable thing. You're a better man than me."

Oh, I didn't think so. "You okay from the other night?" I hadn't had a chance to talk to Kelton in more detail about Lacey's blackout.

"I'll be fine. I'm not doing love, bro. Just not. I have a newfound respect for you and Dad." He kicked a leg up on the couch.

"You'll find that one girl, Kel. And once you do, it won't be about the pain. Because all the good stuff that comes with being in love will overshadow any other emotions."

"So when are you tutoring Chloe? Is it today?" he asked.

"Yeah. I tried to get Wes to postpone it, but she has a math test on Monday, and today is the only day she's available." I filled my brother in about my conversation with Mr. Robinson.

"I can step in, man," he said with a hitch in his voice.

I bet he would. "I'm asking you to stay away from her. At least until things die down. The last thing we need is her father cutting off your balls." I didn't have time to worry about my brother.

Silence stretched for a moment. Then the stairs groaned.

Kelton sat up. My gaze traveled to the doorway. Lacey rubbed one of her heavy green eyes as she wound her way around the couch and the table. I couldn't take my eyes off her. She wore striped sleep pants that hung low on her toned hips while her pink tank hugged all her sexy curves, including her beautiful braless breasts. Every part of me stirred awake—as always— when she walked into a room, but more than that, she erased every thought I'd had before she entered the room.

"I'm out of here," Kelton said as he breezed by Lacey.

Smart brother. An hour alone with my girl was all I needed.

She curled up next to me, her hair brushing over my bare chest as she laid her head against me. "Why is your heart beating so fast?" she asked as her magic fingers slid down below my abs.

I tangled my hand in her hair. "Do you even have to ask?"

"Um, no. Not with Mr. Steel growing in my hand."

I chuckled then kissed her. "Only for you, baby."

She let go of Mr. Steel and traced a path up and down my abs.

I wanted to protest. I wanted to be inside her. I wanted to ravish her gorgeous body, slow and steady. My brothers wouldn't bother us, and my old man had gone up to visit my mom for the weekend.

"Why are you awake?" I asked.

"A lot on my mind. My dad sent me a text last night since we missed each other. He wants me to meet him at the house before school. We were going to talk about his adoptive family last night. He said it wouldn't take long."

I did an imaginary fist pump.

"Why are you and Kelton awake?

"I'd rather not talk." I snaked my hand under her tank top up to her breasts. Her nipples were hard. I caressed one breast then the other, following a lazy path around her hardened nipples.

"Your brothers could come down here."

"Lace, Kel won't, and Kross and Kody sleep through everything." I gently pinched a nipple.

She moaned ever so softly, sending my brain into overdrive. In a flash, I was on my back and had her rolled on top of me. A lazy smile tugged at her lips before she dug her hands into my bare chest. Then she pushed herself to a sitting position as she straddled me. Her lazy smile became seductive as she dragged her nails down my chest to my abs. I bit down on my lip, trying to keep from having my way with her. I wanted to enjoy every touch she had to offer.

She shifted her hooded gaze from me to the waistband of my sleep shorts then back to me as though she was asking for permission. When she pulled at the waistband, Mr. Steel poked out, and she sucked in a sharp breath. My fingers tightened on her bare thighs, rough to soft, and I almost flipped her over and pushed inside her. But I was savoring every soft moan coming out of her mouth as she licked her lips. Then she started to move her luscious hips into me.

My throat became dry, my pulse spiking instantly. I lost all my willpower. I sat up and tore off her tank top. She squealed as my lips found her breasts.

"So soft," I said kissing them.

She arched back, bracing her hands on the sides of my thighs. Her hair fell behind her, grazing the tops of my legs, and the feather-like sensation sent a wave of heat straight to my groin.

Then her breathing picked up and soft mewls and little cries fell from her beautiful mouth. I lifted my head and watched in quiet fascination as she got lost in her own world. I was riveted where I sat. I couldn't look away. Hell, I didn't want to.

My own breathing increased, and I started to break out in a sweat. If I didn't do something soon to tame the animal inside me, I was going to lose it, and I couldn't. Her needs came first. They always did. I made sure of it.

With her head back and her neck exposed, I trailed my fingers up between her breasts to her neck, settling on her lips. She opened her mouth, and I dipped one finger inside before she sucked then bit lightly, her body writhing on me. The way she continued to move, slow and erotic, made my dick harder than concrete. When she righted her head and opened her eyes, my heart practically stopped then tried to beat out of my chest. Lust—and something more—filled her eyes. I knew she loved me, but something deeper than love resided in those eyes. It was as though she'd just opened her soul for me. I knew I sounded like a lunatic, but I didn't care.

"Love me, Kade." Her mouth covered mine, her hands getting lost in my hair.

I pulled my finger from her mouth then nipped on her tongue. She tugged hard on my hair, and I couldn't control myself anymore. I flipped her onto her back, then I stood up.

"Sit up," I commanded.

Her rosy lips split into a smile as she obeyed me. "I love when you get all rough and sexy." Then she reached out to grab onto my shorts.

"Patience," I barely got out. Who was I kidding? My body was on fire as my gaze roamed her toned abs, breasts, pink cheeks, and messy hair and finally fell to her legs.

She held her bottom lip hostage as she smoothed a finger over one of her nipples.

The fire inside me blazed into an inferno. I dropped to my knees then removed her sleep pants. My eyes shot to hers. No thong or panties, and her tattoo was on display.

My little minx just simpered then shrugged as she eased open her legs, exposing the one place I'd been dreaming of tasting.

She whimpered as I stared. I couldn't believe she was all mine. I trailed my tongue along the inside of her thigh, taking my time as I inched upward. I bypassed the one place she wanted me to touch, teasing and tasting over her hip, her tat, then her abs.

She tugged on my hair, wiggling, trying to push me toward her sweet spot. I kept up my assault on every other part of her body until I couldn't take it anymore. I grabbed her butt and pulled her toward me. When I covered her bundle of nerves lightly with my lips, she shot off the couch. I settled into a rhythm, sucking, tasting, and licking. Her breathing grew shallow, her moans louder, the muscles in her legs bunched. I knew she was close, so I eased up. I wasn't trying to torture her. I wanted her pleasure to last an eternity. The problem was that I wasn't going to make it another minute. *This is about her, not you, idiot.*

"Kade," she pleaded.

I slipped a finger inside her and sucked on her clit. She mewed more little noises, moving her hips into me. Every muscle in her legs tightened before she moaned her release.

When she finally relaxed, her moans barely a whisper, footsteps sounded above us. I jerked up my head to find horror painted on her pink cheeks.

I grinned. Between the panic in her eyes and her flushed face, she was downright beautiful. "They're probably going to the bathroom." I kissed the inside of her thighs. The toilet flushed. More footsteps. Then a door closed.

Her features relaxed. I shucked my shorts then crawled up onto the couch. She swung a leg over me and braced her hands on the back of the couch on either side of my head as she straddled me.

I grasped her hips, guiding her down onto Mr. Steel. Once inside her, I stilled.

Her eyelids slid shut. She was warm, wet, and ready. She opened her eyes, pressed her hands to my chest, soft to hard, and began to move. Love and lust washed over her as her cheeks flushed even more. I wanted to give her control, let her drive, but I was dying to thrust hard and fast. She splayed her fingers on my heated skin as she lifted her hips, and when she did, I drove into her, hard. She gasped.

Slow was not in my vocabulary. With my hands anchored to her hips, I lifted her up and brought her down, groaning from the friction our bodies created. She pressed harder into my chest, meeting every movement as I moved faster, taking us higher and higher until our bodies were drenched in sweat. She moaned my name softly. She was mine. All mine.

My rhythm increased as we both got lost in each other. Then she clenched around me, and I exploded, a jolt of heat spreading through my groin then my entire body, the rush roaring through me. She collapsed against me, both of us laboring for air.

I tangled my hands in her hair. "I love the crap out of you."

"This is the best way to start the day," she whispered as she tried to regulate her breathing.

No doubt. I hoped the rest of the day went off without a hitch.

Chapter 19

Lacey

AFTER AN AMAZING RENDEZVOUS WITH Kade, I showered and headed home. With bodyguards tailing me, I kept checking my rearview mirror. A black SUV trailed two cars behind me.

The past couple of days had been a whirlwind. I had trouble processing all of it. Bodyguards following me all the time, a grandfather—who might be responsible for killing Mom and Julie—popping up out of nowhere, Dad supposedly possessing a red ledger that belonged to the mob. And I was more than curious about Dad's past, especially since his past had led to the deaths of Julie and Mom. Maybe his adoptive family had the red ledger. I hadn't thought about that angle until last night. We'd been so caught up in how everyone was going to protect me that we weren't putting our heads together to figure out where this book was. Or thinking about what would happen if we couldn't find it. Lorenzino couldn't keep killing until Dad produced the book. The man would run out of family members.

In my mind, we had to take a step backwards into the past. Clearly, Dad didn't have the ledger. As we were cleaning the house from the break-in, we didn't find anything missing, and we didn't find a red ledger. Dad had given me the nursery rhyme book, and that was the only thing he had from his mom.

I found Dad on the couch in the family room. The news was on, and he was dozing.

"Hey, Dad."

He opened his tired eyes. Boy, he appeared to have aged so much since the funeral. I got comfortable on the couch next to him.

"Good morning." He kissed me on the forehead. "I know you don't have much time." He sat a little straighter. "I know you'll have a ton of questions, and over time I'll answer them. For now, I wanted you to know that my adoptive sister, Gloria, lives in Boston, and she's married to Jeremy Pitt."

"What?" My face had to be twisted up like a pretzel. "The guy Wes works for? The guy who's connected to the mob? That guy?" My mouth was wide open. I seriously couldn't handle any more surprises or information. "Are you telling me you're related to two mob families?"

We could write an epic novel on our lives.

"Her husband is a Harvard grad. He'd been a prominent defense attorney up until a couple of years ago. No one said he was connected to the mob. He runs businesses."

"Dad?"

He held up his hand. "Lacey, put aside for the moment the word *mob*. Please. Frankly, I'm tired of hearing that word. We're humans. We make choices. In the case of both my families, whoever they are, I didn't choose them. And as much as I don't want anything to do with my past, my sister wasn't the one to blame for why I took off. And that's a story for another time," he said sternly. "Gloria and Jeremy are concerned about us."

"You've talked to her?"

"The first time I've spoken to her since I left home was three weeks ago. According to her, she's been searching for me for years. She found me in LA a few months before the murders. And when we moved here, I never sought her out. Her husband discovered that we lived in the area."

My head spun like a spinning wheel spinning yarn. Questions flew through my mind. Yet the one that stuck out the brightest was, "Have you asked her if she has the red ledger? Maybe she didn't give you all of your mother's things."

"Sweet Pea, I will. I'm going to speak with her and Jeremy. Let me worry about this. I know you want to help, but I want you to concentrate on—"

"School and baseball." I was tired of hearing that one. He was right though. I'd worked hard to get to this point, and I did want that baseball scholarship to ASU. But lives could be at stake—Dad's, Rob's, even those of the men who protected me.

"Have you considered that Lorenzino could hurt you?" I asked.

"He won't," he said matter-of-factly. "He needs me to find that ledger. I'm not telling you not to worry, because I know you will. But rest assured Detective Fisher is watching every move Lorenzino and his men make. You should get to school."

Reluctantly, I rose. "Can I meet Gloria?" I was excited to meet someone in Dad's family.

"Let's get through this first."

I guessed I could wait. Concentration on baseball *was* key. Our first game was next week. I needed to be in my zone. Coach was counting on me, and so was the team. A reprieve from all this would help my clouded mind. I kissed him goodbye and headed to school.

I sent a text to Kade once I was in class. I knew he would worry even though I had men tailing me.

He sent me a heart and a smiley face back along with *How did it go?*

I texted him back. *I now could be related to another mob family... lol. Can't wait to hear all about it. See you at lunch.*

I had the urge to laugh out loud. I couldn't wait to see Kade's reaction when I told him I was related to Pitt.

During lunch, Coach Dean requested my presence in his office. When I arrived, I found Shaun and Aaron sitting inside.

"It's short notice, but Mr. Camp has asked if I could send you to the middle school this afternoon. He would like your help with his gym class since most of his players are in gym, and he'd like you to stay afterwards and help his team. He's also asked if I could send three players. Shaun will be going with you. I've already set up passes for you to leave school early. This is a great opportunity for all three of you."

"Coach, why Shaun?" Aaron flicked a thumb at Shaun. "No offense. You're new here, and we do have some great ball players."

Shaun shrugged. "I was curious, too."

"Mr. Camp has pitchers who need work. Shaun has a great change-up and splitter. Lacey has her fastball, curveball, and slider. Gather your things and head over there. He's expecting you within the hour."

I welcomed the change in pace, despite having to work with Aaron. The opportunity to teach my skills to a younger crowd would take my mind off my problems and give my brain a chance to clear.

I trudged to my locker to drop off my books. I was about to dart down to the cafeteria to let Kade know my plans when Shaun sauntered up. His locker wasn't far from mine.

"Can I bum a ride?" he asked. "I don't have my car today."

"Yeah, meet me out in the main lot. I have to do something first." I hurried down the hall, past other students hanging out near lockers, chatting. I rounded the corner and saw Kelton either talking to a brunette or about to kiss her. They were so close that it was hard to tell.

I slowed my pace and cleared my throat. His head came up, and he gave me one of his cocksure grins. "Kade is looking for you," he said, not budging from the girl.

"Can you tell Kade I'll be at Swain Middle? Aaron, Shaun, and I are helping a teacher with gym class and baseball practice."

He stuck his finger in his ear, moving it around. "Okay, I think my ears are clear. Did you say that you and Seever are helping little kids?"

I couldn't remember if I'd ever shared that news with Kade or his brothers. "Shocker, right? I'll send Kade a text as well."

He wasn't going to be happy about Aaron and me working together.

The ride over with Shaun was a non-event. The black SUV followed us and parked in a spot along the road where they could see me. Gym class was held outside under the warm March sun, a welcome change to the cold and snow we'd had last week. The field was clear of any snow, though it was still damp. Eight out of the twenty students were on Swain's baseball team. Aaron, Shaun, and I were working with those on the team.

I was enjoying the fresh air as I worked with a boy, Eddy, and girl, Pam, who were having trouble with their fast pitch. We spent time talking about how to hold the ball, the mechanics of the pitch, and how to breathe when pitching. Aaron had taken four players to a grassy area on the side of the school to work with them on batting. Shaun was working with two boys on their pitching on the other side of the field from me. Mr. Camp, a man in his forties, was holding down the fort with his other students, having them throw a baseball back and forth to a partner. My group was close to a heavyset boy who was throwing to a meek girl with blond hair. From the looks of it, she didn't want to be there.

"God, you're pathetic," the heavyset boy said. "Throw the ball like you mean it."

The tone of the boy's voice caused me to stop and watch. The blonde returned the ball, but it fell short of the boy.

"Girls shouldn't be playing baseball," he said. "Pick it up and throw it again." His tone was condescending.

I swallowed as my face heated. I'd had plenty of boys in middle school tell me the same thing, even though I could throw.

With her eyes downcast, the girl gingerly picked up the ball.

I regarded Eddy and Pam.

Pam said, "Ron is a bully."

I got that. What seeped into my pores, spawning my anger even more, was that the girl was obeying him. I trotted up to the girl. "What's your name?"

She picked up the ball. "Tiffany."

"Can I see the ball?" I held out my glove. "Would you mind if I play catch with your partner?" I didn't want to embarrass the girl. I also didn't want to put her in a worse situation where Ron would lash out at her, thinking she needed a big sister to fight her battles.

She lifted a dainty shoulder.

"Would you also mind if I taught him a lesson? I know you have to go to school with him."

"Be my guest," she said in a soft, low voice. She went to stand with Pam and Eddy.

"Ron," I called. "It's you and me. Show me what you got, dude."

He smirked as though he was about to show me a thing or two about how to throw a ball. He whipped one at me.

I threw the ball back, not hard. We volleyed for several throws. He had a good arm. Then I readied the ball for one of my seventy-mile-an-hour fastballs. One of those pitches in anything other than a catcher's mitt could bruise a hand and sting like ten beehives. When he caught it, he squealed. Pam and Tiffany giggled. Eddy chuckled.

"Is that all you got?" Ron said as he returned the ball.

A few more fastballs and the boy wouldn't be able to hold a glass in his hand. I threw another one. That time his face grew beet red. I didn't want to torture him too much. I also didn't want to be accused of bullying myself.

I jogged up to him. "The next time you call someone pathetic, or tell a girl she shouldn't play baseball, or pick on Tiffany, remember that sting you feel in your hand. You got it?" I whispered so low only he could hear.

His head bobbed up and down fast at every word I said.

When I joined my group, Aaron was walking up with his. "Showing off, Robinson?" he asked.

"Teaching," I responded. I had other smartass comments, but I kept them to myself. I didn't want to come off as a bully in front of my group or Tiffany.

"Is Lacey treating you right?" Aaron asked Tiffany.

"She was great," Tiffany gushed with excitement.

I did a double take. "Relation?"

"Sister," Aaron said as he mussed Tiffany's hair.

I didn't know why I was surprised. Then again, I didn't know much about Aaron's personal life.

The bell rang, and we had about fifteen minutes before we had to shift from gym class to practice with the entire team. I used that time to send Kade a text, figuring he should be getting out of his last class for the day.

Chapter 20

Kade

I PINCHED MY NOSE RIGHT BETWEEN my brows. My fucking headache was back. I stalked into the Ashford Library and scanned the immediate area. I hadn't spotted any black SUV on my way in. I assumed Chloe would show up in one of the black Escalades since those vehicles were standard issue for Wes's team.

A middle-aged lady, hunching behind a semi-circular counter to my right, peered over her reading glasses. My phone vibrated in my hand. It was a text from Lacey.

Sorry I missed you at lunch. I hope Kelton told you. I'm at Swain Middle working with kids.

I texted back. *He did. I'll see you later.*

I wore a hole in the tile floor as I paced in front of the entrance. *You can beat the hell out of me for not telling you I had a date with a gorgeous blonde, a date with your cousin.*

Where the fuck was Chloe? I had at least an hour with her if the knife-like pain in my head didn't kill me first. My headache had slowly been blooming like a damn spring flower since lunch, when Kelton had relayed Lacey's message. Not being able to talk to her before my meeting with Chloe had driven me bat-shit crazy. It was bad enough Lacey was going to be furious that I'd held back so much information. Even more so if she found out I already met with Chloe or someone saw me with another girl.

People talked in this town. Kids from school came to the library. *Smooth move, Maxwell. You're the one who chose the public place.* Well, it was fucking better than a private one. At least if we met in a public place, I could claim that I wasn't trying to hide anything from Lacey. I laughed silently at my reasoning. Either way, I was in the shitter. I should call Mr. Robinson and have him join me. That way we could both take the heat. *For what? He did his part.*

The door opened. Blond, beautiful, and way too happy for my mood, Chloe sashayed through the doors. Her hair draped over her blue blazer and the low-cut white clingy top underneath. She carried herself like a magazine model. *Christ, Maxwell. Get your head out of your ass.* I was going to hell.

I ground my teeth together so hard I swore I heard them crack.

She beamed as she set her sights on me. "Kade, nice to finally meet you. My father was rude in the garage last week. But hey, the situation called for it."

That was rude? I'd call it fucked up. Anyone who had his men hold five guys at gun point for fighting each other had to be insane. "I think he got carried away over his Mercedes."

She drew her body up to mine and planted a kiss on my face.

I jerked back.

"Sorry, habit. Just a friendly gesture."

I was afraid to sweep the room to see who from Kensington was in the library. Since it was Friday, I'd venture to guess not many. "Why don't we get started? I have to meet my girl later." *Or sooner, if possible.* "Let me check with the librarian and make sure we can use that room." I flicked a finger to the empty room adjacent to the main entrance.

"It's free," the librarian said from behind her counter. "Go on in."

I guess there was something to be said for eavesdropping. Chloe went in before me. I was strung as tight as a guitar string as I ambled in behind her.

She removed her math book and a notepad from her leather bag. "So, I suck at math," she said as she settled into a chair at the end of the table.

And I suck at relationships. "Well, let's see what you got." I slid into the chair next to her.

Opening her book, she said, "My test is on logarithms."

I leafed through the chapter on logarithms. After forty-five minutes of explaining and her asking questions, she seemed to be catching on. So, I chose five equations and two word problems for her solve. While she tackled problems, I practiced my speech to Lacey in my head. As I did, I kept fidgeting, squeezing my temples, squinting from the bright light above, and checking the time.

Baby, I've wanted to tell you something. I had to wait until your father... That wasn't a good way to begin. *Baby, I've known something for days now, and I haven't told you because it wasn't my story to tell.* No, scratch that. Either way I was bringing her father down with me, and he wasn't at fault here.

A silky hand touched my wrist. "Are you okay?" Chloe asked. "You look like you're in pain."

I was. My head hurt so fucking bad that I had a knot the size of a nasty volcano waiting to erupt in my stomach. "I have to go out to my truck. I'll be right back." I rushed out into the sunshine and squinted so hard I thought my head would burst. I climbed into my truck to check the console for any aspirin, even though it didn't help my migraines. Maybe taking the whole bottle might. I rummaged around and came up empty. I growled, the small act putting more pressure on my head. I got out of the truck. The parking lot and the cars in it tilted in one direction then the other. Flashes of light followed by patches of dark spots blinded my vision. I lost my footing and fell on my ass. I covered my eyes, pressing my hands to my head in hopes of pushing the pain away.

I wasn't sure how long I'd been on my ass when a soft hand touched mine. I peered up, my eyes barely open, to find Chloe and some hefty dude towering over me.

"Kade, what's wrong?" Chloe asked.

"Head," was all I could say.

"Did you hit your head?" the guy with her asked.

"Don't yell." Every syllable was like a nail to my head.

"We're not," Chloe said. "Al, we should take him to the emergency room."

Chapter 21

Lacey

THE SWAIN MIDDLE SCHOOL TEAM drifted onto the field around two thirty that afternoon. Aaron, Shaun, and I continued with our respective roles. Only this time, I played catcher. Eddy was up first, practicing his curveball.

"All right, let's see what you got." I readied the catcher's mitt.

Eddy wound up and threw the ball. I jumped up and caught his wild pitch. As I returned the ball to Eddy, I spied Aaron watching me from his group down along third base. I stuck him with a glare.

He trotted down the line to home plate. "It doesn't appear your coaching is paying off for the kid."

"Go back to your group. I don't need your advice," I said low.

"You want me to show you how it's done?" His snide tone rode my nerves.

"Do you want to get into a knockout in front of the middle schoolers?" My knee was positioned at his groin. I so had the itch to raise it just a little.

"You just better pray *you* don't pitch like that in our first game." He jogged back to his group.

I silently swore as I put on what I hoped was a winning smile for Eddy and threw him the ball.

Just over an hour into practice, a vehicle screeched to a halt next to the field. I watched it warily.

Kelton hopped out of his truck. "Lacey!" Kelton shouted. His hands were flailing.

My heart rate ramped up. Kelton didn't get nervous, ever. I looked for Mr. Camp.

His sharp jaw dipped. "Go."

I handed the ball to Pam, quickly grabbed my bag, and ran to Kelton. My first thought was Dad. Lorenzino had come into town and hurt my father.

"We need to go." Kelton's handsome face was twisted in fear. "Kade is in the emergency room."

I shut my eyes, shaking my head. I didn't just hear that. A panic attack hung in the wings. *Breathe.* The buzzing started. My legs were quaking.

"Get in." The timbre of his voice was high and firm.

"What happened?" I strapped on my seatbelt. "Was it Lorenzino? Greg? What? How badly is he hurt?"

"Don't know." Kelton sped through the streets of Ashford as fast as the stop signs and traffic lights would allow. "A lady called from Kade's phone and told me to get to the hospital. I tried calling you."

"A nurse. A doctor?" All I could see was Kade hurt with blood all over him. The sunlight dimmed in my peripheral vision. I closed my eyes, held onto the passenger door, and prayed I didn't black out. Kade didn't need me to panic, and neither did Kelton. He'd already seen one of my blackouts, and he didn't need to witness another one.

"Don't know. We're here." He threw the gears in park at the emergency room entrance and jumped out.

I blinked, breathing in deeply. Once I felt I had complete control of myself, I hurried as fast as I could on shaky legs. Thank God for automatic doors.

Kelton strode up to a gorgeous blond girl who was sitting in a chair against the bank of windows to our left. When she saw Kelton, she popped up, and her long hair spilled around her shoulders, framing her porcelain skin.

"I didn't know what to do. Kade had to run out to his truck for something," she said in a singsong tone to Kelton. "When he didn't come back, I went out there. He was on the ground, holding his head. He was conscious, but seemed to be in a lot of pain. I asked my bodyguard to bring us to the hospital. Then I called you."

"I have to call my father," Kelton said, stomping toward a water fountain on the wall.

She set her big brown eyes on me as her pink lips split into a smile. "Hi, I'm Chloe." She extended her long delicate fingers.

My pulse raced. "I'm Lacey, Kade's girlfriend." I gave her my unsteady hand, clenching my jaw tightly. My anxiety and any sense of a panic attack morphed into confusion and anger.

"So, I hear," she said with a sprinkle of disappointment underneath.

Kelton returned, his eyes a little red. Then he swung his gaze between Chloe and me, and the color drained from his face. "Um... My dad is on his way back from the Berkshires."

Before I lost my cool as to who this girl was and what she was doing with Kade, I wanted to make sure he was okay. I scurried over to the information window. "I'm here to see Kade Maxwell." I twirled my hair while the middle-aged blonde typed on a keyboard.

"He's in with a doctor. I'm sorry, you'll have to wait," she said.

Tears pricked my eyes. I wasn't sure how many more surprises, lies, and pain I could endure. I was trying to be strong, except the people I loved were making it hard for me to persevere. I wanted to be an adult and reason and work through a problem. I couldn't do that if I was lied to or treated like I was a fragile piece of glass that would break if someone blew on it.

I chiseled out one last piece of strength, opened my eyes, and went back to Kelton and Chloe. Kelton was on the phone again near the main entrance. Chloe had resumed her seat along the window.

I parked my butt into a chair across from her. "So you found Kade at his truck. Where were you two?" *If she says a hotel, I'll reach out and punch her.*

"We were at the Ashford Library. He was tutoring me. I suck at math, and I have a test on Monday," she said in her flowery voice.

"And how do you know Kade?" *If she says she dated him, I might still punch her.*

"I don't exactly. He knows my dad, Jeremy Pitt."

I seriously was going to have a mental breakdown. I grimaced at

Kelton. He was staring at me as he listened to whoever was on the other end of his phone. After his call, he stalked over to me and sat down one chair over.

"So, you're my cousin?" I asked Chloe.

"I guess your dad finally told you," she said in a silvery tone. "It's about time. My mother has been worried about you and him."

"So, you know Kelton?" I was confused.

"Not exactly. I was at the boxing match last week with my father. Kelton and Kade were there." She tucked strands of hair behind her ear.

Kade hadn't told me that part. I got that he knew of Pitt. The entire city of Boston knew of him. But she had said Kade knew her dad as though they were business acquaintances. I guessed they sort of were, if Kade was tutoring her. Why didn't Kelton react when I said we were cousins, though? Expletives usually flew out of his mouth when something surprised him, and if Kelton knew, Kade must have known, too.

"My dad spoke to the doctor here." Kelton fidgeted with his phone. "Kade is going to be fine. He's having an MRI done. Apparently, he's having migraines again."

Migraines? Again? For as long as I'd known Kade, he'd never been sick or complained of headaches. At this point, I wasn't sure how much anger was stored in me. What else hadn't he told me? With all the information he kept close to his chest, I wasn't surprised the guy didn't have something worse than migraines. Why was it so critical that he keep all this from me? He was not only hurting himself physically, he was hurting me emotionally. He was driving a wedge in our relationship.

Chapter 22

Kade

AFTER MY MRI, I HAD to wait until my father arrived before I could leave. He wanted to take a look at the results of the scan himself. I knew my migraines were a result of stress, but my father was always cautious, and I was grateful he was. There was always that chance my migraines could lead to something else.

My scans were normal. The doctor gave me medication and a prescription before my father wheeled me out to the waiting area. Immediately, my brothers, Chloe, and Lacey converged on me like hungry paparazzi.

"Is he going to be okay?" Chloe and Lacey asked in unison.

I brought my hands up to shield my eyes from the bright lights. The medication hadn't kicked in yet. Kross whipped off his sunglasses and handed them to me. I slipped them on, sighing in relief.

"He's going to be fine," my father said. "I want to get Kade home. He needs some rest."

I thought I'd like a dark, quiet place with Lacey and me snuggled together, then threw out the part about Lacey and me. Her posture quickly changed from rigid to loose to rigid again, and she pursed her lips. I went to grab Lacey's hand, but she backed away. Yep, something was bothering her. She hadn't let me hold her hand after I lied to her in the school parking lot the other day. Hurt wormed its way down into my chest. I had it coming. Until my head cleared, I wasn't in any position to talk about Pitt, the mob, or anything else, except to tell her I loved her. Somehow I didn't think those words would dissolve the friction between us.

"Migraines again, bro?" Kody asked. "Too much of your brain is spent on us and family. You need to get back to working on cars or something other than worrying about loved ones."

Lacey's head whipped around toward Kody. I'd give anything to be in her head right now.

"I have to run," Chloe said. "Thanks for helping." She placed her hand on mine. "I'm sorry about your headaches. We'll talk soon."

Lacey winced when Chloe touched me.

Then Chloe turned to Lacey. "It was nice meeting you. When we have a chance, we'll get together. I'd like to get to know my cousin. If that's okay with you?"

Lacey smiled through the hurt and anger that shone in her eyes. "I'd like that. Maybe by then I'll be in a better mood. Sorry for all the questions."

My gaze shot to my brothers in search of some clue to what had transpired between Chloe and Lacey. None of them gave me any signs.

"One thing my daddy taught me about men," she said to Lacey. "The protectors are the hardest ones to tame, whether they protect your feelings or your life." Then she hugged Lacey before dashing for the door.

Lacey appeared to be mulling over that piece of wisdom. Hell, I was too.

"Come on, Lacey. I'll take you to get your car," Kelton said.

She hesitated before she followed Kelton. She flashed a weak smile at me. "I'm glad you're okay. Can I stop by later on? We need to talk." She looked past me to my father then back to me.

"That should be fine," my father said.

I gripped the arms of the wheelchair, holding back my urge to vault out of it and cocoon her in my arms and make all her anger, hurt, and pain go away. But if I did, she wouldn't listen. Sorry wasn't going to be enough this time. I was certain of that.

The ride home with my father had been deathly silent, which was a welcome relief. The medication the doctor gave me was just kicking in, and my head no longer felt like someone was beating it repeatedly with a sledgehammer.

After a shower, I went down to the theater room, a perfect place for migraine sufferers. No sooner had I sprawled out on the couch than the stairs squeaked.

Lacey padded in with her arms crossed over her chest as she chewed on her lip. "Has your headache gone away?" she asked in a flat tone.

"It's waning." I debated whether to launch into my speech or let her say what was on her mind. "You're upset. And I'm to blame."

"I am upset and confused." She sat down on an ottoman on the side of the TV. "How come I didn't know about Chloe and your tutoring job? Did you know that she was Pitt's daughter?"

In one week our lives had turned to shit. I explained everything, starting with the boxing match and ending with, "I am a dick for not telling you any of this. Your father's adoptive family wasn't my story to tell. In no way is this an excuse, but I was taught not to come in between a family's problems. So I waited for your dad to tell you. I'd planned to tell you about Chloe after school today. You were busy."

Her knee bounced up and down. "I'm not even sure I know who you are. You keep so much from me. Time and time again I've asked you not to. To let me decide what I can and can't handle. Yet you continue to choose what you tell me and when. Am I that fragile and pathetic that you think I'd break into a million pieces?" She got up and paced in front of the TV. "I've lived through finding the dead bodies of people I loved dearly. I've pushed hard in the last year to get where I am. I'm not perfect." She stuck her hands on her hips and pinned a death look on me. "I'll always have memories, nightmares, and symptoms of PTSD." Her face reddened. "How can I heal or face my fears when the one person I love, who's supposed to support me and help me, chooses to make the choices that are not his to make?"

I hopped off the couch and moved toward her. She backed away.

I was about to lose it. I hated that she wouldn't let me touch her. I grabbed my hair with both hands. *No matter what I say, she isn't going to believe me. Sorry isn't going to help either. I've said that a few times. Yet I continue to lie or keep things from her. Trust is huge for her, and I'd broken that sacred vow.*

"And you haven't even told me about your migraines?" Her voice broke.

"Lace." I shoved my hands in my jean pockets. "Tell me something. Are you allergic to anything? Did you have the chickenpox when you were a kid?"

"Huh?"

"Tell me," I said in a hardened tone.

She huffed. "I'm not allergic to anything I know of. I had the chickenpox when I was three."

"Tell me everything else about your life as a kid."

"I see what you're trying to do."

I stalked up to her but didn't touch her. "We both have a past. We both have things in them that we haven't shared. We've only been in a relationship for six months. We can't get mad at each other when something from our pasts surface, like my headaches. I'm not apologizing for not telling you about my migraines. The Pitt and Lorenzino saga—that's a different story. So be mad at me for that. Punch me if you have to." *Just not in the balls.*

Her nostrils flared as her eyes narrowed into slits. "I'll do you one better. We need a break. I need a break." She stomped out of the room.

Chapter 23

Lacey

I RUSHED OUT OF KADE'S AND came home. Crash, bang, and boom, the walls were tumbling down. At least that was the way I felt. The weather matched my mood. Lightning lit up the sky as I sat in my sunroom, gazing out into the night. When the thunder rumbled, I shuddered. I hadn't stayed in the house since the break-in. Even though the automatic lights had been on when I arrived, I'd asked Hunt if he wouldn't mind checking out the house before I ventured in. Then I'd asked him to stay inside with me since he was my bodyguard at night. His partner stayed in the car, watching over us from the outside.

I let my mind wander over everything—Dad, Lorenzino, Rob, Aaron, baseball, ASU, and Kade. I was frightened that my dream of baseball and attending ASU could be in jeopardy. How could I concentrate on the game when every time I turned a corner I had a fast pitch flying at me?

If I was building a relationship with Kade, I wanted to be his partner. I wanted him to confide in me, ask me my advice, and let me make my own decisions. I never once doubted his love for me. I couldn't keep going if he kept shutting me out. Maybe we weren't cut out for each other. Maybe he needed someone who accepted his way of protecting a loved one. Lies might protect, but they can certainly destroy, and he was destroying our relationship more than protecting me.

I also worried about Dad's and Rob's safety, as well as my own. I was on alert with Aaron, and I'd been wracking my brain about where that ledger could be. *The box of keepsakes.* I uncurled my legs from the chair.

"Lacey?" Hunt called.

A bolt of lightning split the sky, and Hunt's reflection shone in the glass of the sunroom.

"Your dad has been trying to call you. Here." He came into the sunroom and gave me his phone.

"What's wrong?" Dad asked. "Where's your phone?"

"Nothing. My phone is up in my room." I was upset with Dad, too. He could've told me sooner about Lorenzino, his mom, his adoptive family. Maybe we could've put our heads together earlier to uncover the ledger. Plus, we could use more family members around us. I surely could. Whether Dad was home or working, I felt alone. Friends were great to have, but they didn't replace family. Kade was the closest person I'd consider family.

"Are you sure you want to stay in the house tonight?"

"Yes." *No.* "I'm a big girl. Hunt is here." Kade must've called him and tattled on me.

"I'd prefer if you stayed at Kade's," he said.

"That's not happening." Kade needed as much space to think as I did. If we were in the same house, it would be difficult to think straight.

"Sweet Pea, please reconsider."

"Dad, I have to live here. I can't let fear drive me. I promise if I feel I can't stay, I'll have Hunt bring me to Kade's. Besides, you've met Hunt. He's a monster of a guy." I winked at Hunt.

He puffed out his chest.

"Oh, and I talked to Gloria today. I invited her, Jeremy, and Chloe over for dinner after your game next week."

"Really? That sounds great." It was the first piece of good news I'd had in a while. I'd like to get to know his family, including Chloe. She seemed nice and bubbly, a trait I could use to rub off on me, although I wasn't sure of her intentions with Kade.

"I got to run. Love you," Dad said.

When I hung up, Hunt's phone rang. Kade's name came across the screen. I handed it to him. Despite my anger with Kade, I was also concerned about him. I'd never experienced a migraine. My mom had had them. They'd knocked her down for the count. It wasn't only migraines; stress overall wasn't good for anyone's health.

"Hey, dude." Hunt answered the phone then left me alone, his voice trailing down the hall. "She's fine. Man, get some rest. Stop worrying."

I trudged up to Dad's closet. His bedroom was simple, with a bed, a dresser, a chest at the foot of the bed, and an old worn-out red chair he cherished. It was the first piece of furniture he'd owned. In our California home, the red chair had been tucked in a corner in Dad's office.

I dug my feet into the soft white carpeting of his walk-in closet. Like the bedroom, the closet was sparse. Shirts and pants hung from the rods, another dresser lined the back wall, and four pairs of shoes sat on the top shelf.

I snooped in all the drawers in both dressers and came up empty. I set my sights on the chest. Mom had always stored blankets in it. I opened it, and the scent of lavender filtered up—Mom's favorite fragrance. Aside from the nice smell, several items were neatly packed inside—Mom's jewelry box, our baby albums, old car magazines, music CDs, my parents' wedding album, and a shoe box. But no ledger. I sifted through the jewelry box and flipped the top off the shoebox. In it were greeting cards that Dad and Mom had exchanged over the years along with some keepsakes—Dad's old watches, cuff links, and an engraved bottle opener with Dad's name on it. As a last resort, I did a once-through on the entire room.

Disappointed, I padded over to my room and flopped on my bed. Dad was right. How could we produce something we didn't have? The book of nursery rhymes sat on my nightstand. I snagged it and flipped through the pages. The book's cover was shiny and thick, and the pages were made of a cardboard like the cover's, only of a thinner gauge. The pictures beneath the rhymes were raised slightly off the pages. I found "Humpty Dumpty" and read as I traced the outline of the colorfully dressed egg boy. Tears burned my eyes as I thought of reciting the rhyme to Kade at the airport. As I stared at the page, my dam of emotions opened and I let the tears flow.

I stood on the mound waiting for the batter, who was talking to his coach, to pony up to the plate. Over a week had gone by. I'd been sleeping in my own bed with Hunt babysitting me. The first night, I'd cried myself to sleep. The nights following got a little easier, although I wasn't so focused on someone breaking in as I was about Kade, the ledger, and baseball. I'd seen Kade in school. He'd tried to talk to me a few times. I brushed him off. I wasn't ready yet. Aside from the disappointment of not finding the ledger or any clues in Mom and Dad's keepsakes, I was excited to meet Gloria and spend time with Chloe. Maybe Gloria would open up more about Dad's mom and whether she'd missed something that belonged to Dad. Through all that, baseball had been first and foremost as I got ready for our first game of the season.

We were up by one run against Kennedy, and I was hoping to close the game with a win. The stands were packed with kids shouting and whistling. Since it was a home game, most of the school was watching, including the media. A local station was lined up on the sidelines with their camera pointing at us. I couldn't say I was surprised. Renee and I were the first two girls to play again since Mandy's death, and we were the only two on any of the teams we were playing this season.

Mark Wayland, our catcher, came running out to the mound. "Okay, three outs. That's all we need to win this game." His red hair stuck out of his ball cap.

The infield joined us, huddling close.

Finn, who played first, tapped my glove. "You got this."

Tim, our second baseman, did the same as Finn then said, "What he said."

Both returned to their positions.

"Let's win this, Robinson," Aaron said. "Maybe I won't harass you so much."

Kelton pushed Aaron. "Watch it, Seever."

"Stop it, both of you." I glared at Aaron then Kelton. This wasn't the time to compare who had the bigger penis.

Mark gave me the ball and trotted back to home plate.

"In and tight," Aaron said nicely before returning to third.

I turned the ball over in my glove, confused as to why he was acting like my best friend. I discarded the thought. I had to concentrate on my pitching and striking out the next three batters.

"My mom would be so happy if we won." Kelton skimmed the stands behind home plate.

"Your mom is home?"

I'd wanted to meet her, but I'd never pushed the issue. Mr. Maxwell had said in due time. He'd been apprehensive about how she would react to strangers. I was okay with that. I didn't know a great deal about mental health issues, except my own, and when I did meet her, I wanted it to be a warm and happy experience for her.

"Just for one night. If you would talk to my brother, you would know. He may be stubborn, but he does"—his face twisted in pain—"love the crap out of you."

"Did he tell you to tell me that?" Kade had instructed Kelton to tell me that during tryouts last fall to help ease my nerves. I was more focused on his mom and that I hadn't known she was home. This wasn't the time for family matters, or love, or anything else, even though a pang of hurt was stuck in my chest.

"Fuck no. You two have to work out your own shit."

I looked to the bleachers. Kade, Kody, and Mr. and Mrs. Maxwell were sitting in the second row. Mr. Maxwell brushed his wife's long black hair away from her face. She leaned into him and said something. Mr. Maxwell grinned from ear to ear like a little boy who was flirting with his first love. Then she sat up straighter, adjusting her large dark sunglasses. She reminded me of a movie star who was hiding from the paparazzi—beautiful, elegant, and poised.

"No pressure," I mumbled, wishing my own mom was here. She'd cheer for me louder than anyone.

As Kelton slipped back to shortstop, I stole one last glance at my dad, who was sitting behind the Maxwells with Tyler and Becca. He'd invited the Pitts to the game and dinner, but they hadn't been able to make the game. My dad touched the bill of his Kensington High ball cap, a gesture he always did to let me know he was cheering for me.

I dug my cleat in the dirt around the mound then set my sights on home plate. The top of Kennedy's line-up was batting. The lead-off hitter had gotten a double off my first pitch in the first inning. I stretched my neck as the batter got into position. Finally, Mark gave me a signal for a curveball. I went through my routine, checking the infield and outfield, making sure everyone was ready. Satisfied, I relaxed my shoulders, placed my index finger on the ball, aimed at my target, and threw.

"Strike one," the umpire called with his right thumb up in the air and his index finger pointing outward as though he was shooting at someone.

On the next pitch, the batter swung and missed. The crowd was on their feet, shouting. One more strike. Kicking one foot out of the batter's box, the lanky batter rolled his neck one way then the other, looked down to his third base coach, then stepped back into the batter's box. Mark gave me the curveball signal. I readied the ball in my glove, wound up, and fired the ball into Mark's glove.

"Strike three," the umpire's voice boomed before the home crowd roared.

The batter stormed away, banging his bat against the ground.

I got in a groove, my confidence and zone tightly reined in, and repeated the same pitch three more times. Now, with two outs, my heart raced with excitement. One more batter, and the first game would be in the record books—my first full game pitching for Kensington High. For a second, I couldn't believe I was standing on the mound, pitching again.

Mark jogged out while the next batter took practice swings. "We got this. You got this. We win and the other schools will get wind that a girl struck out ten batters in a game. They'll be running scared." He placed the ball in my glove then tapped my shoulder with his catcher's mitt. "Three strikes." He trotted back.

If I could strike out the short stocky guy at the plate, then it would be my all-time best. Stocky Guy crouched low, back elbow high in the air, and waited. I tossed a glance over my right shoulder. Aaron punched his glove. I checked on Kelton. He nodded. Tim and Finn did the same. Kross was in left, Renee in right, and Dave in center. All three of them pounded their fists in their gloves. My stomach churned with a nervous excitement in anticipation of winning. A sense of warmth spread through me knowing we were a team. At that moment, I felt like I belonged there.

The crowd was on their feet, chanting my name. Mark gave me the signal for a slider. Back in September when I was trying out, my slider had been horrible. I'd had no control over it. Six months later, it was better than my curveball.

I held the ball a tad off center, cocked my wrist, and threw. The ball landed in Mark's glove with a thud.

"Ball," the umpire said, deep and loud.

Argh. I stretched my neck one way then the other, and, out of habit, checked Finn at first. Then I wound up, raised my left leg, and released the ball. In slow motion, it traveled down to home plate. The batter swung at air as the ball thudded into Mark's glove.

"Strike," the umpire called.

The fans were still standing. I stepped off the mound and caught the ball Mark threw. I returned to the mound, released a breath, settled into my stance, and threw another slider. The batter swung, and the ball popped off his bat behind Mark.

"One ball and two strikes," the umpire announced.

One more strike, I chanted to myself. This time Mark signaled a fastball. While my fastball was the bomb, my slider was working with two strikes. However, Mark was one of those great catchers that could read a batter. Since he was expecting another slider, Mark had a point. The dude wouldn't be expecting my fastball.

My gaze drifted to Kade. He angled his head. My eyes shifted to his mom then back to him. My hand trembled in my glove as I thought about Julie and Mom.

"Something wrong?" Aaron's voice drifted in amid the crowd's chatter.

Yeah, my life. Your life consists of baseball. Focus.

"Robinson, get your head out of your ass." Aaron's tone was snarky and hard.

I despised him, but his voice snapped me back. So I threw the pitch.

"Ball," the umpire said.

Damn it. I circled the mound.

Mark returned the ball. Aaron jogged up, as did Kelton.

S.B. Alexander

"Get back, Maxwell. I'll handle this," Aaron said.

Kelton pressed forward.

"It's fine, Kelton," I said. Aaron wasn't about to do anything stupid.

Kelton hesitated a minute before he returned to his position.

"I want this win. You want this win. Pitch the ball like you have been. In and tight. Got it?"

I hadn't expected any of those words out of his mouth. I was waiting for *I'll break your arm if you don't win this game.* "Yeah."

He jogged back to third base.

I did want this win, and letting my team down because of my problems wasn't an option. With all the energy left in me, I gripped the ball and let it fly. I didn't hear the umpire. All I saw was the batter swing at air, and the next thing I knew, I was in someone's arms and they were lifting me up. The way the guy was squeezing me, I thought it was Kelton until I went to smack him and locked eyes with Aaron. Oh, my word. Aaron Seever was holding me like he hadn't seen me in ages and wanted to kiss me.

Shock rocked my body. I immediately squashed it. I wanted to savor this moment for all kinds of reasons. I'd pitched my first complete game. I'd reached my all-time best. We won the game. Aaron was lifting me high in the air, and I was on top of the world. For all the bad that had happened, the game and the win gave me hope that I was back. The last time I'd felt that elated had been when the coach at Crestview, my old school in California, had put me in to close a game with one out. The first batter I'd pitched to had popped out, and the second kept fouling the ball until he swung at one of my curveballs and struck out. That game had clinched the playoffs for us.

But within seconds of Aaron picking me up, Kelton snatched me from him with unease flashing in his blue eyes. I almost told him to chill. Then I remembered Chloe's words of wisdom: you can't tame a protector. And Kelton was just as protective as Kade.

After we celebrated as a team on the field, Coach came up to me. "You did good, Robinson." He proceeded to pat my head.

The last person to bump fists with me was Renee. "Awesome, Lacey." Her lips curled with one side of her mouth turned upward, reminding me of my sister, Julie. The resemblance was so uncanny that it had

150

caused me to black out when I first pitched to Renee at tryouts last fall. Now I felt as though Julie was with me in spirit.

"You were awesome, too, girl." She'd batted in a run and hit a home run, giving us two of our three runs to win the game.

I searched for Dad. He was standing with the Maxwells. He said something to Kade, who had been talking to his mom. Dad touched the tip of his ball cap, and Kade waved with a somewhat cheerful smile. When he said something to his mom, I tore my gaze away. My anger over his deceit had transformed into despair, and I was close to tears. I didn't want to ruin the high I had over the win.

Renee and I walked off the field. The media barricaded us, firing off a barrage of questions. *How does it feel to win your first game, Lacey? Renee, how does it feel to be responsible for two RBIs? Ladies, how did it feel to show the boys on the other team you could play like them?*

Before I could answer, Aaron came up alongside me, mumbling under his breath. I couldn't make out what he was saying. I was certain that he didn't like us getting all the attention. After all, he'd hated when the media had paid attention to the last girl on the team, Mandy Shear.

"The win feels great," I said. "The real credit goes to my teammates, though. I couldn't have pitched a good game without them." I wrapped one arm around Renee and the other around Aaron. He tensed. "These two are great ball players, especially our captain." I flicked my head at Aaron. It was the truth. The guy could field a ball every which way, and he could hit. He was responsible for the other home run.

"So, how does it feel to be playing with two girls?" an attractive brunette reporter asked, shoving the microphone in Aaron's face.

This I had to hear.

He moved away from me, flipped off his ball cap, then combed his fingers through his sweaty hair. "I see them as just one of the players on the team. Gender doesn't play a role on the field." He jutted out his chin.

Renee had a wildly surprised look, and I imagined I did as well. What the hell? Given the confidence in his tone, I couldn't decipher if he was telling the media what they wanted to hear, or if he was sincere. Whatever. I wasn't going to complain, at least not right now.

When the reporter asked Aaron about college, I tuned them out and lifted my gaze back to Dad. It landed on Kade instead. He waved again, only this time with a wider smile. I went to return the gesture when out of nowhere Tyler came running onto the field. He lifted me up in his arms like Aaron had, squeezing me.

"Is that your boyfriend, Lacey?" a reporter asked. "Star pitcher dates star quarterback. Great headline."

"Give me a break," Aaron murmured, brushing past me.

"Tyler, you're embarrassing me," I said. "Please put me down." I didn't mind a hug from Tyler. When I'd told him that Kade and I were on a break, he'd given me a hug, telling me that Kade and I would work things out. I didn't want to draw attention away from the win and the team to become a reporter's headline, though.

He grinned, his blue eyes sparkling in the sunlight. "I love your slider. You've gotten so much better."

At that moment, Kade appeared. "Put her down, Langley." His voice was rough as he emphasized each word.

"You're dating a Maxwell, too?" the reporter crooned.

Renee rolled her eyes. "Seriously?" she said to the reporter before she followed Aaron off the field. "See ya, Lacey."

The reporter was worse than the gossip mill at school. As Tyler slowly released me, he planted a kiss on my lips. Next thing I knew, someone had pulled me away from Tyler, and Kade's fist was flying into Tyler's face. Tyler returned a punch to Kade's chin.

"I told you to stay away from her," Kade growled.

"You're not dating her anymore. I told you you'd screw things up with her." Tyler kept his hands clenched at his sides.

"Are you getting this, Frank?" the female reporter asked in a jaunty voice.

The cameraman was filming the scene playing out like it was a soap opera. Our great win was squashed by two guys fighting over me. The headline wouldn't be about how Lacey Robinson pitched a great game or how a girl shut down an entire team of boys. It would read that two men had vied for the attention of the star pitcher. No one would take girls seriously in the game.

Heat clawed its way up my neck to settle in my face. If I yelled at either one of them, I'd only add more substance to the juicy story the reporter was developing.

Kelton and Kross came over. Kelton pulled Kade away, and Kross stepped in between Kade and Tyler.

"Bro, not here. Dad has eyes on you, and he's not happy. And let's not forget Mom," Kelton said.

Kade tore his arm from Kelton and stalked off the field. I sought out my dad. This wasn't the place to give Kade and Tyler a piece of my mind. So I gathered my gear and met Dad at the base of the stairs to the parking lot.

When we were alone in the car I blurted out, "Men."

"Sweet Pea, Kade loves you. It's my fault he didn't tell you about Chloe sooner."

"Don't take the blame for him. He could've told me everything, and when it came to who Chloe is, he could've just said he'd let you tell that part. Then I would've bugged you and you would've told me. I've been upset with you, but not as mad as I am at him. I want to make my own decisions. I want to feel like I'm his partner and not his daughter or a fragile person who can't handle anything."

"You're right. I always viewed your mom as my partner, asking for her advice and including her in my decisions. A relationship is about being partners, no matter what. I'll do my part to include you in family matters."

Finally, a breakthrough. "Thank you."

Another mission ahead of me was to get Kade to come to the same conclusion, only as my boyfriend. But I wasn't sure he could.

Chapter 24

Kade

I PACED IN LONG FURIOUS STRIDES inside my garage. I couldn't go into the house knowing my father wanted to tear me a new one. I'd shamed the family in public. I'd acted out in front of my mom. A searing pain shot through every limb in my body. I couldn't face her at the moment. I would crumble into nothing if I'd upset her.

Tyler was right. I'd pushed Lacey right into his arms. I didn't know how to fix our relationship. We couldn't pick up where we'd left off. I'd dug a hole so deep that crawling out of it wasn't enough. Not this time. The only good thing was that she was safe. I'd been calling Hunt every night to check in with him. Part of me was jealous of my best friend. He was spending time with her, eating dinner and watching movies.

I rubbed the back of my neck. The side door opened, and my father came in on a gust of wind. His expression was blank, which was never a good sign.

"Should we suit up and get in the ring?" I asked, nodding to the ring Dad had put in so Kross could work out.

"Is that what you want? You want to feel pain, son?" He pinched his chin.

"It's better than the pain inside here." I tapped on my chest.

"Hitting someone isn't the answer, Kade. Not even in a jealous rage. I've taught you better than that."

"Well, I've never been in love before." I smoothed a hand over my hair, fighting the urge to pull it out.

He wandered up to the boxing ring. "You remind me a lot of myself. I hated when men looked at your mother when we were dating. I wanted to wipe every last suggestion of lust off their faces. But that wouldn't have accomplished anything."

"How did you handle it?" *Give me something to take away the pain clawing in my chest.*

"I tried not to show your mother any outward signs of jealousy. It was extremely hard. When you're in love with someone, it's hard not to display your feelings. You have to trust your relationship. You have to communicate with one another about how you feel. Men are going to gawk at Lacey. Women will do the same to you. Talk about how it makes you both feel."

"Tyler is in love with Lacey."

"So?" He shrugged. "She's not in love with him."

"She confides in him." I joined my father as we both sat on the edge of the padded floor of the ring.

"Maybe because he listens. Or maybe she feels like he gets her. I don't have the answer. Son, open up to her more about your feelings, and I don't just mean love. Tell her what makes you mad, sad, happy, what you're afraid of. You get my drift."

He had a point. I knew Lacey was happiest on a baseball field. I knew what made her mad. But aside from her PTSD triggers, I didn't know what else frightened her. For me, spiders were high on the list. I'd wrestle a bear over a spider. I hated the feeling of a spider crawling on me.

He patted my leg. "There's a lot going on. It's time to relax a little and enjoy your senior year. You only get to live this time in your life once. Why don't you boys have a party down by the lake?"

"How can we? We're still watching over Lacey. Until we know what Lorenzino is up to, relaxing's hard." And I certainly hadn't done anything to help the situation. She didn't want to talk to me. I wasn't sure what I could do. Maybe a party would be a way of breaking the ice with Lacey.

"Let law enforcement do their job. Shake off your anger then march into the house and apologize to your mother. She's a little shaken up that Tyler hit you. She's in the formal living room with the triplets."

Fuck. If I'd ruined any of her progress toward coming home permanently, I wouldn't be able to live with myself. My pulse beat rapidly as I went in search of my mom.

A lamp glowed on the table near the bay window in the living room, and a fire crackled in the stone fireplace along the back wall. The triplets were scattered around Mom, who was sitting on the couch. All heads turned when I walked in.

"Are you hurt?" Mom's voice was soft and delicate, her blue gaze drifting down to my jaw.

"I'm not. I'm sorry you had to see that." I grasped one of her hands gently as I settled next to her.

Water filled her eyes.

"Guys, can you give us a minute alone?" I asked.

"Sure thing, bro," Kody said.

One by one they kissed Mom on the forehead before leaving.

"I can't handle seeing any of you boys hurt. Karen can't either." She brushed a strand of hair off my forehead, a single tear sliding down her cheek.

"I promise. I'm not hurt. I love you and Karen. Will you tell Karen that for me?" My own eyes clouded with tears. My entire body should burn for upsetting my mother.

She blinked, a tear catching on her eyelashes.

I had to get my jealousy and anger—and everything else in my world—under control or else I was about to screw up my family circle and hurt those I loved the most.

Chapter 25

Lacey

I BARELY HAD ENOUGH TIME WHEN I got home after the game to change and freshen up before our guests would arrive—let alone think about Kade and Tyler's feud. Apparently, they'd had words prior to today. I buried that for now. I didn't want to dwell on anything that would sour my mood in front of Dad's adoptive family.

An enticing aroma floated through the house. Dad had prepared beef stew in a crockpot with the help of one of Mary's recipes. It would've been nice to have Mary here to cook one of her amazing lasagna dishes along with her famous red velvet cake, but the stew smelled delicious. My stomach grumbled.

The doorbell rang just as I was brushing out my hair. I was curious how Dad would handle himself given he hadn't seen Gloria in ages. I was also interested in meeting the infamous man of Boston. I checked myself one last time in the mirror then started downstairs.

Chloe bounced in as beautiful as ever. Behind her was a petite lady who wore her blond hair up in an artfully messy style, and on her heels was a tall man with dark eyes and dark hair with graying sideburns. He wore an open collar shirt underneath a black blazer.

"James," Gloria said. "It's so good to see you, and I'm so happy you called." She hugged Dad as her husband closed the door.

"Smells amazing," Chloe said as she waved at me. "Lacey, did you win?"

Her bubbly personality was the medicine I needed to take away my sour mood. "First game, first win." I beamed from ear to ear.

Dad appeared relaxed as he shook Jeremy's hand. Chloe hugged Dad then me. The girl had a touch fetish. When she'd touched Kade's hand in the emergency room, a pang of jealousy had whipped through me. I guessed touching people was in her nature.

Gloria wrapped her arms around me and squeezed. "I've heard so much about you," she said. "Sometimes I wish Chloe had taken up a sport. It would've toughened her up."

"Mom." Chloe rolled her eyes.

Their interaction reminded me of my mom. She had always said just the opposite. *I wish Lacey had a little more interest in girly things.*

"Lacey." Jeremy and I exchanged a loose hug, his suit jacket smelling like cigars.

Once the pleasantries were out of the way, we made ourselves comfortable around the dining table just off the kitchen. Dad had everything prepared so that we could serve up the bowls of stew ourselves, making the atmosphere casual. Jeremy and Gloria sat on one side of the table, and Chloe and I were on the other. Dad sat at the head of the table.

"A girl pitcher, huh?" Jeremy said as he placed his napkin on his lap. He raised an eyebrow. "And how fast is your fastball?"

"Seventy-five miles per hour."

"No kidding? I'd like to see you pitch."

Dad swallowed a bite of stew quickly and said, "Then come to a game. She did so well today. She's worked really hard despite what we've been through. I'm extremely proud of her."

Warmth radiated through me to hear Dad's declaration. I had worked my butt off. I couldn't have gotten to this juncture without him.

"One of the reasons for my call"—he glanced at Gloria—"was to reconnect. I also wanted to share with you that Lorenzino could be my father."

Now I was proud of Dad. He dove right in, not mincing words or wasting time.

"Wes told me," Jeremy said with no sign of emotion.

Chloe and Gloria sat regally, postures straight, left hands in their laps as though they'd been to a Miss Manner's school of proper etiquette. I graded my own posture. My left elbow was on the table, and I was hunched over my bowl. Not wanting them to think I hadn't been taught properly, I straightened my spine and placed my hand in my lap. Mom and Dad weren't strict on perfect table manners. Mom's pet peeve had been talking with food in your mouth. Apart from that, we ate, talked, laughed, and fought over the last piece of bread or the last of the mashed potatoes.

"And you're okay with that?" I asked. Dad was related to two mob families. I didn't know much about the mob. Mostly what I'd learned was from movies or TV shows, but I didn't think mob families aligned with each other, especially if one was Russian and the other Italian.

"Why wouldn't I be?" Jeremy asked. "You're family. I'm not sure what you're implying."

Dad glared at me.

"Well, can two mafia families get along?" I took a bite out of my bread.

Jeremy laughed heartily. "The bigger issue here, Lacey, is finding that ledger Lorenzino is after and stopping him from harming anyone in the process."

"What is so important in a ledger that someone would kill over?" I chased down my mouthful of bread with iced tea.

Jeremy wiped his mouth with his napkin. "Names, dates, burial grounds, money laundering information, tax evasion. Could be anything."

"Information like that is old news," Dad said. "The ledger has to be at least forty years old."

"True. And the statute of limitations has probably expired on most of the criminal activity associated with whatever is in the ledger. However, burial grounds are not just for bodies. Harrison Lorenzino's great-grandfather was tied to several bank robberies. He was known to bury money to hide it from the Feds. That ledger may list the places where some of that money is still buried."

"We've looked everywhere for that ledger." Dad swiped his fingers across his forehead.

"Do you think you missed something when you sent my dad the package from his mom?" I asked Gloria.

"Sorry, sweetie. We don't have anything else and neither does my mom. I went through all her belongings after her funeral a couple of years ago. If we had anything of your father's, I would've put it in the package. And our father passed away four years ago."

Wow! Dad's past slowly unfolds. "How did he die?"

Dad grasped his spoon. His knuckles became white.

Gloria regarded Dad before she said, "My parents weren't the healthiest. My mom died of heart disease, and my dad had a bad liver."

"Gramps drank a lot," Chloe said. "I always try to get my dad to cut down on his whiskey."

My dad was about to bend his spoon in half.

"Here's how I see it," Jeremy said. "Lorenzino is waiting and watching. The LAPD have been questioning him, so he's being cautious. If he is your father, I don't think that matters one way or the other. Greed can drive some men over family."

"I'm not his family, and I want nothing to do with him," Dad stated firmly. "If he did kill my family, then I want to see him pay dearly for it."

Dad couldn't catch a break. I had the urge to hug him. We were talking about one father who was dead and another who might've killed Mom and Julie.

"Can we talk about something else?" Chloe asked. "Better yet, can Lacey and I be excused?"

Maybe it was a good idea to talk about something else and give Dad a chance to breathe before he converted that spoon into a piece of art.

"Take your dishes to the sink first," Gloria said.

Chloe shot off the chair with her bowl in her hand, her ankle boots scuffing the wood floor.

"I have one of my men looking into Dennis Weeks's background. Kade mentioned him to me the other day," Jeremy said to Dad. "Do you know that name?"

Jeremy sounded like he and Kade were old friends. Kade had told me everything they'd discussed. Hearing it from Jeremy, though, made the deliciousness of the stew turn sour in my stomach.

"No." Dad released the spoon. "The LAPD apparently has a confidential informant. I guess Weeks's name was brought up. Detective Fisher has been silent about what type of lead he has."

"I'll let you know what I find." Jeremy sat back and draped his arm on the back of his wife's chair. "I have feelers out on Lorenzino, too."

Dad smoothed his fingers across his mouth. "Mmm. When I stopped my research on my mother, the detective I'd hired had given me a report with names of people my mother was associated with. I could reach out to them."

Another avenue to investigate.

"Not a bad idea. Just be careful those people aren't connected to Lorenzino," Jeremy warned.

Chloe returned. "I'm sorry to hear that you and Kade broke up."

"Chloe," Gloria said. "Don't pry. Where are your manners, young lady?"

"It's okay," I said. "It's true. How do you know?" I took my bowl to the sink with Chloe on my heels.

"I called him to tell him I passed my math test. I was supposed to have another tutoring session with him, but his mother came home and he wanted to postpone."

"And he told you we broke up?" I filled my bowl with water as I tried to imagine a conversation where Kade told someone other than his brothers or Hunt that we'd broken up.

"I asked about you." She twirled her hair in both her hands. "He said he messed up. I don't know what's going on. I do know my daddy is a very demanding man. He wanted to feel Kade out and see how well Kade knew your family. Like I said, my mom was worried about both of you. Your dad didn't want to talk to my mom, and I desperately needed a tutor. That was Daddy's way in."

"Young lady." Jeremy's deep voice reached us from the table.

"She needs to know. You could be responsible for their breakup." She frowned at her father.

It still wouldn't change anything. Our problems went deeper than Jeremy and his scheming ways.

"Anywho," Chloe whispered. "Is Kelton dating anyone?"

"Kelton?" I didn't know how to answer that one. *Do I warn her away since Kelton is a playboy? Do I play matchmaker so she doesn't set her sights on Kade? Or do I stay completely out of it?*

"He's yummy." She tucked strands of her hair behind her ear.

The triplets were definitely handsome. I shut off the water. "I'm not a good matchmaker. I suggest you talk to Kelton yourself." Kelton's playboy ways or who he was dating wasn't any of my business, and I barely got anywhere with him when I tried to talk to him about love. The Maxwell boys didn't kiss and tell either.

"I already left him a message," she said.

Wow. She works fast.

Gloria brought her dishes to the sink. "Chloe's right. My husband can be overpowering," she whispered. "You and Kade will work it out."

"Does Jeremy keep things from you?" I asked.

"When we first met he did. It drove me crazy. But beneath his tough exterior is a man who loves and cares deeply for his family. He'd do anything to protect us."

"How did you handle it? I mean, Jeremy keeping things from you?" I rested my hip against the counter. I could use all the advice I could get.

Chloe was texting. The men were in their world talking about the statute of limitations.

She swept my hair over my shoulder, her brown eyes searching my face. "At first, I had to walk away. But I realized that wasn't the answer. We both loved each other. He isn't perfect, and neither am I. Look, sweetie. You can't get mad every time Kade keeps something from you. Understand his reasons. You have to meet each other halfway. Decide what you can and can't handle and communicate with him."

I hadn't even given Kade a chance to explain, and I certainly didn't understand his reasons, except the part about Dad's adoptive family not being his story to tell. I'd assumed he didn't tell me because he didn't want to worry me.

"Gloria," Jeremy called. "We should get going. I have an early meeting."

"Daddy, I barely got to spend time with Lacey."

"There'll be time for that later," Gloria said.

Chloe huffed.

It had been a long day. I was tired both mentally and physically.

Jeremy and Dad agreed to swap information if they had anything of substance regarding the ledger, Lorenzino, and Weeks.

After they finally drove away, I asked Dad, "Are you okay?"

"I am," he said as we cleaned up the kitchen. "I never had a problem with Gloria. Now, my father was a different story. He and I never got along. He always treated me like I was a male Cinderella. Over the years, he drank more and more to the point where he took out his drunken frustrations on me. He was very abusive. One night when I was seventeen, I came home past curfew. He was waiting up for me. We had words, then it got out of hand. We both ended up in the emergency room. After that I took off." He loaded bowls into the dishwasher.

"I'm so sorry, Dad." I stopped wiping down the table. "I know that had to be hard for you to tell me." I wasn't about to ask for details. The fact that he'd told me that much was a win in my book. Frankly, that was all I needed to know. The details would only serve to anger me more, and I couldn't take out my anger on a dead man.

"I don't like talking about him. I don't even like thinking about that time in my life, though it did feel good to say it. But let's concentrate on the future."

Great idea. "So when are you going to call those people your mom was associated with?"

"I want to talk to the private investigator I hired first. Jeremy's right. We need to make sure the names in that report are not associated with Lorenzino."

"I can do an internet search while you talk to the PI. Better yet, I can have Kody help. He's good with finding things on the internet." Kade had once told me Kody was a whiz with Google searches and computers in general.

"Tell you what," Dad said. "Let me read through the report and talk to the PI, and then we can put our heads together on a plan of action. Deal?"

I smiled so wide, my cheeks hurt. It was the first time I'd felt like an adult with Dad, and I was excited that we had another avenue to search.

Chapter 26

Kade

ODY AND I SAT ON my tailgate down by the lake watching our friends and family enjoying themselves. My brothers and I had liked the idea of having a party. In my mind, it was a way to let loose and maybe reconnect with Lacey. During the past week of school, it had driven me fucking insane not to be able to sit with her at lunch or talk to her or touch her. Something had changed in her since the night of her first baseball game. She seemed happier. Maybe it was her first win. Maybe she wasn't mad at me anymore. Or maybe she was moving on with her life. The last thought gutted me. I grilled Hunt for information since he spent nights with her. All he said was that she was happy she was finally getting to know about her father's past. *Please let it be that and nothing more.*

Not surprisingly, news of the party had zipped through the school halls like a damn rocket. Anytime anyone was having a party, the entire school seemed to show up. I hadn't gone to many. At the ones I had, people had been packed in like sardines in the kitchen and open areas of the house. Not my scene. The lake—and the breathing room that came with it— was the perfect venue for me.

The night air was fresh and crisp as the campfire crackled and threw the occasional spark. "Chasing Cars" by Snow Patrol blared from speakers that Kelton set up on the deck of the boathouse my father had renovated into a game room. Lacey had dubbed it the funhouse. Tents dotted the landscape. Anytime we had parties, we set up our tents and told others to bring theirs. Battery-powered lanterns hung from tree branches, giving the lake area a dim glow. Guys were snuggled up with their girlfriends around the fire, including Kross and Becca. I'd give anything to have Lacey cozied up to me by the fire. Instead, I hung with Kody, drinking a beer. I didn't drink all that often, and I was hoping the alcohol would ease my nerves. I was mainly waiting for my baseball beauty to arrive. My plan was to play it cool. Not suffocate her. Keep it casual. Hunt texted me and said she was on her way.

"Your girl might want my help doing some fancy Google searching. Her dad has a couple of names of people his mom knew. They might be able to shed some light on uncovering her or the ledger."

I growled. *I* should be helping her, although Kody was the computer mastermind. He could find a needle in the haystack that was the net.

"Are you ever going to talk to her?" He also had a cup of beer in his hand.

"And say what? I already apologized. That's not enough."

"Grovel then. You're brooding." He finished off his beer and burped.

"Says the brooder."

He nudged me, flicking his chin toward the path leading down from the garage. Lacey glided down it dressed in tight jeans and knee-high boots, her hair flowing behind her and a smile on her gorgeous face. Heat unfurled inside me, sliding down to my groin as I pictured her on the stairs in nothing but her thong as she caressed her naked breasts. That seductive image vanished in an instant when Tyler trotted down the path.

"Lacey," he said. "Wait up."

I tightened every muscle in me. *If he so much as touches her, the cold lake has his name written all over it.*

Kody held out his arm. "You can't let him bother you. She'll always have guys checking her out or vying for her attention. Trust her. Trust what you guys have together."

I wasn't sure we had anything at the moment.

Tyler planted his hand on the small of her back as they found their way to the campfire.

I cussed under my breath, and every one of my muscles vibrated.

"Easy, tiger." Kody slowly lowered his arm.

I gulped a large mouthful of beer, my eyes glued to Lacey and Tyler.

Becca and Kross scooted closer to Shaun, who was the only guy in the circle without a girl. Lacey sat cross-legged next to Becca. Tyler scanned the grounds. When he found me, I tipped my cup to him. Restraint burned a path through me. Fighting wasn't the way back into Lacey's good graces. I had to be the bigger man. I had to show her I was in control, even though I envisioned throwing Tyler into the lake. He said something to her, and she nodded. I tracked his movements to the cooler then back to Lacey. He handed her a can of soda.

She swept her hair over her shoulder as her eyes met mine. I waved casually. She set down her soda and pushed upright as my phone buzzed.

A text from Hunt. *Sullivan is here on crutches. You want me to stop him?*

I showed Kody my screen.

"What the fuck?"

I typed my response. *Is he alone?*

Seever and his girl, Tammy, are with him.

Nah. Let him walk among the wolves.

"You sure, bro? This can't end well, and it's not a way to win your girl back. Although I'd love to have a go at Sullivan again."

"He's not here to fight if he's on crutches." I was curious why he was here.

We hadn't seen or heard from Sullivan since he'd been shot. It had only been a few weeks since the ordeal. He had to be recovering still. I texted Kelton, who was in the funhouse playing poker, and copied Kross on the message. The music died. Kelton flew out of the funhouse. Kross stretched to his full height, keeping his sights on the path down from the garage.

Lacey began her trek toward me. At the same time, Sullivan emerged. Seever and Tammy were by his side. Kody hopped down, meeting Kross and Kelton as they converged on Sullivan. The kids around the campfire scrambled to their feet. Others at the water's edge did the same. Shaun and Becca sidled up to Tyler, who swung his gaze from my brothers to me. He angled his head and opened his palms.

I shrugged. I wasn't moving. My brothers could handle the situation. I'd intervene if need be.

A light scent of citrus floated in the air as Lacey propped her hip against the edge of the tailgate. "Hi."

Her sugary tone sparked goosebumps on my entire body. "Thanks for coming."

"A party, huh? When I first moved here, I remember some kid at school bragging about how off the hook the Maxwell parties were. Seems tame to me."

"Well, give it an hour or two. The brave and drunken ones will be throwing themselves in the lake." I searched her face, my gaze landing on those glossy lips that I was dying to capture between mine. Hell, I wanted to devour them, slide my tongue into the warm cavern of her mouth, and taste her.

"You're not going to read Sullivan the riot act?" Her eyebrows knitted.

"Nah. My brothers can handle it," I said easily.

"Are you sure you're really Kade Maxwell?"

I stretched out my hand. "I am." I wanted to touch her so bad. "You must be Lacey Robinson. The school is abuzz about this great pitcher who pitched two more winning games this week."

She placed her hand in mine. "Nice to meet you, Kade Maxwell."

When her fingers landed in my palm, tingles shot up my arm. I lowered my head and planted a soft kiss on the back of her hand. "It's my pleasure."

She blinked, her long lashes fanning out over her silky skin as a slow ball-squeezing smile materialized.

Our quiet, pleasurable moment died when the bane of my existence hobbled toward us with Seever and Tammy flanking him. The triplets had wry smirks plastered on their faces as they stalked up behind them.

"It seems they need your help," she said.

"Will you stay? I need backup." *Give her the choice.*

She lifted a shoulder. "Sure. I've been known to kick butt." She climbed into Kody's spot on the tailgate.

Tammy, Seever, and Sullivan settled in front of Lacey and me. I felt as though we were the king and queen of the land. My brothers crossed their arms over their chests, never losing their annoyed expressions. Tyler wormed his way up to stand next to Lacey, and Shaun and Becca ponied up to Tyler. Our other guests clambered closer, and hushed whispers buzzed around us. Sullivan hunched over his crutches as his dark and insolent gaze fixated on Lacey and me.

Tammy Reese waved at me with a flirtatious smile. In spite of her sweet façade, the girl was downright trouble. Before Lacey, she'd been the only girl I'd dated at Kensington. Tammy and I had had dinner once, and one time was all I fucking needed with her. She babbled non-stop over a dinner she didn't eat about wanting marriage and babies as soon as she graduated. That wasn't for me. Sure, a family was definitely in my future, but not when I graduated high school and not with her.

Lacey scowled and mumbled under her breath.

Seever shoved his hands into his Kensington letter jacket. "Hear my cousin out before you go ape shit."

"I need your help," Sullivan said. His beady eyes narrowed.

"Do you want me to put you out of your misery?" I couldn't help it. My enemy, the one who'd almost killed Kody, wanted my fucking help.

Snickers, snorts, and other derisive sounds echoed through the crowd.

"Ha, ha. Seriously, Maxwell. You know it had to take a lot for me to come to you for help."

"What do you think, Lace? Should we let him speak?" I didn't take my eyes off of Sullivan.

"Why not? He is outnumbered." Her tone dripped with sarcasm. "You have the floor, Mr. Sullivan."

He regarded Lacey with a cold, clinical expression.

"You heard the lady. Speak," I said.

"How much do you know about Jeremy Pitt?" Sullivan spoke the words slowly as though he was rethinking his decision to come here.

Dead silence, except for the crackling of the fire.

A smile flirted on Lacey's lips as our eyes met. She licked them as though she was hungry to tell him the answer to his question. A rush of adrenaline charged through me. Since Pitt had threatened both of them about touching Lacey, I was eager to see Sullivan and Seever's reaction.

I bowed to Lacey. "You have the floor again, Ms. Robinson."

Chapter 27

Lacey

SURPRISE SHIMMIED ALONG MY SKIN. Kade hadn't barked out orders at his brothers or me. He'd given me the choice to stay by his side. He'd asked for my opinion on Greg. He wasn't throwing his fist into Tyler's face or Seever's or Sullivan's, and he'd allowed me to address Greg's question.

I squared my shoulders and stared at Greg. "Mr. Sullivan, shouldn't you know about Jeremy Pitt? After all, you and Aaron are the ones who've been conspiring with two of his men to hurt me."

The partygoers let out a collective gasp.

"We weren't going to hurt you. We knew Tyler was listening that day at the restaurant. We knew he would bring that back to the Maxwells. It was a way to get under their skin and get them to react."

He was as crazy as Aaron. "How did you want them to react? By putting you in the hospital?"

Kade's jaw flexed. "Or maybe kill you? Did you not get enough pain from Kross and Kody?"

"Let me get this straight. You were trying to use me to get to the Maxwells. Is that right?" I asked.

"Something like that," Sullivan said firmly.

Kade groaned.

I raised my eyebrows. He'd told the truth. First step in the right direction. Okay, this could be fun. Aaron was here. Greg was here. My beef was more with Aaron. Maybe if I caught them off balance, one of them would accidentally reveal something about what had happened to Mandy. It was a long shot.

"So, Aaron, what's your story then? Are you trying to hurt me or are you trying to use me to get to the Maxwells? And if I were you, I would choose your answer carefully."

He inclined his head, his green eyes appraising. "I'm not sure what you're implying."

"Cut the bullshit," I said evenly. "When we ran into each other in the hall at school, you told me you wished my plane had crashed on my way back from California. Did you not? Oh, and you threatened to break my arm if I made the team. And let's not forget about the psychological game you instigated where you had Tammy steal my gear before tryouts then return it, making it appear like I was the one who was crazy." I had never been interested in the drama club or acting. Yet, I felt like I was on stage as the partygoers were all gathered around watching and listening intently.

"You threatened her again?" Kade asked. "You truly are psychotic."

The triplets pressed forward. Tyler mashed his lips into a thin line. Shaun had no expression at all, and Becca sent Aaron a death glare. The crowd around us whispered and gasped.

Tammy smirked at her boyfriend. I wanted to smack the amusement from her face.

I held up my hand as though I was a judge presiding over a criminal case. Adrenaline cascaded through me. I was enjoying this way too much. The sounds died. The triplets held their ground. Aaron glowered.

"I came here for help," Greg said. "I didn't come here for you to grill my cousin."

"You should've thought about that before you stepped into your enemy's lair," I said.

"What's your deal, bitch?" Tammy asked.

Becca sidled up to the tailgate and said to Tammy, "Shut the hell up. You're just as bad as your boyfriend."

Tammy lunged for Becca. Tyler wedged in between them.

"Cat fight," someone in the crowd shouted.

Aaron snagged Tammy's arm and pulled her back to his side.

"Tsk, tsk. Such a pretty face." I said. "Such a shame you ruin it when you open your mouth. No wonder Kade didn't want to date you anymore."

Kade whispered, "Are you sure you're really Lacey Robinson?"

"New and improved," I said.

His lips tilted up into one of his famous Maxwell grins. "I like new and improved."

"Fine, you want to do this here and now? I was fucking with your mind," Aaron said, holding his head high.

"Like you always do, fucker," Kelton muttered.

Aaron's jaw hardened. "You're a good ballplayer. So good it pissed me off. Is that what you want to hear?"

"No." I raised my voice. "I want the truth. If we're going to win games and work as a team this season, I want to get all our cards out on the table." I waved my hands around to encompass everyone who was watching. "If it has to be in front of the whole school, then so be it." I didn't like airing my dirty laundry to strangers. But I had enough to worry about and no time to wonder if and when Aaron would strike. "You want to win. Right?"

He let go of Tammy. "I did my homework on you when you first arrived."

"You don't have to do this," Greg said.

Aaron continued. "I asked Coach about you too. He showed me tapes of your games at your last high school. I'd never seen a girl pitch like you. You're the best girl I've ever seen play. No offense to Mandy. She was good, but not like you."

Kody mumbled but kept himself in check.

"I was afraid any scouts who showed up this season wouldn't pay attention to anyone but you. I hated you. I wanted you to go away. Then two things happened. I saw how you helped my sister, Tiffany, with that bully, Ron." He shrugged. "I knew then you were a team player and not someone who was out for herself."

Or maybe he'd *learned* a lesson about being a team player.

He scratched his head. "Then after our first game when you pitched your ass off and we won… I don't know. I didn't want to start the season with an attitude that would bring down the team. Shit, it's my senior year, the scouts will be at games, and as captain I need to keep things positive. I know with your pitching that we'll go to the playoffs. Both you and Shaun"—he gave Shaun a cursory glance—"have been great so far."

"Thank you," I said. "Does this mean all your psycho games are over and we can play ball without all the snide comments and threats?"

"My goal is to win games and win State. Plain and simple." A sheen of sweat coated his face.

The crowd applauded, whistled, and shouted.

A boy in the back yelled, "You got balls, Seever. I admire you for that."

A girl said, "Way to go, Lacey."

Aaron sounded sincere, and for him to spill his guts among his peers was better than a simple *I'm sorry*. But I wasn't going to bask in glory just yet. Words were great. Actions were better. We had more games to play, and he was standing amid the Maxwells, who wanted to let loose their fury not only for his threats against me, but because Aaron was one of Greg's co-conspirators.

I angled my head at Kade. "What do you think?"

"That was a great speech, Seever," Kade said. "Time will tell how sincere you are. It's your turn, Sullivan. Are you willing to come clean like your cousin? Maybe apologize to Kody for putting him in the hospital?"

Kody's blue gaze was drilling a hole in the back of Greg's head.

"This was a bad idea on my part," Greg said. "I'm out of here."

"You came here to ask for help," Kelton said. "You're here now. So talk."

The triplets still had their arms crossed over their chests and were blocking Greg from leaving. He scratched his black greasy head.

"Just ask the question," Seever said.

"Why? So we can stand here and go through another round of questioning from a girl who thinks she's better than us?"

"I hate to break it to you, Sullivan. She is better than you," Kade said. "Lacey is better than most people I know, including me. She doesn't go around bullying people. She doesn't go around calling people bitches. She doesn't threaten to break someone's arm just because they might be better than her on the ball field." Kade glowered at Tammy, Aaron, and Greg.

Again, surprise wound through me. Kade wasn't the type of person to brag about anyone or anything, and definitely not in public. Part of me wondered if the change in him tonight was a one-time occurrence designed to help us resolve our differences.

"You don't have to defend me to them," I said to Kade.

"You're right. But if I don't, I'll put Sullivan in the hospital along with Seever." He turned to Greg. "I've heard enough tonight. Say what you came here to say, then get the fuck off my property. We're trying to have a party."

Everyone clapped again.

"My father doesn't believe Pitt's men shot me," Greg said. "I thought I could ask for your testimony as to what went down that night. If you recall, the police didn't question you or Kelton or Hunt. There is no police report, and Pitt won't take my father's calls."

"That's not our problem," Kelton said.

"I'm confused." Kade hopped off the tailgate and got in Greg's face. "You want us to tell your father what? That you and Seever ambushed Kelton, tried to beat the shit out of him, and pulled a knife on me? Is that what you want? I'd be more than happy to do that."

Greg straightened, adjusting his crutches. "And how Pitt's men shot me."

"Why?" I asked, climbing down to stand next to Kade.

"Without a police report, I can't prove anything, and I want Pitt to go down for what he did to me."

"Aaron isn't the only one with balls," Kross said. "How dare you ask us for help when all you've ever done is cause us trouble? Unless you're willing to spill the truth about your involvement in Mandy's accident, then I suggest you leave before I break your good leg."

Kody's chest rose, and his nostrils flared.

"Or," I said, "I could ask my Uncle Jeremy for a meeting in exchange for your testimony about your involvement in Mandy's accident."

"Come again?" Greg said. "Are you telling me that *the* Jeremy Pitt is your uncle?" His seedy features were scrunched up in ten different ways.

"That's what the lady said." Kade grinned smugly, as did the triplets. "Do you still want to bargain?"

The buzz in the crowd grew louder.

At my back, Tyler said, "I didn't see that one coming."

Aaron said, "Shit."

The others also spouted words in surprise, but my attention was on Greg.

He considered his options, then he said, "I'm out of here. I've told the police and you a million times I had nothing to do with Mandy's accident."

"Didn't you see her at the same gas station just before she died?" I asked. I remembered Kody telling me Mandy called him when she'd seen Greg at the gas station.

"I told the police that," Greg said.

Kody was riveted to his spot. Kelton and Kross were on either side of him.

"What did you say to her?" I asked.

The light went out in Greg's eyes as though he knew he'd never leave unless he came clean. "You would never believe me if I told you. So why bother? You already have me down as guilty regardless of what I say."

"If you know more, just tell them so we can all move on," Aaron said.

If it weren't for the rustling of the tree branches, we could have heard a pin drop. I held my breath. Kelton and Kross drew closer to Kody. Kade watched his brothers.

Greg blew out all the air in his lungs. "I was getting gas. Mandy pulled in to fill her tank. All I said to her was that it was a great day for a bike ride. She hurried to get gas. She called someone on her phone, then she peeled out of the gas station."

Kody flew at Greg, knocking him to the ground, and drove a right hook into Greg's face. Then another right hook. Left jab. Then another round. "I don't believe you," he yelled.

Greg tried to cover his face. "I swear to God," Greg shouted. "I swear."

Tyler, Aaron, Kross, and Kelton peeled Kody off Greg. Then Aaron helped his cousin to his feet.

Kody was breathing heavy. "Get the fuck off our property. And no, you don't get our help, ever. Whatever your beef is with Pitt, handle it yourself. If I ever find out you aren't telling the truth—whether it's next week or ten years from now—I'm hunting you down like an animal and killing you."

"One last thing," Kade said as he stalked closer to Greg. In a blur, Kade rammed his fist into Greg's gut. "That's for the night in the garage when you pulled a knife on me."

Greg bent over, grunting.

I pushed my tongue against my teeth. *So much for Kade not fighting.*

Tyler, Shaun, Kross, and Kelton escorted Aaron, Greg, and Tammy off the property.

"Becca," Kade said. "Can you do me a favor and cue up some music?"

"Sure thing." She jogged down to the funhouse.

Within minutes, music was blaring and the crowd had dispersed somewhat, talking amongst themselves and gathering around the fire again.

Despite Kade's last act, I stood dumbfounded at how the night had turned out. Kody clenched and unclenched his fists as he leaned against the tailgate. Kade joined him. I shuffled up to the other side of Kody.

The moon shone down over the lake, lighting up the ripples on the surface of the water.

Kody was still breathing heavy, his knuckles bruised and bleeding.

I slipped my hand into Kody's. He closed his fingers around mine. "It hurts to hear Mandy's name. It still fucking hurts."

God, my heart split into so many pieces. "I know the feeling."

"You know what hurts the most? I wanted Sullivan to pay. I wanted to believe he was the one who forced her off the road."

"Kody, nothing's fair," Kade said. "Our sister's death wasn't fair. The deaths of Lacey's mom and sister weren't fair. We don't control fate. We can only control our actions, our decisions. I know you miss Mandy. Just like we all miss Karen, and Lacey misses her family. At our age, we shouldn't have had to experience the hurt and pain of death. But our experiences make us stronger so we can face what's ahead." Kade's voice broke. "I love you, Kody. I'm always here for you."

"You're not alone." I threw my arms around Kody.

When Kade joined in on the hug, tears spilled down my face, and I felt as though I was part of a family again.

Chapter 28

Kade

I PASSED HUNT AND HIS PARTNER, who were parked in their Escalade on Lacey's street. When her father was home, they gave the Robinson's some privacy, although Hunt checked in with Mr. Robinson every hour.

The bay doors of Lacey's garage were open. Today I was spending time with her to hopefully mend our relationship. After the party had resumed, I'd hardly had the chance to talk to her. Kids had been chatting her up about how awesome she was and asking her if she really was related to Jeremy Pitt. She hadn't divulged much except to say that Jeremy's wife and her dad were siblings.

"Hey, Mr. Robinson?"

He poked his head out from under the hood of Lacey's car. "Oh, Kade. Lacey should be in her room. Or at least she was when I came out here."

"Problem with her car?" Please say no. The last thing we needed was for her to get stuck somewhere.

"Just changing the oil." He wiped his hands on a towel. "Have you two worked out your differences?"

"Not yet. I didn't want to ruin her fun at the party last night. We agreed to talk today." A boulder sat heavy in my stomach. Hell, my nerves were all over the place. I'd practiced my speech on the way over, but I wasn't sure words were the key to resolving our conflict. "I never thanked you for doing your part in telling Lacey about your adoptive family before my deadline."

"I know it didn't help your case with her. You're right. My daughter is strong, and we both need to be more open with her."

If only you could've seen her last night. Strong was an understatement. My girl was the star of the show. She was strong, calm, determined, and had nerves of steel. As I'd watched and listened to her interaction with Tammy, Seever, and Sullivan, I'd been spellbound. Usually she was the type of girl who acted out her aggression with knees to guys' groins and fists to girls' faces. Last night, though, physicality as a way to tackle a problem had gone out the window. Her words and fortitude had been brilliant. She'd not only earned respect, she'd commanded it in such a way that everyone either feared her or revered her.

Unlike me. It had taken everything I'd had not to fly off the tailgate and drown Seever in the lake after hearing what he'd said about wishing Lacey's plane had crashed. My restraint was short-lived when I punched Sullivan with every ounce of strength I had. Years of pent-up hatred for the guy and what he'd done to Kody and the hell he'd put us through was all I'd been able to think about as Kody had unleashed his wrath on Sullivan. I'd caught the way Lacey had recoiled and how her face had blanched. I knew she didn't agree with what I'd done, and I might've ruined my chances with her.

I nodded at Mr. Robinson. "I agree." I left him in search of Lacey, thinking I had to take a page out of her playbook for our conversation.

The house smelled of something delicious. As I passed the island, I spied a pan of blueberry muffins on a wire rack. I thought of my mom as I climbed the stairs. She loved to bake cakes. She had a knack for decorating them with flowers and other designs.

"Hey." Lacey's voice drew me back to the present. "I thought I heard you."

I dragged my gaze up to a beautiful creature in low riding sweatpants and a Dodgers T-shirt that sat a little higher on her waist, exposing her fabulous abs. *Don't go getting all horny. You're here to talk. Tell that to your dick.*

I followed her like a puppy dog into her room, where she flopped on the bed. All I could think about was tackling her, stripping off her clothes, and devouring her. I got as comfortable as I could on the edge of her bed with one leg underneath me. "Studying?"

"Chemistry test tomorrow." She twisted her hair up on her head and stuck a pencil in it.

I looked away. Otherwise I wouldn't be talking. I'd be showing her how sorry I was. My gaze landed on her nightstand. "Is that the infamous nursery rhyme book?"

She gave me an impish grin.

Yeah, I was thinking of "Humpty Dumpty," too. "I've been a complete ass to you during this Pitt and Lorenzino mess."

"Kade?"

"No, it's my turn to talk." *If I don't, you'll be naked in the span of a minute.*

She crossed her legs and gave me her full attention.

"You said some things that day in my theater room that I've been turning over and over in my head. I know the pain from the death of a loved one. I also know how far you've come in the six months we've been together. I'm not perfect either. We'll both have nightmares and memories of our turmoil. But, Lace, I don't have PTSD. I'm learning about the symptoms and how to support you. I want to protect you from everything, including your PTSD. I know I can't. I know it's up to you to heal. I also know I need to support you and not shut you out." I exhaled. "Baby, please, never for one second believe that I think you're pathetic. I'm sorry if I made you feel that way and for everything else." My practiced speech came out easily.

She folded the corners of the pages of her chemistry book. Her eyes were downcast. A brittle silence dangled.

Say something. Anything. The quietness drove the nausea to churn inside my stomach.

"It's..." Her voice broke. "This is hard for me." She kept her eyes on her book.

My pulse went into overdrive. I'd so fucked up. My heart skipped several beats. I couldn't lose this girl.

She lifted her soft green eyes, worrying her bottom lip. "I have so much going on that I don't know how to process it all. I could be in danger. I have a new family, albeit a mob family. I have baseball. I want that baseball scholarship to ASU. I have an illness that stops me in my tracks and causes others to freak out along with me. I don't want anyone's pity or sympathy. The only way I can do that is to tackle a couple of things at a time." She pushed out all the air in her lungs as her cheeks puffed.

Please don't say it. Please don't say it. I was squeezing the energy out of every one of my muscles.

"But..." She held my gaze. "I know you're sorry. I know you love me. But until my other problems are behind me, I can't work on a relationship. I just can't."

"So that's it? You're breaking up with me?"

Her shoulder came up to her ear. "I guess. I guess I am."

The blood drained from me. My tongue was frozen to the roof of my mouth. I'd been too cocky and comfortable in our relationship. My brothers were right. Hell, Tyler was right. "For all that we've been through, not even let's take it slow?" My lungs burned with the need for air.

"You need someone who is okay with you shutting them out. You need someone who doesn't question your motives. I want a partner, not a boyfriend who thinks he knows what's best for me. I have my father for that."

"I didn't shut you out last night." She was drawing my heart out of my chest in tiny pieces, and an emptiness engulfed me.

"I'm not sure one night is enough," she said. "I'm not even sure you know how to solve problems without using your fists."

I was about to say that Sullivan had deserved it, but then I remembered my father's words—*no one deserves to be beaten.* I slowly got to my feet on the shakiest legs I could remember having. I could argue with her all day about all the reasons why we were good for each other. The set of her jaw and the determination stamped in her eyes told me she wasn't budging, and if I didn't get out of there, my lungs were about to collapse. "For what it's worth, my intentions and actions were out of love. I hope you at least understand that part." I crossed the room to the door. Somehow I had to show her she was my partner.

"You'll always have a place in my heart," she said.

I gripped the doorjamb before stalking out of the room and then the house.

Chapter 29

Lacey

As soon as Kade left, something snapped in my brain. I picked up my chemistry book and tossed it across the room. It smashed into the wall with a resounding thud, knocking a framed poem to the floor. Tears poured out of me. I'd thought long and hard about our relationship after the party last night. He'd been more reserved than normal, especially with Sullivan showing up. He did ask my opinion about Greg. He didn't attack Tyler. He did defend me in public, which for Kade was out of character. We also enjoyed a great moment with Kody after Greg left. Yet I wasn't sure if the events at the party were enough to repair our relationship. Not to mention that he'd let loose on Greg. Kade had always said he wouldn't throw the first punch, and last night he had.

When I'd seen him on the stairs, I'd had to reel in the urge to pepper kisses all over him. The more he'd talked, though, the more I kept wondering how many more times he would lie or keep me in the dark. I didn't want my heart to hurt any more than it did, and with all the challenges I was facing, I was having a hard time concentrating.

I screamed and started grabbing at everything around me. I snagged the nursery rhyme book and tore a page out of it. Then another. Then another. At the third page, something shiny fell out.

Footsteps battered the floor. My father came running in. "What's wrong? What are you doing? What is that?" He pointed to what had fallen out of the book. It looked like a key.

I picked it up. "I don't know. I'm so sorry I ruined your book. I'm so sorry. I don't know what got into to me."

"Give me the book and the key." He said it calmly, as if I had a gun in my hand.

I sat on my heels, wiping my eyes.

"Since when do you throw things?" Dad asked. "Kade couldn't have made you that mad."

No. I was the one who had the problem. I was the one who was so confused. I was the one whose brain was filled with mob families, ledgers, killers, school, and everything else. A knot formed in my stomach. I was the lunatic who'd just ruined a precious gift given to Dad by his mother.

I sniffled. "The key, Dad. What is it?"

The bed groaned when he sat down. I watched as he examined the book and the pages. A piece of paper had been stuck behind the large raised illustration of a tree on the page with the poem "Here We Go Round the Mulberry Bush." "This looks like a safe deposit box key," he said. The name *Erica Lukin* was written on the paper, along with a phone number with a Boston area code.

We shared a light bulb moment.

"Who is that?" I asked as I hiccupped.

"I don't know. I flipped through this book a million times. Could this be?" His voice was heavy with disappointment.

"Where the ledger is?" I dared to ask.

"Yeah. Nah. Can't be."

"Why not? We've been searching for a red ledger. This book is yellow, and the pages with the raised pictures don't have any data about victims and burial grounds or whatever Jeremy said would be in a ledger." My pulse was singing a tune like we'd just found a million dollars. Maybe we had. Jeremy had said Harrison's great-grandfather had something to do with bank robberies. "Call the number." Roots of hope sprouted inside me.

Dad stared at the key and the name as though he was deciding whether to put the key back into the book and close it. "What if it's a trap?" Dad asked. "Why would she hide a key in a children's book? A large part of me thought the ledger would never be found. I didn't think my mother wanted it to be found."

"If she didn't, wouldn't she have destroyed it? We're getting ahead of ourselves. We don't know if that name and key lead to the ledger. And how would it be a trap? She gave you the nursery rhyme book. Maybe she knew you would do the right thing. Maybe she was afraid to take the ledger to the police. Only one way to find out."

He removed his phone from his back pocket and dialed the number. I scooted closer to him and braced my hands on my knees.

Dad tapped the speaker picture. The line rang three times.

"Hello," a soft female voice said.

"Hi, Erica?" Dad asked.

"Who's calling?"

"My name is James Robinson. This may sound odd. I have a safe deposit box key and a piece of paper with your name on it."

"Where did you find it?" she asked evenly.

"Again, this is going to sound crazy. My sister gave me a nursery rhyme book that belonged to my now-deceased mother, Lorraine Newbury."

A thick silence ensued. Dad and I kept our eyes on the phone, willing her to speak.

"What picture was it behind?" she asked.

"The mulberry bush." The tips of Dad's fingers bloomed red as he gripped his phone.

"She did love to read that particular one while she was pregnant with you," Erica said.

Dad and I shared a holy-crap-on-a-cracker expression. His mom had mentioned that in her letter.

"Who is your sister?" she asked.

"Gloria Pitt," Dad responded.

"What were your adoptive parents' names?"

"Celia and Todd."

"Does the key belong to a safe deposit box?" I asked. I bit on a nail.

"Who is that?" Erica asked.

"This is my daughter, Lacey." Dad said. "Well, does it?"

"One final question. If you are Lorraine's son, then you can tell me the shape and place of your birthmark."

I scrunched up my face.

Dad regarded me with wide eyes. "I have a triangular birthmark on my inner thigh near my groin."

She sighed. "Very well. Is there anyone else in the room with you besides your daughter?"

"No. What's with all the questions?" Dad asked.

"I'm doing what Lorraine instructed me to do. She was a very, very dear friend. She was also an extremely secretive person. She wanted to ensure that if anyone came forward that they'd have to prove their identity. Since we are speaking via phone, I'll still need to verify that birthmark in person."

I snorted at the image of Dad pulling down his pants and showing a stranger his privates.

"Um," Dad said. "When can we meet? And does the key belong to a safe deposit box? And if so, what's in it?"

"Where do you live?" A small child called for her granny in the background.

"The Boston area," I said. "Can you come by today?" I clasped my hands together on my lap.

"Unfortunately, I can't. I don't live in Boston."

"But your area code is Boston." I slumped.

"A phone number can be forwarded. James, the phone you've called from—is that a good number to reach you?"

"Yes," Dad said. "We'd like to get this taken care of as soon as possible."

"I realize that. The key does belong to a safe deposit box. I'm not privy to its contents. I'm authorized to access it. Lorraine thought the less I knew the better. I will contact you within two weeks with a date, place, and time."

"Two weeks?" My voice hitched. That was too long. I didn't think Lorenzino was going to be patient for much longer.

"I'm sorry. I have responsibilities of my own. I will do my best to shave off some time. We'll be in touch." The line went dead.

Dad and I shared another puzzled moment.

I collapsed on the bed, disappointed that we couldn't get into the box now. "What do you think?"

He flipped the key over and over in his hand then removed his wallet from his pocket and tucked it into a compartment along with the piece of paper. "The best place for this is on me. If anyone gets wind of this, they'll have to go through me to get it."

Great! Dad had become even more of a target. "Have you thought about what you're going to do with the ledger?"

He dragged his fingers across his chin. "If I hand the ledger over to Lorenzino, it will only get him out of our lives, not answer any of our questions. If I hand the ledger over to the police, it could make our lives worse. There was a reason my mother kept it all these years. Either way, it doesn't solve who killed your mom and sister."

Dread set in as a chill tiptoed up my spine. We were in a catch twenty-two situation.

"I'll check in with Jeremy and bring him up to speed. We'll see if we can find out anything on Erica, too," Dad said.

I propped my head in my hand. "You're going to show a complete stranger your birthmark?"

"Sweet Pea, whatever it takes to find the ledger. So, tell me why you went into a rage. What did Kade do?"

"I broke up with him."

"Why?" he asked, angling his head.

I sat up. "I don't want to get hurt any more than I am now, and I'm not sure he'll change."

"Do you want him to change? Is that your goal? And turn the table. Don't you think he would like to see you change in some way? A relationship is about growth, working through each other's differences, and moving forward together." He kissed me on the forehead. "I have some calls to make." He padded to the door. "Don't let your head get in the way of your heart."

"You mean like Kelton does?" Oh, my God. Did I just say that? Great, because Kelton's such a good role model.

Chapter 30

Lacey

BECCA AND I WERE SITTING in the courtyard, soaking up the warm April sun during our free period. I had my head back and my feet up on an empty chair, trying to clear the cobwebs from my brain so I could think about my pitches and ASU and nothing else. Baseball was in full swing, and the ASU scout was attending my game tomorrow. Any nerves I had had to be directed at baseball and not at Dad, the ledger, or anyone or anything else. But it was difficult.

Well over a week had gone by since Dad and I had spoken to Erica, and two nights ago she'd called to set up a time to meet with Dad at a bank in Boston tomorrow. Dad and I had been on pins and needles, and now excitement and fear and apprehension swirled inside me as the clock ticked away. Since I had a baseball game, I couldn't go with Dad. Our school policy stated that I had to attend school the day of the game. Otherwise, I couldn't play. And Dad said the safest place for me was in school. He and Jeremy had a plan. Two of Jeremy's men would shadow Dad just in case Lorenzino was watching or got wind of what was going down. Wes had done a background check on Erica and hadn't found anything suspicious.

"The school is still buzzing about the Maxwells' party," Becca said, tossing her low ponytail behind her. "I know I was proud of you and glad that you worked out your differences with Aaron."

"Me too." Aaron had been a new person at practices and games.

He was all about baseball. He didn't dish out snide remarks. We talked about strategy and pitches and teams and which batters to watch for since he knew most of them.

"So, Kross told me Kelton is dating Chloe Pitt. I'm shocked that Kelton is dating anyone." She played with her earring.

"We'll see how long it lasts."

"Have you talked to Kade since your breakup?"

So much for clearing my head. "No." I was surprised the triplets hadn't cornered me to play matchmaker like they had last fall. This time when I saw them, we talked about everything other than their brother. "We're cordial to one another. I do miss him." Every time I saw him in the cafeteria or in psychology I wanted to take away the sadness in his eyes. I'd thought about all the advice Dad and Gloria had given me. The one thing that stuck in my head was something Gloria had said about her relationship with Jeremy. *He isn't perfect, and neither am I.*

My goal wasn't to tame him or to make him out to be someone he wasn't. Neither of us was perfect, and I didn't want someone who was. I just wanted Kade to let me deal with my own emotions and let me decide what was best for me.

"Maybe a change would help." Becca looked past me. "He's kind of cute with the curly hair."

I peeked over my shoulder. She'd been looking at Shaun. He was sauntering over. "Last thing on my mind, girl."

"He seems like a loner, doesn't he? It's kind of sad. It's also odd that I haven't seen him hang with any guys. He seems to be attached to us."

A lot of kids in school were loners. I didn't see that as a big deal. I lowered my voice since several kids were hanging out, soaking up the sun like Becca and me. "Maybe his thing is to hang with girls."

She leaned in. "You think he's gay?"

"You're asking the wrong person." My ex was gay, and I hadn't picked up on it.

"Hey," Shaun said as he folded himself into an empty chair and opened his laptop. His unruly blond hair was a little oily today.

Becca and I said *hi* at the same time. Then we both dissolved into laughter. It felt good to release some tension.

"Laughing at me?" Shaun gave Becca and me a cursory look.

My phone rang. "Hey, Dad. Is everything okay?"

"Yeah. After I get done at the club tonight, I'm going to crash here since I have to be back in Boston in the morning. I've already spoken to Hunt. I'll check in with you when everything is done and I'm in Pitt's office like we talked about. Okay? Maybe you should stay at Kade's tonight."

I moved to an empty table. "That's not necessary. I stay at the house with Hunt for most of the night anyway. A few more hours alone won't matter." Dad usually got home from the club just past two in the morning. "Call as soon as you have the box. I'm dying to know if the ledger is in it," I whispered, scanning the tables. Everyone seemed to be absorbed in conversations or books.

"Love you," Dad said.

I stared at the pavement for a minute then went back to our table.

"Everything okay?" Becca asked.

"Yeah." I smiled, but my insides didn't.

"Do you want to grab a bite after practice today, Lacey?" Shaun asked. "We can talk pitches and make sure you're ready for the scout."

That wasn't a bad idea. I didn't have anything to do. It would keep my mind focused on baseball. "Sure."

Becca gaped at me.

A minute or so ago she had been suggesting Shaun and I get together. "What? We're teammates. It's food."

Shaun half grinned. "And we're friends. Nothing more."

School and practice came and went, albeit slowly. Shaun and I decided to meet at Wiley's Bar and Grill. I drove with the window down, letting in the warm night air. The music was turned up high as I sang "Thinking out Loud" by Ed Sheeran. There was nothing like a beautiful night, good music, and a dark country road for singing at the top of my lungs. Oncoming headlights shone in the distance. I switched off my high beams and flicked my gaze to my rearview. Two cars trailed me. I knew one was Hunt and his partner. I wasn't sure about the other. I thought it was Shaun since he'd pulled out of the practice lot behind me. I kept singing, but then the words died in my throat as my eyes widened. The oncoming vehicle was in my lane. I squinted just to be sure. Panicked, I blew the horn and flashed my lights. If I swerved right, I might go off the embankment. If I went left, the other car might too, and then we would still crash head on. So I swerved right and started to careen down the embankment. Just as I did, the oncoming car veered back into his lane. With my heart pounding in my chest and my hands gripping the steering wheel, I cut the wheel hard to my left and maneuvered my Mustang back onto the road before pulling off to a small clearing.

The car behind me screeched to halt. Hunt ran up to my car. Then Shaun came running too.

"Lacey! Are you all right?" Hunt asked. Shaun echoed his concern.

Hunt reached in and pried my hands from the steering wheel then turned down the radio. "I'll be right back." He trotted to his black Escalade and said something to his partner as the car that had swerved into my lane faded into the distance.

"That was close," I said in a trembling voice.

"Um. Yeah, it was. Probably someone texting or playing with the radio." Shaun opened my door, squatted down, and rubbed my arm. "By the way, who's the guy?" He jerked a thumb at Hunt.

"A friend of Kade's." I inhaled and exhaled to regulate my heart and the buzzing in my head.

"Does he always follow you?" Shaun asked.

No one knew about my bodyguards. They were supposed to blend in. I glanced in the rearview. The Escalade was headed in the opposite direction while Hunt strode back.

"I'll drive," Hunt said. "Kade's house isn't far. Let's wait there for my guy." His tone was decisive.

"Hi, I'm Shaun," Shaun said to Hunt as he rose.

Hunt towered over Shaun. "Thanks for stopping. I can handle it from here."

"Hunt, I'm fine," I said. "Shaun and I are grabbing a bite at Wiley's." There was no reason to go to Kade's, and I didn't want to draw too much attention to Hunt and why he was guarding me.

"It'll only take five minutes. I need to speak with Kade anyway. Lacey will meet you at Wiley's," Hunt said with finality.

"Go ahead," I said to Shaun. "If anything changes, I can text you."

"You sure? You can ride with me." Shaun considered Hunt before he slanted his gaze to me.

Hunt's booted foot was halfway into the car.

Shaun and I swapped numbers. Then Hunt slid in. I had no choice other than to climb into the passenger seat.

"I don't need to see Kade," I said when the car began moving.

"I do."

"Why? Can't it wait?" My good mood was turning bitter. I didn't want a confrontation with Kade. I didn't want to drum up a conversation about our breakup or our relationship in general. Not tonight.

"Lacey." His tone hardened. "The big day is tomorrow. I don't know what just happened back there. I hope my partner can get the car before we lose him. I need to make damn sure that wasn't a threat or an attempt to kidnap you, and right now, the safest place until my partner calls me with some information is Kade's."

Chapter 31

Kade

CHLOE AND I SAT AT the kitchen island going over slopes and other algebraic equations. We'd changed the tutoring venue from the library to my house since it was quiet and free of onlookers or gossipers. Since I wasn't with Lacey anymore, the rumor mill was in full force. I got tired of hearing the whispers around school about why we'd broken up. It went from *Lacey showed him who wore the pants in the relationship at his party* to *she was in love with Tyler*. How they came up with those reasons was beyond me. All I knew was I missed Lacey like a crack addict missed their injections.

I also didn't try to push Lacey into talking. When she was ready—*if she was ever ready to talk or give me another chance*—I'd be ready to listen. I wasn't aloof about the breakup. I didn't want to agonize and make myself sick or bring the mood down around my brothers. I saved my moping for nights alone in bed.

I also kept apprised of the Lorenzino situation through Hunt. I knew the big day of Mr. Robinson's meeting was tomorrow. I'd asked if I could help and join in on tailing Mr. Robinson. Jeremy had said no, and so had my father. The best place for me was in school, making sure Lacey was safe.

Kelton waltzed into the kitchen and flipped on a switch. The kitchen lit up like an airport runway, the fluorescent lights glinting off the gold-specked black granite countertop on the island that my mom had handpicked when we moved into the house. "How can you two see?"

I had the pendant lights on over the island, which were enough for me. "Do you mind? I don't need all those lights."

"Are your migraines back?" Chloe asked.

"No, it's just better on my eyes when the light is directed at the book."

"You two almost done? I'd like to steal Chloe," Kelton said. "By the way, your girl pitched like a star during practice today. I think she's ready for those ASU scouts tomorrow."

I snarled as he mentioned Chloe then grinned at the news about Lacey. Chloe and Kelton had hooked up about the time Lacey and I had broken up. Chloe had called him, and before I knew what was happening, they were snuggled up on the couch in the theater room just before one of her tutoring sessions. Part of me wanted to pry Kelton away from her. I had my own problems, and they were adults. I didn't know what Pitt would think if he found out. Hell, maybe he knew.

On the other hand, I was stoked to hear Lacey was ready for the scouts. Her dream was close, and that sent a wave of warmth and a pang of fear through me. If I couldn't make amends with her before she left for ASU, I might never get her back.

The doorbell rang.

Kelton made himself useful while Chloe finished her last problem. She'd been doing well. She was smarter than she thought. Her issue with math was that she tried to do everything in her head rather than work the problem out on paper.

Kelton returned with Hunt and Lacey. Her stiff body posture told me something was wrong.

"What happened?"

Hunt had one of his mean grizzly looks like he wanted to punch a wall.

Chloe jumped up. "Lacey." She glided over to her cousin and threw her arms around her. One thing about Chloe—she liked to touch people. She often used her hands when she talked, either to wave them around or to touch someone.

"Hi," Lacey said. "Math test again?"

Chloe beamed from ear to ear at Kelton.

"Well, that's my cue to steal her," Kelton said in a husky voice. "Come on." He grabbed her hand. "We have time before your bodyguard whisks you back to Boston. I want to—"

"Kelton," Hunt and I said together.

Chloe waved at Lacey as they left. "We'll talk soon."

Lacey removed her ball cap, her hand quivering. "I hate to say this, but I'm glad to see Kelton with someone who may give him a run for his money."

"Or maybe he'll get his private parts chopped off," I said.

Lacey smiled weakly.

"What's going on?" I asked, not moving from my barstool. I was afraid if I did I would carry Lacey off to my room, lock the door, and not come out until we were a couple again.

She blew out a breath. "A car came at me head on, on Meyers Road. Hunt thinks it might not have been coincidental, with the timing of tomorrow."

I arched an eyebrow at Hunt.

"I don't know," Hunt said as he scrolled through his phone. "Hopefully Mike will track down the car that took off."

Lacey went over to the sink and got herself a glass of water. "It was probably someone doing something that distracted them from the road. Can we go now? I'm meeting Shaun for dinner." She peered at Hunt over the top of her glass.

Keep it together, Maxwell. Between the almost accident and dinner with Shaun, my insides were going haywire.

"It's best if you cancel, Lacey." Hunt's tone was unyielding. "I'm responsible for your safety, and my gut is telling me something's not right."

She dragged her gaze from Hunt to me. I wasn't about to take anyone's side, at least not out loud. I agreed with Hunt. Precaution was the name of the game. I blanked my face as best I could.

Lacey gulped down her water then texted someone. Shaun, I imagined.

Hunt's phone rang, and he walked out.

"Are you okay?" I swept my gaze over her, slow and steady. I hated to be so obvious, but she was standing in my kitchen, sweaty and way too sexy. My libido was fighting for control while my protective side wanted to comfort her.

"I'm good." She lifted her chin.

No, she wasn't. She was trying hard not to show how flustered she was. "Are you ready for the game tomorrow?" I hated small talk and the awkwardness behind it. However, if it kept Lacey here and talking, maybe the topic would shift to our relationship.

"Nervous about the scouts. Nervous about my dad. I hope by the time I take the mound everything is over with and he has the ledger. But then the question becomes what next? He's not certain what he's going to do with it yet. If the ledger is even in the safe deposit box."

Everyone was assuming that the ledger resided in that box. "I'm sure if it's there your dad will make the right decision."

Hunt came back. "Mike was able to get the license plate of the car before he lost track of it. We'll check into it."

"Again, it was probably a false alarm," Lacey said, sounding as though she was trying to convince herself it wasn't the mob trying to kill her.

Hunt growled.

Any other time I would've smacked anyone who growled or snarled at Lacey. But Hunt had every right. He was on edge. He had a job to do. She didn't need to be riding him for protecting her.

"I'm going to use the bathroom then say goodbye to Chloe." She marched out of the kitchen.

"Breathe, dude," I said, finally stretching my legs. "She's nervous too."

"How much do you know about Shaun, that new guy on the team?" Hunt asked.

"Not much. I know his name is Shaun Spears. Lacey mentioned he moved up from North Carolina. He likes to hang with her and Becca at school. He's a good pitcher. I don't like that Lacey was meeting him for dinner. But that's my own jealousy coming out. Why?"

"No reason. I'm just making sure I have all bases covered. He was following behind us, but they were headed to Wiley's. Keep an eye on her at school tomorrow. It's a home game, so she shouldn't have any reason to leave school property. The bodyguards will be on extra alert too." He scratched his neck. "When are you two going to kiss and make up?"

"Now, if she'd let me."

"She's a great gal. You can't lose her," he said.

Don't I know it.

Chapter 32

Kade

AFTER SEEING LACEY LAST NIGHT, sleep was impossible. Every part of my body ached. I craved to have her in my arms again—to feel her velvety skin against mine, to taste her watermelon lips, to feel her fingers in my hair, to hear her soft mewls of pleasure as I kissed and licked every inch of her body. Fuck, I was torturing myself.

I got up and took a cold shower. By the time I'd dressed, a ray of morning light beamed through the barely open curtains. I buckled my belt as I padded to the kitchen. I grabbed a container of juice from the fridge and closed the door as my father walked in. His footsteps were heavy on the wood floor.

"You're not working today?" I asked, snagging a couple of glasses from the cabinet adjacent to the sink.

Normally, he'd at least be dressed in his suit pants and not sweats. He rubbed his eyes as he straddled a barstool. "I'm working from home this morning, then I have a full afternoon of patients."

I poured juice in both glasses then gave him one.

"Have you thought about what you're going to do after graduation?" He drank his juice, his gaze fixed on me.

Where did that come from? When something was bothering my father, he didn't beat around the bush. I didn't question him, and it was too early to argue with him.

"I haven't. I was hoping Mom would come home, and I'd get to spend some time with her. With you working, I could help by taking care of her and the house."

He scrubbed a hand over his unshaven jaw. "Son, I appreciate how dedicated you are to this family. I love the man you've grown into. It's time to stop worrying about us. It's time to let your brothers make their own mistakes. I know you want your mother home. God, I do too, more than anything. But live your life. Find something you want to do. It doesn't have to be college, although I'd love it if all my boys went to college. But sometimes a year or two out in the world gives you time to decide. Has Lacey been accepted into Arizona State?"

"Dad, remember we're not together anymore. I do know she submitted her application a couple months ago." Lacey would be heartbroken if she didn't go to ASU, and even more so if she didn't get the baseball scholarship.

"Son, give it time. She'll come around. In the meantime, why don't you think about taking a year to travel? It would be a good experience for you."

The idea of wandering around the country had a certain appeal—even more so if Lacey could join me. But that was unlikely. "I'll think about it."

"Good. Let me know how things go with Mr. Robinson and how Lacey does at her game."

I trudged back to my room to brush my teeth. On my way, I noticed a faint light coming from the guest bathroom. I poked in my head. A cell phone sat on the sink, lit up with an incoming text message. Lacey's phone.

I jumped out of my truck and hightailed it into school. I had five minutes to find Lacey and give her phone to her before the bell rang.

The smell of fresh cut grass hung in the air as the sun's rays beat down. I hurried past a slew of kids and through the main entrance into school. The halls were jammed. Normally, I'd find Lacey either at her locker or hanging outside of her homeroom class, talking with Becca.

But when I reached her locker, she wasn't there. I went down two doors to her homeroom class. She wasn't inside. Becca wasn't around either.

I called Hunt. "Lacey at school yet?"

"She's running late. I took extra time turning over my shift to the bodyguards. I wanted to make sure everyone was on their game."

"I have her phone."

"You were my next call. She realized it this morning. I'll let her know."

"The bodyguards ready then?" I asked, blowing out a breath.

"Chill, dude. I'll check in with you after I get some sleep."

I had no reason to worry. Up to this point, Hunt and his partner had done a great job on the night shift, and the dayshift bodyguards were great too. Given that today was the big day, I'd feel better when I knew Lacey was in class. With her running late, I anticipated she wouldn't get into school until midway through her first period. The bell was about to ring for homeroom. Since she had English after homeroom with Kelton, I sent him a text.

Lacey will be late. Let me know when she comes in. I have her phone. You got it.

By the time my first period class ended, I hadn't heard from Kelton. So I dialed him. Kross came out of class behind me.

"Did Lacey show up?" I asked into the phone.

"No, bro," Kelton said.

My body went ice cold. I checked the time. Even with traffic lights and stop signs, she lived—at most—fifteen minutes from school.

"What is it?" Kross asked. Lines were stitched in his forehead.

I was trying to stay calm while my system wanted to slam the panic button. "Lacey isn't in school yet. I have her phone. Hunt said she'd be late, but I didn't think he meant over an hour."

A river of kids filed up and down the hall as Kross and I huddled against a bank of lockers.

"Call Hunt," he said.

"Nah. He's probably home sleeping by now." I called Steve, one of the bodyguards on the dayshift. "Steve, where's Lacey? She's not in school."

"Kade? What do you mean?"

"Where is she?" My hand gripped the phone like a vise.

"I'm not on her detail today. We have Pitt's personal guards on her."

I shut my eyes, praying so fucking hard he didn't mean the steroid twins. "Not the one with a scar on his face?"

"Yeah. Jerry and his partner, Paul. I'll call them then call you back." *Motherfucker.*

I counted to ten, my mind racing. "Let's go," I said to Kross. "Hunt didn't tell me they switched out her normal bodyguards today."

"Why?" Kross hitched his backpack on his shoulder.

Fuck if I knew. I'd specifically asked Wes not to put those morons on her detail. "No idea. Let's check the parking lot. Can you call Kelton and tell him to call us if Lacey shows up?" I had to keep my line open for Steve.

Kross got out his phone and filled Kelton in.

A pain latched onto the back of my neck as Kross and I went in search of Lacey. We drove around the school's main lot and the lot of the sports complex. No sign of Lacey's Mustang. We phoned Kelton again. Still no sign of Lacey. Then Steve called back. He couldn't get ahold of the steroid twins. I was resisting the panic button as best I could, but the stabbing pain in my temples made it hard for me not to smash the damn thing.

My stomach felt like Kross had used it as his punching bag as we drove through the streets of Ashford. I knew Lacey's route from her house to school. I also knew she liked to stop at a coffee shop in town to get a latte beforehand.

"Red light." Kross braced his hands on the dash.

"I see it." I braked then scanned the street up ahead.

Shops lined the small town of Ashford on both sides. The coffee shop was up on our left. People were going in, and a girl with long brown hair hurried out. I did a double take, but when I focused, it wasn't Lacey.

"Green, dude."

Swallowing the razors I had stuck in my throat, I pressed on the pedal as gently as my nerves would allow.

A side parking lot cut a path in between the coffee shop and the local bookstore. I eased into the lot and circled around back. My blood froze, and a pounding beat in my ears.

"She's here," Kross said excitedly.

Somehow I didn't think so. The scar-faced twin stood next to Lacey's Mustang, talking on his phone and waving wildly with one hand. I jerked the gearshift into park and jumped out. My hands were balled into fists and my jaw was glued together as I stalked up to him.

Kross caught my arm. "Wait."

"Kade just showed up. I'll call you back," Scar Face said.

"What the fuck is going on?" I peered inside Lacey's car. Her backpack was on the passenger seat. "Where is she?" I was about to fillet him like a fish.

"What happened?" Kross asked Scar Face in a placid tone.

Thank God he was calm.

"Paul and I lagged one car behind her as she came into town. Out of nowhere a delivery truck stalled in the intersection, blocking us. When we finally got around the truck, she was walking out of the coffee shop. So we parked here, and Paul got out to make sure we had eyes on her. By the time he got around to the front of the building, she was gone. We've searched the area and talked to everyone inside. Paul is in the coffee shop now checking again with anyone who might've seen Lacey or anyone with her."

"Steve tried to call you." I got in his face. "Why didn't you answer?"

"Back off." He pushed me. "I was doing my job, trying to get answers."

I lunged at him, pinning him against his vehicle. "You're a fucking moron."

Kross peeled me off him.

"She's long gone, asshole," I snarled. "You can't even do your fucking job. Why the fuck does Pitt trust you two?"

"Bro, direct your energy elsewhere," Kross said. "This isn't helping to find Lacey."

I shrugged off my brother and marched onto a side street, swearing. I called Wes. No answer. I called Hunt. No answer. I called Pitt. No answer. I was about to throw my phone when Kross drove up in my truck. I hopped in.

"That other dude, Paul, came back," Kross said. "An employee in the coffee shop remembers waiting on Lacey, but she didn't see anyone with her. No one did, according to everyone they spoke to."

Nausea rolled in violent waves in my stomach, and I had the urge to puke up the orange juice from breakfast. "Head to Boston." I punched the dashboard.

After a long, agonizing ride, I strode into Pitt's skyscraper in downtown Boston like I owned the building. I didn't stop at the security desk. I counted to three, waiting for the rotund guard to say something. As if I cared. I was on a mission. I wanted answers. Why did Wes change the bodyguards? Did they know where Lacey was? Did her father get the ledger? Did he know Lacey was missing?

With Kross at my side, I stabbed the button on the wall.

"Sir," the guard said, his voice booming in the sterile lobby. "Do you have an appointment?"

I pressed the button again, willing the elevator doors to open. I was going up to Pitt's office whether I had an appointment or not. Yeah, I was about to blow. I'd tried to call Wes and Pitt several times on our way in. I'd given up on Hunt. The guy was sleeping.

"We do," Kross lied. "Jeremy Pitt is expecting us."

I smiled over all the rage bursting free inside me. I could always count on my brothers to have my back. I was glad Kross had come with me. Of the triplets, he was the levelheaded one, and he was the muscle I needed in the event things got physical.

"I have to clear—"

The elevator dinged, and Kross and I jumped in. I hit forty on the panel, and as the doors slid shut, the security guard's voice trailed off. Then the car started its ascent, a little too slow for my liking. I stretched my neck in all directions then rubbed the back of my head.

Since I couldn't get ahold of Wes or Pitt, I didn't know if they were in the office. I knew if everything went off without a hitch for Mr. Robinson that he was scheduled to meet Pitt in his office.

The floors ticked by.

Kross was as calm as if it were a normal day with the sun shining. He tucked his hands in his pockets. His blue eyes had a quiet intensity that usually helped to steady my nerves, giving me the strength I needed at times like this.

The car stopped, the doors opened, and the receptionist's head bobbed up from her desk. She was the same lady who'd turned shades of red when Hunt had embarrassed her. Kross and I stepped out of the elevator. I barely acknowledged her as I hung a left. Kross didn't miss a step.

When I reached Pitt's closed door, I stormed in. Mr. Robinson was leaning against the bar, fear written all over his face. Wes had a red book in his hands, and Pitt said into his desk phone, "That's okay, Sarah."

I had every intention of punching Wes's lights out first, but given the dismal atmosphere and what Wes was holding, I had to take a step back and regroup for a second. My rage wouldn't help find Lacey, and Mr. Robinson now had the ledger.

"Where's Lacey?" I asked no one in particular.

"They have her," Mr. Robinson said in a despondent tone. He crossed his arms over his chest.

"Who?" Every muscle in me cramped. I didn't want to assume. Hell, a Mexican cartel could have her.

Kross made himself at home next to Mr. Robinson. I ponied up to one of the wingback chairs.

"Lorenzino," Wes said as he placed the ledger on the desk. "James got a call soon after he arrived here."

"Why didn't you call me? And why are you guys standing around this office then?" I clamped down on the inside of my cheek, drawing blood, the metallic taste smearing my tongue.

"We just got the call ten minutes ago. We're waiting for a time and place to meet to exchange the ledger for Lacey," Pitt said. "In the meantime, Wes has a team of men in Ashford working with the police, and I've alerted my contacts at BPD."

I couldn't stand there with Mr. Robinson about to break down, Wes acting like it was another day at the office, and Pitt staring blankly. I had to keep moving. I had to do something. I assumed Lorenzino wouldn't hurt Lacey as long as we gave him the ledger. Still, my stomach lurched with a bad feeling. After all, we were dealing with the mob.

"How does Lorenzino know you have the ledger?" I dug my fingers into the leather chair.

"Lorenzino probably had a tail on James." Pitt held his chin in his hand. "We always suspected they were watching."

"How did they know today was the day though? And they kidnapped Lacey at the same time her father was getting the ledger?" I believed in perfect storms, but they were rare.

"Did anyone know Lorenzino was in town?" Kross asked. "Wasn't the LAPD watching him?"

Another good point.

"I checked with Detective Fisher after I got the call from Lorenzino." Mr. Robinson was frozen in the same position. "He tracked him to a private airstrip in LA yesterday morning but couldn't get access to the flight plan."

"And what about that Dennis Weeks guy? Is he involved?" I was about to poke a hole into the chair.

"We haven't been able to find out much about him except what his police records show, which isn't much—several robberies, a handful of stints in jail, and three ex-wives," Wes said. "He was on Lorenzino's payroll until a year ago, when he disappeared. We're still digging into his background."

Mr. Robinson's phone rang.

Chapter 33

Lacey

AN AGONIZING PAIN THROBBED IN the back of my head as a faint male voice bled into my consciousness.

"It's almost show time," the male voice said.

My head bobbed. I blinked several times to clear my vision. I tried to wipe the drool from my mouth, but my arm wouldn't budge. Panic set in as I tried to move my other arm. I realized I was tied to a wooden chair, and pain dug into my wrists as I thrashed one way then another to get my arms free.

"Still fighting," the man taunted. "I told you this would go easier if you didn't."

I lifted my head. Two men were lounging against a bar, the soft glow from pendant lights above spotlighting their features. The man to my left had gray hair and a gray beard. He was the man in the photo I'd found in Dad's office—Harrison Lorenzino. The man to my right had red hair, and pockmarks dotted his face. He was the man in the photo that Detective Fisher had shown us—Dennis Weeks.

I twisted again, snarling at my captives. Suddenly, the memory of what I'd done to Weeks in the car returned to me.

I'd barely gotten out of the coffee shop when a man grabbed my arm and said into my ear, "This will go easier if you don't fight." I had no time to react, and my latte splattered to the ground. His large hand covered my head, and he shoved me into the back of a black sedan that was parked at the curb. No sooner had the door closed than the car sped away. I was barricaded in between two men. I'd seen pictures of both, and one I knew without a doubt had had something to do with Julie and Mom's murder.

"It's you. You killed my family," I said. His cologne smelled of insect repellent. It was as strong as it had been when I'd entered the garage the night I found Julie and Mom. A rage of adrenaline rushed through me. I balled up my hand and swung, hitting his face with the back of my knuckles. Then I quickly got in his lap and pulled on his wiry hair as hard as I could, screaming, "I'll kill you," over and over again.

His hands were on my arms, trying to push me off, but I wasn't letting go. Not until he felt pain and lots of it.

"Get her off me, Harrison. Don't just sit there like you're enjoying this," Weeks's voice blared in my ears. His fingers slid down to circle my wrists.

I spit in his face then slammed my forehead into his nose, drawing blood.

"Goddamn," he said. "Stop your screaming."

I screamed louder before I sank my teeth into his fingers. As he swore, something hard struck the back of my head, and blackness colored my vision.

Weeks laughed hauntingly, the sound severing my trip down memory lane. I clenched my eyes shut for a brief moment, panic and rage starting off the buzzing in my head. I opened my eyes and did a quick scan of my surroundings. Tables peppered the floor. A stage banked the wall to my right, and a stale odor burned the hairs in my nose. I was in Dad's club, Rumors.

"Where's my dad?" My words broke apart.

"If he doesn't do anything stupid, he should be here momentarily," said Harrison, who was nursing a drink.

Did Dad have the ledger? I cleared my throat. "He doesn't have what you want, and even if he did, he wouldn't give it to you."

Harrison let out a smug laugh. "Oh, he has what we want. My sources wouldn't lie."

I guessed Erica had spilled the beans. It didn't matter. I was sitting here tied to a chair with my life hanging in the balance.

"And he'll give us the ledger," Weeks said. His voice was gritty and disgusting as he cleaned his nails with the tip of a long blade. "Otherwise, I may have to use this knife. It hasn't seen action since your sister and mother."

Oh, my God! I felt like a box of nails had gotten stuck in my throat. The buzzing in my head increased. Adrenaline began to pump through every vein at warp speed. "So you admit you killed my family?"

His dead gray eyes glinted.

A phone rang. Harrison swiped it off the bar. "Yeah. Is he alone? Make sure he isn't wearing a wire." He hung up. "Get her ready," Harrison said to Weeks. He narrowed his green eyes at me. "No funny business."

I prayed Dad had a plan. I wanted both of them to pay, but since I didn't have my phone, I couldn't record the conversation. More than that, I salivated for a chance to rip out Weeks's eyes. To make him feel pain for what he did. In that moment, I understood why Kade hated Greg Sullivan so much and why he wanted revenge for him putting Kody in the hospital.

Weeks circled behind me, the light shimmering off his blade. Once my arms were free, I sprang upright but stumbled.

Weeks yanked me to him. He brought the tip of the blade up to my chin. "If you fight me, you'll be in pieces by the time your father walks in," he said, deep and deadly. "Better yet, I'll gut out your pitching arm. I hear you're quite the pitcher." He traced the knife's edge along my right shoulder then down.

Someone was feeding them information. At the moment, I didn't care. "You know, I should've taken up football. I'm a great punter." My calm voice belied the tacks poking the lining of my stomach.

"Girls always think they can play a man's sport."

"I don't think. I know." I kicked out, my foot connecting with his crotch.

He doubled over, letting out a guttural sound. The knife dropped, sounding a loud bong as it hit the hardwood floor. Weeks clutched his balls. Red rage bloomed in the pockmarks on his face as his features distorted in pain.

I ran, dodging tables. I pumped my legs and arms as hard as I could to reach the main exit, which was at least thirty feet away.

A hand landed in my hair and jerked me backwards. "You don't listen well," Harrison said.

"I don't take orders from killers." I elbowed him in the gut as he hauled me back to Weeks.

Weeks's nostrils flared as he retrieved his knife. I smirked at the murderer, even though my nerves were singing a scary tune.

Weeks twined my hair around his hand and wrenched back my head. With his other hand, he positioned the cold, razor-sharp blade at my jugular. "Step out of line again, and I'll slit your throat."

An image of me bleeding out made me freeze. He shuffled us toward the entrance to the back hallway then stopped. Harrison returned to the bar.

Footsteps clomped across the floor. Dad came into view with a red book in one hand. He froze, swinging his gaze from me to Harrison. "Let her go," he said, his voice thunderous. "This has nothing to do with my daughter."

"Hand over the ledger. Once I have it and I'm safely to the airport, *then* I'll let your daughter go." Harrison scrubbed a hand over his beard.

"Not a chance. She leaves here now, and when she's safely in the hands of family, then I'll give you the book." Dad held up the ledger.

Weeks's puke-smelling breath breezed over my neck. It took every ounce of my energy not to choke.

"She is with family. Aren't we family?" Harrison asked.

"You'll never be my family," Dad said in a brusque tone.

"If I had known Lorraine was with child, I would've taken care of her and you," Harrison said without any emotion.

"So instead you kill my wife and one granddaughter. And now you're threatening another. Is that how you take care of family?" A valley-sized crease formed between Dad's eyebrows. "No wonder my mother disappeared."

"An unfortunate accident," Harrison said. "No one was supposed to get hurt."

"And yet they did," I said, gulping in air slowly.

"Shut up." Weeks pressed the blade harder against my skin.

A trickle of warmth slid down my neck. I squeaked, my pulse racing, the buzzing in my head blaring. "Dad, do what he says." So what if we gave a ledger to a mob guy? It was his after all. I didn't care if it led him to buried money. Sure, I wanted revenge, but I wanted to get out of this alive. I wanted to get to school. I wanted to play ball later today, and I wanted to impress the hell out of the ASU scout.

With his gaze sharp on Harrison, Dad flung the ledger at him. Harrison fumbled to catch it. When the book soared behind the bar, Weeks loosened his hold on my hair.

I threw my head back, hitting Weeks in the mouth. The knife clanged to the floor.

Dad launched himself at Harrison, and I spun around. Weeks dove for me, and I dove for the knife that lay between us. Weeks's hand landed on the blade. The sound of grunts and groans peppered the room behind me.

"I enjoyed killing your family," Weeks said. "I can't wait to filet you into pieces." Hunger swam in his eyes.

Fear slithered down my back, but anger cleared it. "You have to catch me first." I sprinted down the darkened hallway for the back door. Thank God for the smidgen of light from the exit sign.

Heavy boots thudded behind me, cutting through the buzzing in my head. Long, gnarly fingers seized my arm. Turning, I punched and kicked, landing blows to his stomach and groin. On my last punt to his crotch, he drove the knife into my right leg just above my knee. I wailed as the stinging pain shot up my leg. I yanked the knife out, and blood oozed from the wound. Weeks bent over, grasping his balls again. This time his face turned an ugly purple.

Cracks, snaps, groans, and grunts filtered in from the barroom.

Weeks launched his fist into my face. The blow sent me hurtling backwards. My head landed against the door with a loud thwack. The pain ignited a blinding fury. I lunged for Weeks, drove the knife into his abdomen, removed it, and then stabbed him again and again. I couldn't stop. His eyes bulged out as he staggered backwards, falling to the floor with a heavy whump.

A gust of wind swept in from the back door along with a blinding light and several heavy footsteps.

The knife slid from my bloody hands as my legs wobbled then collapsed under me.

"Lacey?" Kade's voice trickled into my ears.

I squinted at two men with guns in their hands, but no Kade. Maybe I was hearing things. Then a gurgling came from my right. I swung my attention to Weeks. He sat up, and his hand snaked out toward the knife. His white shirt was slowly turning red. There was so much blood. Blackness crept across my vision. I couldn't pass out. As I labored for air, Weeks attacked me, the gleam of the blade masking the darkness.

"Lacey!" Dad and Kade both shouted my name before a gunshot echoed.

Weeks crashed to the floor.

I jerked my head to the left to find Kade pushing the men with guns out of the way.

Kade's warm, strong hands cupped my face. "I'm here, Lace. I'm here, baby. You're safe now." His voice was music to my ears.

"My dad. Where's my dad?" I blinked, once, twice, trying to ward off the darkness that was hell-bent on taking over my vision.

But my body had other plans.

Chapter 34

Lacey

I SHIVERED AS I WOKE. Déjà vu blanketed me as beeps and pings echoed from the medical equipment around me.

"Sweet Pea." Dad jumped out of his chair. Bruises and cuts covered his face. He threw his arms around me. "God, I was so worried."

"You're okay?" I hugged him back, but it hurt to move. My body felt like it had been through the rinse cycle several times. "Why am I in the hospital? Where's Kade? Is Weeks dead? Did Harrison get the ledger?"

"Slow down." He smoothed a hand over my head. "You passed out. More than likely from a combination of your head injuries, blood loss, and the trauma of the scene."

I touched the back of my head and found a lump and stitches. "Oh, my God. They shaved my head?" A small bald spot sat at the base just above my hairline. I felt the rest of my hair, making sure they hadn't cut it off. I sighed heavily when I found I still had long hair. "Did Harrison get the ledger? Is Weeks in jail? He admitted killing Julie and Mom."

"Harrison is in the custody of the Federal government. And they confiscated the ledger. Weeks is dead."

I slapped a hand over my mouth. "Did I kill him?" I remembered stabbing him several times after he'd punched me. I prodded the lump on my left cheek gingerly. I also remembered the men with guns and hearing the gunshot and then Kade practically knocking the men out of the way.

"You did him some damage, but no. The BPD SWAT team actually killed him. Weeks was about to stab you. One of the SWAT guys shot him."

I couldn't say I wasn't relieved. The man had murdered my family. "Where's Kade?" I would've thought he would be in the room with Dad.

"He's in the waiting room. I didn't know if you would want to see him," Dad said, his tone matter-of-fact.

I guessed I couldn't argue too much with his explanation. "You did tell him I was okay?"

"Of course. Besides, he wouldn't let go of your hand when you arrived until the ER doctor pried him off you."

A knock sounded, then the door cracked open. "Can I come in?" Coach Dean asked.

"Oh, my God. Baseball. The scout." Since there weren't any windows in the room, I couldn't tell if it was day or night. I swung my legs over the side of the bed and winced at the soreness in my right leg. Hell, in my entire body. My heart pounded.

Dad guided me back onto the bed. "You're not going anywhere. The game ended about an hour ago."

I glanced at Coach. He had an *I'm sorry* expression painted on his face. My breath halted. *Please don't tell me my dream is gone.*

He loped over to my bedside. "How are you?"

"I missed the scout. Didn't I?" Tears threatened, and my stomach suddenly hurt.

Coach mashed his lips together and nodded. "Your life is definitely more important than any game. I'm relieved that you're safe and alive."

"Any chance he'll come again?" A tear escaped, trickling down my bruised cheek.

"I explained the situation. He's sorry, but he won't be returning to Kensington."

The faucet opened. Tear after tear poured out. Dad and I had moved here so I could do everything possible to get on the ball team for Kensington and work hard to get the baseball scholarship to ASU. I'd accomplished the former, but I wasn't able to bring home the latter. Losing the chance to play for ASU hurt like I'd lost my one true love, but the end result—I was alive, and my family's murderer was in custody. Both were worth more to me.

Coach touched me lightly on my shoulder. "I know you had your heart set on ASU, but if I'm not mistaken, what really matters is baseball. UMass Boston and Colby College up in Maine are interested in you. I know they aren't your first choice, but they're both great schools. Why are you dead set on ASU?"

I sniffled. "My brother graduated from ASU. And they were interested in me. I guess I feel connected to them. They wanted to give me a second chance after everything I'd gone through with my family's deaths." If they hadn't, I wouldn't be here, and I certainly wouldn't have met Kade.

"Now you have more schools interested in you. The other option is you could always attend ASU and see if the coach will take you as a walk-on."

I'd hadn't thought of that. A small window of hope opened. "Did we win tonight?"

"We did. Shaun pitched a no-hitter. He and Aaron wanted to be here to share the good news. I told them you needed rest. I better run. You'll probably be out for two or three games. I'll let UMass and Colby College know when you'll be pitching again."

If I had my way, I'd be pitching at the next game. But somehow I didn't think the doctor would give me the all clear that soon, considering I had two head injuries and a stab wound.

"I'll get Kade," Dad said.

"Wait."

"You don't want to see him?" Dad asked as he touched a cut on his cheekbone.

"Yes, but are you disappointed in me about ASU?" I felt along my leg as a memory of me pulling out the knife surfaced.

"You've been through hell. You've also worked your tail off. Don't think for one second that I'm upset. I'm proud of you."

I wasn't proud of myself. I'd blacked out yet again. I might've worked hard to get on a ball team, but I hadn't worked hard enough to overcome my PTSD. "Do you think I'll ever get to the point where I don't pass out?" I desperately longed for the day I wouldn't freak over a dark house or lots of blood or anything else that reminded me of Julie's and Mom's dead bodies.

"Oh, Lacey. Your illness isn't something that can be cured overnight."

I had a sneaking feeling that the memory of stabbing Weeks and him stabbing me had set me back in my recovery.

"One more thing before you get Kade. Are you planning on staying in New England after I graduate?"

Dad sank down onto the bed. "We can talk about this another time, but something in your eyes tells me you're worried about me. Don't be. If you want to take a chance as a walk-on at ASU, then go for it. I was planning on asking your opinion. What would you say if I told you I wanted to stay in New England, at least for the foreseeable future?"

"Really? What about Eko Records and Zepplins and Rob?"

"Well, I want to reconnect with Gloria. I've been thinking about selling the record label and Zepplins. Rob wanted to tell you himself, but I think this is a good time to let you know. Rob has signed with the Dodgers. They approached him again last week."

I squealed with delight. "Really?" Rob had given up his dream to play for the Dodgers when Mom and Julie died. "I'm thrilled that you want to stay in New England, and I'm so excited for Rob." I couldn't wait to talk to him.

Dad patted my leg, and his mouth curved into a handsome smile that reached his green eyes. "Don't think too much about colleges or your future right now."

I had one last question. "Was there anything else in the safe deposit box?"

"There was another letter from my mom that basically said she never gave the ledger to the police because she knew Harrison had friends in high places within the government. And she knew if she did, the trail would lead back to her and eventually me. She couldn't bear Harrison finding out about me. She didn't want me to live that kind of life. She went on to say she often thought about burning the ledger, but she wanted to see the Lorenzino family pay for breaking the law. Apparently, Jeremy was right. The ledger detailed exact locations where millions of dollars of stolen cash were hidden. But it's time to put all this behind us and focus on living again."

I agreed. One thing was nagging me though. Lorenzino had said he knew Dad had the ledger. I knew it didn't matter anymore, but I was curious.

A young male orderly in red scrubs came in, carrying a tray of food. He set the tray down on a table next to the bed then wheeled it over to me. The smell of the food wafted through the air.

"I'll let Kade know he can come in. Why don't you eat something?" Dad kissed me on the forehead and left the room.

At the mention of Kade's name, any hunger I'd felt left with the orderly.

Chapter 35

Kade

I CHOMPED MY NAILS DOWN TO their nubs as I paced a packed waiting area of the hospital. A baby cried. A man kept coughing. A small child scampered around a line of chairs as his mother chased him. My gut twisted as my head shot up every time the double doors to the secure patient area opened.

I'd been waiting all fucking day to see Lacey. The doctor didn't want a ton of people in her room, and Mr. Robinson thought it would be best to wait until she woke up. Since we weren't together anymore, he didn't know if she would want to see me. I'd almost punched him, but he was doing the right thing. I couldn't bulldoze my way into Lacey's life, and I didn't trust myself. I knew if I were in the room with her I wouldn't be able to keep my hands off her. And if she rejected me, I'd definitely lose my shit.

I found an empty seat, sat down, and bounced my knees, watching the same little boy run around the chairs. I chuckled as his mom continued to chase him. He reminded me of when my mom had chased the triplets if we were out somewhere. She'd catch Kelton first and threaten to take away his pet lizard if he didn't behave. By the time she was finished scolding Kelton, Kross and Kody were in their seats acting like perfect little boys.

I was trying to be perfect. I was trying to keep my emotions in check. Every long, tortuous minute that passed found me thinking that if only

I had guarded Lacey myself like I'd wanted to, none of this would have happened. Or wondering whether she would have been kidnapped if Steve, Lacey's daytime bodyguard, had been on her detail this morning. Wes had told me he would find out exactly what had happened with the steroid twins. I also strained my mind to think how Lorenzino had known Mr. Robinson had the ledger when Mr. Robinson didn't even know if there was a ledger in the safe deposit box. Not to mention that if Weeks had been watching the Robinsons, then why hadn't any of Lacey's bodyguards noticed?

In between my heart stopping and starting when I pictured Lacey hurt, I continually replayed the scene after Mr. Robinson had gotten the call from Lorenzino. I'd torn out of Pitt's office like a madman on a mission, only to be stopped by Kross and Mr. Robinson. I'd fought my way through them and gotten on the elevator. Nothing in the world was going to prevent me from saving Lacey, until, just before the doors shut, Mr. Robinson called, "You'll only get her killed." At that moment, I'd dug my palms into my head and sworn several times. I couldn't wake up to a world without Lacey in it. I also couldn't give up control to someone else or to fate. That wasn't in my playbook, particularly when it came to someone I loved.

The little boy let out a high-pitched giggle, bringing me back to the present.

I checked the time. I was giving Mr. Robinson five more minutes. If he didn't give me the green light, I was storming into Lacey's room. All day my emotions had vacillated like an out-of-control sine wave—fear, rage, desperation, relief, worry. When I had heard her scream, nothing could have stopped me from barging into the club to save my girl. Then when I saw the point of the knife heading for Lacey, my heart had stopped cold. I'd almost ripped the gun from one of the SWAT guys and shot Weeks myself. Thankfully, they'd reacted just in time.

The swooshing sound of the doors drew my attention away from the little boy. Mr. Robinson emerged. His face looked like Kelton's had after he and Seever went several rounds.

In five strides I met him at the information desk. "Well?"

"You can go in," he said. "I have to take care of some things at the club. I cleared it with the nurse for you to stay past visiting hours. The doctor wants to keep Lacey overnight for observation. She's in room two."

Mr. Robinson was still talking, but I was already striding through the doors into the long cold corridor that seemed like ten miles of nothing but gray walls. My heart thrummed as I thought about what I was going to say to Lacey. I knocked then entered, and I was met with a dazzling smile that overshadowed her swollen cheek, her bloodshot eyes, and her matted hair. Even still, my breath caught in my throat as goosebumps jumped to attention on my arms. I didn't move. I probably looked like a large buck frozen in the headlights of an eighteen-wheeler.

"Kade?" Her soft voice glided over me like baby oil. "Are you okay?"

"I am now." I was surprised my voice was even. Hell, I was surprised I could talk. I was even more surprised my legs worked as I crossed the short distance to settle in the chair next to her bed.

She swept her gaze over me. Long thick lashes framed her tired green eyes. Yet a ray of happiness shone through like a beacon on a foggy night. "I'm okay."

I let out a nervous laugh. "I was so worried." *Man, is that all you've got to say to the girl you love?*

"I don't bite." Her voice was breathy. Her long wavy hair framed her soft features.

Butterflies fluttered in my stomach. "I know." I wiped my clammy hands on my jeans. "I don't know what to do. I want to kiss you. I want to hold you. I want to hug you. But I'm afraid. I'm afraid you'll reject me. I'm afraid I won't let go."

"Please sit with me." She moved, creating a larger spot next to her as she patted the bed.

I traded the hard chair for the softness of the mattress, and hopefully for her touch. She snaked out her hand and placed it on my leg.

I covered her hand with mine, cold and soft to hot and rough. I licked my dry lips. My pulse slowed then sped up. "I was so fucking scared I'd lost you. I haven't been the best—"

"Please. Let me talk." Her eyes were downcast, her smile gone.

My pulse sped up.

"Since Julie and my mom died, I've struggled through nightmares, anxiety attacks, blackouts—the list goes on." Grief marked her tone.

"The one constant since I've moved here has been you." She lifted her gaze, her hand trembling underneath mine. "You understand death. You get my illness. I never told you why I got my tattoo or why I got your initials inscribed on the paws. I'm in love with you, Kade. But the tattoo is a symbol of how you've helped me through my darkness. I know you try to protect my emotions because of my PTSD. Please don't."

Warmth spread through my chest. "Even after I've been a complete ass, you're still in love with me?"

"I've never stopped. But I need you to promise me you'll be honest and open and treat me as an equal, not a person who you think will crumble over bad news." Her tone was velvety, yet a hint of hardness edged each word.

"I'll do my best, but I can't promise I won't fuck up. And I need you to promise that you won't walk out or break up with me every time we have an argument. Because we're going to argue and disagree on things. Sometimes, Lace, you don't see past your anger."

Tension sucked the air out of the room as we locked eyes.

"Um... Do we shake on it?" Her sensuous mouth curved.

I kissed her hand.

"I'd rather you kiss me here." She placed a finger on her lips.

"If do, I might not stop."

"That's okay. As long as you don't squeeze me or touch the back of my head."

"How about I just hold you?" I adjusted my position so she was able to lay her head on my chest. I seriously wouldn't stop kissing her if I started, and right now, feeling her against me was all I needed.

"Your heart is racing," she said.

I buried my nose in her hair, inhaling her orange fragrance. "I wish I could've barged into the club sooner."

"It's over with. I don't have to worry or wonder who killed Julie and my mom. Weeks admitted he did it. But I keep wondering about how Lorenzino found out my dad had the ledger. He's said his sources wouldn't lie." She pressed a cold hand underneath my shirt.

"I've been thinking about how he knew, too. You were taken about the time your dad was scheduled to meet Erica. That wasn't a coincidence. Wes had changed your bodyguards. My gut tells me they might be involved. Maybe one or both of them was secretly working for Lorenzino. Or maybe Erica had a tie to Lorenzino."

"Wes checked her out. And if it was Erica, then why didn't she say something to Lorenzino when my dad's mother died? Also, the way she was grilling my dad over the phone leads me to believe she wasn't his source." Her fingers danced their way up to my chest then back down. "Not to change the subject, but UMass and Colby College are interested in me. Coach also said I could take a chance as a walk-on at ASU."

"Is that good?" Both subjects were sensitive.

"Ask me later. I might need months for my mind to clear."

"How about we just lie here and sleep?" I could use some sleep, particularly now that Lacey was safe and back in my arms. As my eyes grew heavy, I made a mental note to follow up with Wes on the steroid twins.

Chapter 36

Lacey

A WARM MAY BREEZE BLEW IN through the cracked open window in my bedroom. I kicked off the blankets and down comforter. I'd been lying awake for hours, listening to the crickets outside sing their nightly tune while Kade slept soundly next to me.

I sat up and plucked ASU's letter from my nightstand. I switched on the bedside lamp and read through it again.

Dear Ms. Robinson,

Congratulations! We are pleased to inform you of your admission to Arizona State University. Your admission to ASU is evidence of the Admissions Committee's confidence in your potential.

I continued to read through it, willing the words to say I'd been selected by the Sports Committee to play baseball for ASU. No such luck. I'd cried the day I'd missed the scout. I'd bawled again like a baby when I'd opened the letter two days ago. The finality of it cut deep. The good news was that I had choices. I'd pitched my best for the UMass scout last week, striking out eight batters. I couldn't say I pitched a great game for the scout from Colby College yesterday. I struck out three batters and walked four. Physically, I was back to normal. My head and leg had healed, and the stitches were out. I did miss four games in April. I'd been practicing almost every day since the doctor had given me the all clear. We were winning games. We'd only lost three this season, and as a pitcher I was only responsible for one, yesterday's. Maybe my attitude hadn't been right or maybe my heart hadn't been in it. I was, however, into the guy next to me.

I rolled over and stared at Kade. He looked so peaceful, sleeping with one arm above his head and the other on his bare stomach.

My fingers itched to trace the deep ridges of his toned abs. I didn't want to disturb him. Dad had asked Kade to help out at his club, and he'd been working late most nights. I didn't mind. When I wasn't practicing or there wasn't a game, I'd been going into the city with him and spending time with Chloe and the Pitts. I enjoyed getting to know Gloria. She was slowly becoming more of a mom figure for me, giving me advice on love and college, something Mary had done when she was living with us. I missed her and owed her a phone call to see how she was doing.

Kade moved. I couldn't take it anymore. I trailed my fingers over his scruffy jaw then over his lips. Before I could blink, he was sucking my fingers into his mouth.

He groaned. "Tastes good."

"I didn't mean to wake you." Maybe I did a wee bit.

He shifted onto his side, facing me. "Hi, stranger. It feels like I haven't seen you in ages."

"Is sucking on my fingers your new thing? I thought you liked my ears and abs?"

"Baby, I crave every part of your body. If I've been negligent, I'll just have to fix that."

I closed my eyes, relishing the erotic sensation. I didn't get many chances to sleep with Kade. And since Dad was back in California working with his lawyer on the sale of Zepplins, I didn't want to be alone. I'd gotten used to Hunt or someone being in the house.

"I'm not complaining." I slipped a leg in between his.

He snaked his hand over my hip to rest on my butt. I went in search of Mr. Steel, who was fully awake.

Lust burned in his eyes. Then he was on top of me, crushing his lips to mine. His tongue pushed through. I moaned as our tongues fought each other in a heated tango. Desire coated my body, raising goosebumps on my skin.

He broke the kiss, sucked my lip, then made his descent down my neck, chest, and stomach. When he reached my sleep shorts, his fingers dipped inside the band. With hooded eyelids, he slowly removed my shorts, his chest rising and falling. He flung the shorts somewhere behind him. He grabbed my hands and pulled me to a sitting position then knelt between my legs, reached out, and tugged on the hem of my tank top.

I raised my arms as though I was programmed to do so. Like with the shorts, he took his time removing the garment, treating the act like he was unwrapping a Christmas present, careful not to mess up the bow.

I almost whined then thought better of it. While I usually wasn't patient when I wanted something badly, I knew complaining would only make him go slower, infinitesimally slower since he had the patience of a saint and liked to tease me. The air of the room breezed over me as he exposed my breasts, and my nipples hardened. I lowered my arms as he tossed my tank over his shoulder.

"You're fucking beautiful." His voice was sexy and needy.

I raked my gaze over him. His stomach muscles tightened as though he was holding back a sea of desire. The four hearts tattooed over his chest rose with every intake of breath. He softly caressed one of my breasts before moving to the other.

Electricity jumped between us, the intimacy growing thick, driving us both to explore each other as though it were our first time together. His hands moved effortlessly over my entire body, stopping to spend precious time exploring my abs. I traced the thin line of hair that snaked down below his belly button until I was inches from Mr. Steel, and oh, boy. Mr. Steel was more than ready to play. Kade's eyes fluttered closed as he groaned.

I shivered with the need for him to consume me. I wanted his arms around me, his lips everywhere and anywhere on my body, and Mr. Steel inside me. But I'd learned with Kade that touching was more sensual, more intimate than a kiss. Touching evoked tingles, shivers, butterflies, and a sensual feeling that traveled from head to toe, front to back, and side to side. His fingers dipped lower, brushing up one leg then the other, yet never touching the one spot I craved him to. I knew he wanted to savor the moment to heighten his arousal and mine.

"Anticipation heightens the senses," he'd once told me.

My anticipation was at its peak. I knew one way to break his resolve. I scraped my nails along his scalp then tugged hard on his hair.

In an instant, I was on my back and he was hovering over me. With his eyelids at half-mast, he stared down at me with love blazing in his eyes. "I need you, baby." His tone emerged vulnerable, desperate, and with a sprinkle of sadness.

A pang of hurt gripped my heart. Since we'd started dating again, we'd gotten along great. He'd asked my opinion before he gave my dad his answer about working for him. He'd apologized to Tyler. He was cordial to Aaron. I wasn't in danger. So why was he sad? "I'm yours, Kade Maxwell," I said, hoping to assure him of my commitment to him, to us.

I sucked in a quiet breath. My declaration had unlocked something in him. My hard-core, protective, badass alpha boyfriend had water in his eyes. I couldn't recall ever seeing Kade with tears in his eyes before, at least not while we were lying naked, making love, and for some reason, it was powerful to see his emotions so exposed in such an intimate setting.

Lightly, I dragged my fingertips along his jaw. "I don't know what's going on in your head." I brushed my lips over his, warm and soft. "But I love you." My heart beat like a rock-and-roll drummer.

He plunged his tongue into my mouth as he rolled us over so that I was on top. His hands were everywhere as our tongues fought for control. When I moved against him, he growled, grasped my hips, and gently guided me down onto Mr. Steel. I broke the kiss with a moan. The pleasure of him inside me was pure and explosive, shooting a bolt of lightning up to my core. Flattening my hands on his chest, I pushed up to a sitting position. We began a rhythm. Up then down, slow and steady.

"Polar bear," he said as he traced the tattoo on my lower left hip.

He flipped me onto my back again.

He pinned my hands over my head. "Seeing my initials on that bear drives me crazy." His ab muscles bunched as he snuck his hand between us, feeling for my clit.

My breathing ramped up, and I squirmed beneath him. When his magical fingers touched the sensitive spot, I cried out. His mouth slammed against mine, hungry and greedy, masking the groans coming from me. He released my hands, planted his on either side of my head, then began rolling his hips. Sweat coated our bodies, making the glide against each other slick and smooth. I dug my nails into his butt then his back. He growled, plunging in and out harder and faster. Then he slowed. His gaze was intense, as though he was trying to hold back, trying not to let go.

"Don't hold back."

"I want this to last." He lowered his head and sucked on one breast then the other, his hips rolling forward then back.

I wanted it to last too, but I wanted that exhilarating high that came with the feeling of falling off a cliff even more. So I tapped on his sculpted butt, harder than I'd intended.

His head came up. His eyes flared in shock before one side of his mouth turned upward, and he drove into me, in and out. A fire started to build inside me, spreading wild flames down my stomach to settle between my legs. My mind became foggy as his heady scent covered me. With each thrust, he took me closer and closer to the edge.

"Put your legs around me," he said.

As I did, he grabbed my butt, pushing in deeper, harder, and faster, ratcheting up my arousal. The world around me disappeared, then suddenly I was falling into pure white-hot bliss. My body quaked as I rode the wave.

"That's it, baby." Thrusting one last time, he growled before his body tensed then stilled. A bead of sweat dripped from his forehead onto me.

"I'm not sure I can move." I didn't want to.

Untangling our bodies, he moved to lie on his back with me on top of him. I rested my head on his chest, placing my hand over his racing heart. My head bobbed up and down as he tried to regulate his breathing.

"Did you just slap my ass earlier?" he asked with amusement in between breaths.

The fire transferred from my legs to my face. I was glad I wasn't looking at him. "I didn't mean to."

"It was kind of hot." He traced circles on my back.

My mouth fell open. Okay, that was a first. I'd known he liked it when I pulled his hair. "You're into pain, aren't you? Wait, don't answer that." My face felt like an inferno.

"You're more beautiful when you're embarrassed." He massaged my butt.

I snuggled into his chest. "Have you thought about what you want to do after graduation?"

He let out a huge breath. "College isn't for me right now. My dad suggested I take a year and travel around the country. I don't know though. My mom has been doing better with her new medication. It might be nice to be around."

Sadness washed over me. If I went to ASU, I'd be leaving Kade and Dad. I didn't know if I was ready to be out in the world on my own with all my fears and PTSD triggers. I could ask Kade if he wanted to come with me. But I wouldn't. His family was in Ashford. His brothers were staying in the area after graduation. There was a possibility his mom could come home to live with them, and that was Kade's dream. I thought of my own mom and our mother-and- daughter moments where we'd talked about boys and life. I would never have that again, which was why I'd never take the chance to spend precious time with his mom away from Kade.

Besides, I was a strong girl. I fought a killer and won. I fought my demons and rose out of a deep depression to play ball again. I couldn't let my illness drive my decisions. I had to do what was in my heart. Gloria had counseled me on that.

"What time is it?" I asked.

He reached over and snagged my phone from the nightstand. The light on the phone lit up his relaxed features. "Five a.m. Plenty of time for round two before school."

I dug my chin into his chest. "Or sleep." I was sleepy all of a sudden.

"Are you having nightmares?" he asked.

"A couple. Nothing to worry about." I'd always had nightmares. I didn't think they would just vanish, and even with Weeks dead and Lorenzino in jail, I was still a little paranoid. I had the sense someone was following me. It was probably my own paranoia. Even so, I'd asked Dad how Lorenzino had known he had the ledger, and he'd said Lorenzino had probably had men watching us.

"Baby, your nails are like claws."

"Sorry." I removed my hand from his shoulder. I hadn't realized I'd been gripping him so hard. "Pitt's bodyguards aren't following me anymore?" I knew Hunt wasn't. He'd taken a job at one of Pitt's clubs in Boston.

"No. Why?"

"I thought I saw an SUV following me home from practice last week. But it's probably nothing."

Chapter 37

Lacey

I STOOD OUTSIDE WILEY'S BAR AND Grill, texting Kade to let him know that I was hanging with Becca, Tyler, Shaun, and Renee. We were meeting to celebrate our win and our last game of the season. I also owed Shaun a rain check for bagging out on dinner the day of my almost head-on collision. Hunt had suspected the mob was responsible for running me off the road, but when he'd finally located the driver of the vehicle, he discovered it was a high school student from Lancaster Christian. The boy's phone had fallen to the floorboard, and when he'd tried to pick up it up, he'd swerved into my lane. It didn't matter to me who was behind the wheel. I was just relieved that no one had gotten hurt.

After I sent the message, I scoured the street. I couldn't shake the feeling that someone was watching me. When I'd mentioned my unease to Kade, he'd checked with Wes to see if Pitt had ordered his guards to babysit me. Since Pitt was family and he had a bodyguard on Chloe, we thought maybe he had one on me. But that wasn't the case. Even so, Kade asked if I wanted protection. I declined. There was no reason for me to think I was in danger. He agreed, although he was still scratching his head as to the timing of my kidnapping and Dad getting the ledger. The same question sat in the back of my mind, but I didn't dwell on it. I had decisions to make about my future.

Except for people window shopping or ducking into a pizza place across from Wiley's, no one was around. And my internal radar gave me the all clear, so I marched into Wiley's. Utensils dinged, patrons chatted, and someone shouted in the bar. A Red Sox game was on the large TV screen that filled the entire backdrop of the bar. I checked the score. The Red Sox were up by two runs against the Oakland A's. I wasn't a big fan of either team, but since I lived in Red Sox Nation, I quietly rooted for them unless they were playing the LA Dodgers.

"Lacey!" Shaun waved from a table in the dining room.

I skirted around packed tables, inhaling the varying aromas of the delicious foods, especially the plate of nachos a waiter was carrying.

Shaun and Tyler rose like gentlemen as I approached.

"Sit with me." Renee patted the empty chair in between her and Tyler.

"Where's Becca?" I knew she wasn't with Kross. He was at a boxing gym in Boston with Kody.

"Restroom." Tyler took his seat then draped an arm over my chair.

Shaun arched an eyebrow. "No Kade or Hunt tonight?"

"Kade is working at my dad's club in Boston." I'd never explained to Shaun why Hunt had been following me the night of the accident. I guessed it wouldn't matter now. Everyone at school knew I'd been kidnapped. "Hunt was my bodyguard for a while. Since my kidnappers are no longer a threat, I don't need protection anymore."

"I'm glad you're okay." Shaun's gaze probed deep as though he was trying to figure out if I was telling the truth.

Tyler leaned his elbows on the table and said to Shaun, "You pitched a great game tonight. Any plans for college?"

I looked past Shaun and spied Becca gliding our way.

"Dude, I asked you a question." Tyler's innocuous words did nothing to mask the bite behind them.

The tension grew thick. Renee kicked me under the table.

"Hi," Becca said, taking the seat beside Shaun. "What did I miss?" Her bubbly personality was a welcome relief.

"I'm sorry." Shaun switched his attention to Tyler. "No plans as of yet."

A haggard-looking waiter came over to the table. We ordered a pizza and a round of soda.

S.B. Alexander

"Is your father doing better?" I asked Shaun. His father had been in some sort of work accident not too long ago. I'd asked him about it, but he'd brushed it off.

"He's fine. I'll be right back." Shaun excused himself.

"What was that all about?" Becca asked as she scooted into Shaun's chair.

"It was weird the way he was staring at Lacey." Tyler unfolded his napkin.

I appreciated Tyler playing big brother. If Kade were here, he would've been talking with his fists.

"He definitely likes her," Renee said.

"Um. I'm right here," I said as I tucked my hair behind my ear. "And he seems lonely." There'd been a sadness in his hazel eyes when he was gawking at me.

"Here he comes," Renee whispered as her gaze roamed the restaurant.

"Sorry, I got to run," Shaun said. "Something came up with my dad. See you in school on Monday." He darted out of the restaurant like he had a fire to put out.

A veil of silence hung over the table for a second before Becca piped up. "Way to scare him off, Tyler."

Tyler shrugged. Then Renee launched into a conversation about the playoffs followed by Becca telling us about the nursing program she'd been accepted to at NYU, and Tyler shared his excitement about his football scholarship to Florida State.

The waiter delivered the food. We each grabbed a slice of pizza.

"Any idea what you're going to do, Lace?" Tyler asked.

"Not really. I'm waiting to hear from Colby College and UMass. But I'm considering walking on to the ASU ball team." I picked at a pepperoni.

Tyler wiped his mouth with his napkin. "Baseball is your passion, and walking on isn't a sure thing."

"I know." My conundrum was that for so long I had thought only of ASU when I thought of playing college ball.

Becca started in about some movie she wanted to see. Not long after we'd finished eating, we said our goodbyes. I wanted to get home anyway. Dad had been gone for over a week, and he was due home from California tonight. I couldn't wait to tell him that we'd made the playoffs.

I hurried to my car. Once inside, I set my phone on the passenger seat, turned on the Red Sox game, and headed home.

Ten minutes later, I wheeled into my driveway, and my world blurred into immediate panic. The house was dark. Not one light was on. Dad's Impala was parked in the driveway, and the garage doors were wide open. All the air left my lungs. The only sound in my car was the buzzing in my head. I envisioned Mom and Julie's dead bodies. *Breathe.* I inhaled the vanilla freshener that hung from my rearview mirror.

Why was the house dark if Dad was home? A voice somewhere in my subconscious whispered beneath the buzzing. We have automatic lights. They should be on. I argued with myself. *Maybe the electricity cut out. That has happened during storms.*

I closed my eyes. That was it. The electricity went out. No, I remembered passing the other houses on the street. They had their lights on. Why was I worried? Weeks was dead. We didn't have the ledger, and Lorenzino was in jail.

On that note, I cut the engine but kept the headlights energized. I opened my door and climbed out slowly. I rolled back my shoulders and stuck out my chin. A full moon sat high in the sky. I scanned the yard— for what, I wasn't sure. Maybe someone had broken in again. I should call Dad or Kade. *No, don't call Kade. You want him to stop treating you like you're fragile. You're his hero. Show him. Buck up, and push forward.*

I laughed out loud. I was always giving myself pep talks. Sometimes that was the only way to get through a scary situation. Then I laughed again. I was going to need more than my own subconscious to help me with the dark, ominous scene before me.

I dialed Dad's number. With every ring, my heart beat harder against my ribs and the buzzing in my head grew louder. On the fifth ring, a loud boom rang through the night.

My brain went blank, and my body was in motion almost before I realized it. I dropped my phone and sprinted into the house.

Chapter 38

Kade

I DIDN'T KNOW WHY I'D AGREED to work for Mr. Robinson. I hated the club scene. The place stank of sweat, booze, and cigarettes. The signs that hung on the wall above the mirror over the bar warned that there was no smoking.

I carried a large bucket of ice from the storeroom to the bar. Kid Rock pumped from the overhead speakers, not loud, since the Red Sox game was on. The club didn't perk up until about eleven every night. Until then, local patrons floated in to drink and watch their favorite sports team. Once the band set up, the old timers found their way out while the younger crowd drifted in.

I dumped the ice into the silver bin next to the bar sink.

Leo, the tattooed bartender, who was flipping the cap off a bottle of Coors, said, "Thanks, man."

"Do you ever take a night off?" I asked. Since I'd been working there, I'd never seen the man *not* tending bar.

"Come on, Kade. You've been here at the height of the hour. What better way to meet some fine chicks? Or are you blind and celibate?"

"Dude, seriously?" I shut the lid to the ice bin. Granted, I'd seen one or two pretty girls, but none who compared to Lacey.

Leo placed the bottle of Coors in front of a guy in a black business suit. "I need the money, and I need to get laid. Two things crucial to a guy's survival."

I'd go crazy if I spent every day in a bar. I liked the awesome bands, but the sweat-soaked bodies, couples on the dance floor gyrating together as if they were having sex, and the smell of the puke from people who couldn't handle their liquor wasn't what I would call fun. Thankfully, the job was only temporary until Mr. Robinson had time to search for a permanent hire.

The businessman chuckled. "He's got a point."

The only part of what Leo said that had resonated with me was the getting laid part.

"What's wrong, dude? You bat for the other team?" Leo asked, swiping a towel off the sink.

"Fuck you, man." My phone vibrated, and I fished it out of my pocket. Glancing at Hunt's name on the screen, I said to Leo, "I got to take this." I pivoted on my heel and wound my way into the hall from the bar. "What's up?"

"Hey, I have Wes here with me, and you're on speaker," Hunt said. "Where's Lacey?" Unease wove through his words.

"She's hanging out with friends at Wiley's. Why?" Dread squeezed my throat.

"If you recall, I told you Weeks had three ex-wives," Wes said. "The day Lacey was kidnapped, I also mentioned my team was still digging into Weeks's background. Well, we may have found how Lorenzino knew James had the ledger. Weeks has a seventeen-year-old son, Barry, who's been living with him. So, I contacted Detective Fisher to reach out to the ex-wives who live in LA. One of them confirmed her son was living with Weeks. She described him as having blond curly hair and hazel eyes. I'm waiting on a picture."

Fuck me. I punched the wall. Pain shot up my arm, but I welcomed it to keep myself grounded in the moment. I flexed my fingers a few times then dug around in my front pocket for my keys, storming down the hall to the back exit.

"Kade, Kade!" Hunt's deep voice blared through the phone.

I slammed my hand on the metal bar and pushed open the heavy door. The muggy night air enhanced the sweat beading on me. I jogged to my truck, jumped in, and started the engine. When I did, my Bluetooth connected.

"Kade, are you there?" Hunt's panicked voice came through the truck's speakers.

"I'm in my truck. I'm headed back to Ashford." My voice sounded calm even though my stomach was twisted into a big fucking knot of fear.

"I know that description sounds a lot like that new guy at school, Shaun Spears, but we don't know for sure," Hunt said.

"I'm not taking any chances. Her text earlier said she was meeting Shaun at Wiley's. The dude hangs around her all the time." Fuck if I wasn't going to be there to protect my girl. "I got to call Lacey."

I slowed to a stop at the red light on the corner outside Rumors. I dialed Lacey's number, and it rang, and rang, and rang until her voicemail picked up. "Lace, baby. I need you to call me as soon as you get this message," I said as calmly as I could. I hung up. Dialed again. Again, the line went to her voicemail. I waited a minute and tried one more time. If I kept calling and she didn't pick up, I'd drive myself crazier than I already felt.

The light finally changed to green. I gunned on the gas, turned left, and made my way toward Lacey's as fast as I could behind cars that were slowing to let people cross the street and through more traffic lights. I dialed Mr. Robinson's cell phone. He was flying in from California today, and he should've been home by now. The line rang repeatedly until it connected to his voicemail. I tried the house phone. No answer.

"Fuck." I banged on the steering wheel.

My next phone call was to my father. I knew he was home, and if he saw it was me calling, he'd pick up. He was the closest to Lacey's and Wiley's. My brothers were in Boston, and I didn't want to worry or bother them.

He answered on the first ring. "Hey, son."

"I need your help, Dad. Remember that guy, Dennis Weeks? He has a son who's been living with him. If it's who I think it is, he's been hanging around with Lacey. He's at Wiley's with her. Can you get over there? I'm at least fifty minutes out."

"Slow down, Kade. You're not making much sense."

"Dad, please? I'm worried. He might want to hurt Lacey. His father killed her family. Why would he stay here? What if he wants revenge for his father's death?" I gripped the steering wheel so fucking hard my hands were vibrating.

I heard a beep through the phone. "I'm getting in my car. Wiley's is fifteen minutes away at the most. Have you tried calling her?"

"Yes. No answer. I even tried Mr. Robinson. I'll try calling Becca or Tyler or Renee. They were supposed to be with her. Call me when you get there?"

"Son, as hard as this may be, I want you to take a breath and get here safely. I've seen too many soldiers die in battle because they panicked. You're not helping anyone if you get hurt, and you could also hurt someone else if you get into an accident. Now, I've got this. I'll call you when I get there. Understood?"

Calm wasn't remotely possible at that moment, but he was right. "Yes, sir." I pressed the end button on the steering wheel, only to press the call button immediately.

"Call Tyler." Even though it still ate at me that he loved Lacey, I knew he'd watch out for her.

One ring. Two. Three.

Pick up. Pick up. I eased up on the gas, slowing my speed from ninety to seventy. The last thing I wanted to do was hurt someone else.

On the fifth ring, the line connected. "Hello."

Thank God. "Tyler, is Lacey with you? Are you still at Wiley's?"

"Dude, what's wrong? You sound like—"

"Is she with you?" I didn't give a fuck what I sounded like.

"No. We finished dinner about thirty minutes ago."

"So she's not with Shaun either?" I held my breath.

"No. He didn't stay for dinner. Something came up with his father."

Shaun could've been waiting for Lacey outside the restaurant and kidnapped her. I wasn't going to breathe easily until I knew Lacey was safe.

I barely said thanks as I hung up. Rage and fear were a lethal combination, not only for me but for Shaun. If he so much as touched her, I was going to kill him. I knew I was jumping to conclusions. I also knew there was a remote chance I had the wrong person. But I knew my gut wasn't wrong.

Chapter 39

Lacey

I PLOWED THROUGH THE DOOR IN between the garage and the kitchen, my pulse slamming in my ears and my head buzzing. "Dad!"

Please don't be dead. Please don't be dead.

The house was eerily quiet. I knew I hadn't imagined the sound of a gun going off. I scanned the kitchen and the sunken family room from where I stood near the refrigerator, thankful for the full moon and its light spraying in from the windows in the breakfast nook. After a sweep of both rooms, all the air I'd been holding in came rushing out in relief that there weren't any dead bodies.

"Dad!" I called again.

Buzz. Slam. Buzz. Slam. That was the sound in my head—a foreboding tune.

I walked around the island to the wall between the family room and kitchen and snatched the first thing I could find—a frying pan that had been sitting on the stove. Gripping the handle like a baseball bat, I continued to the light switch. Broken glass crunched beneath my flats. When I turned the lights on, a shadow skated across the floor.

Icy fear washed through my veins, and that tune in my head reached a crescendo. The edges of my vision blackened. I dug deep within me to stay in the moment. I had to find Dad. My body wasn't listening. My breathing was off. I shook my head back and forth, but no matter what I did, neither the fog nor the noise was fading. The head shaking only served to make me dizzy. I stumbled and caught onto a barstool to steady myself. The pan banged against the stool, severing the deadly silence that had filled every corner of the house.

The shadow grew, emerging from the family room and growing into a body—a male body that was pointing a shotgun at me. "Glad you could join us. Do you like how I set the scene for you?"

I clenched my eyes shut then opened them. I was in a dream. I had to be. Otherwise why would Shaun be standing in my house with a weapon and a bloodthirsty expression on his face?

"Oh, I'm sorry," he said. "Let me introduce myself. My name is Barry Weeks."

A nervous laugh escaped me. "Come again?" I sounded like I'd just inhaled a tank of helium.

"You heard me. I've been waiting weeks to get my revenge." Disdain rang through his voice.

The frying pan became heavy in my hands as I tried to meld Shaun the gentleman with Barry the hungry revenge-seeking stranger. "Revenge?"

"Lacey, you're a smart girl." He kept the gun steady, the barrel aimed directly at my chest. "But let me spell it out. You killed Dennis Weeks. My father."

Sweat broke out at the base of my neck. "Your father? I didn't kill anyone." I had to do something other than stand there like a human flypaper. I pushed off the stool, hoping I could walk without crumpling. "Your father killed my mother and sister." I rolled back my shoulders and raised the frying pan as though I was standing in the batter's box.

Shaun's lips curled into a diabolical grin as he stood near the breakfast nook, the glow from the moon displaying his new features. Gone were the shaggy blond hair, quiet demeanor, and friendly personality. I was now in the presence of a predator with slicked-back hair tied at his nape into a short ponytail. He wore black gloves, black jeans, black boots, and a black T-shirt like he thought he was some cool cat burglar.

"I've always liked your spunk, Lacey. I particularly enjoyed the show you put on at your boyfriend's party. But tonight, I'll be the star of the show." He moved forward. "I'll never see my father again because of you."

My heart thumped fast and furious as my brain thawed. "So, you were helping your father? You were Lorenzino's source? How did you know my father had the ledger?"

He stopped three feet from me, gun ready. "I didn't. I overheard your conversation with your dad that day you, me, and Becca were sitting in the courtyard. You said something like you hoped the ledger was in the box."

Suddenly, I remembered the conversation between Becca and me before Shaun had sat down with us. Becca had said that he'd seemed attached to us.

"You've been stalking me the whole time?"

"It's time to end this. An eye for an eye." He closed the distance between us.

I swung the frying pan. It dinged off the gun, sending a vibration up my arm before the pan crashed to the floor.

His expression was caustic with a hint of smugness shining through as he pressed the shotgun into my chest. The cold metal awakened my subconscious, reminding me of advice Coach Dean had once given me. *Facing your fears scares the demons away.* If I was ever to overcome my fear of the dark and get past my PTSD, now was the time. I couldn't stand around waiting for that gun to go off. I had to find my dad.

I puffed out my chest. "So you're here for revenge?" I shifted my glance from his narrowed gaze to the block of knives on the counter near the stove. I shuffled toward it.

With a quick turn of his head, he followed my line of sight. "You think those knives are going to overpower a shotgun?" He laughed, low and lethal.

"Where's my dad?" I swallowed, but it was more of a loud gulp.

He laughed again, raising the hairs on my arms. "Daddy is taken care of. Now it's your turn."

I sucked in a sharp breath and halted in my tracks. The buzzing in my head was as loud as a jet engine. The room grew darker as my body quivered. I wobbled before my legs gave out. Tiny pinpricks of pain poked into my hands and knees as I tried to push upright. Pain seized the leg where Shaun's father had stabbed me. I sat on my haunches as I pulled a shard of glass from my knee.

Shaun set the barrel of the gun underneath my chin and guided my head upward. His mouth moved, but I couldn't hear him. Tears pricked my eyes.

Get ahold of yourself. Stand up. Dry your tears, and do something about this jerk. I didn't have any weapons. I had nothing to fight with except my body and a small piece of glass. *Then fight. Outsmart him. Use your self-defense training. Do something other than sit on your ass and wait to die. Your father wouldn't want you to give up, and neither would your mom and sister.* There'd been too many deaths, too many tears, too many nightmares.

I held the shard of glass in one hand, planted the other on the floor, and pushed to my feet, the gun still firmly pressed underneath my chin. I had no idea of my next move. *Keep him talking, and think.* Self-defense wouldn't help against a weapon. *Why not? Go for his balls. At least a hit to his groin would slow him down long enough for you to get out.*

Once I was standing on shaky legs, I released a quiet breath, and with it some of the buzzing dissipated. I could stick the glass into his leg to slow him down.

"Pathetic. You're making this too easy." His voice sounded muffled.

Something thumped somewhere in the house.

Shaun flinched, and I took the opportunity to kick him in the crotch. He bent over and groaned loudly. As he did, I drove the glass shard into his thigh.

"Fuck," he said through gritted teeth.

I tore out of the room, running down the hallway. "Dad! Dad!"

A beacon of light spilled out into the hall from the glass-enclosed sunroom. Again, I was grateful for the moonlit night.

"Lacey." Shaun said my name as if it tasted like rotten fish. Then two clicks sounded, sending severe chills down my spine.

I went rigid, one foot in front of the other, my heart jackhammering. Slowly, tentatively, I pivoted to face the creep.

"Now, running wasn't nice." He stalked forward, his face contorted in pain as his eyes flashed with fury.

"This isn't either." I dove into the sunroom.

A blast rang out.

Chapter 40

Kade

I DROVE UP TO LACEY'S HOUSE, slamming on the brakes right behind her Mustang. Her car door was open, and the headlights were shining on a scene that reminded me of something out of a horror movie. Pure raw panic set up camp in my gut as I took inventory of the house and its surroundings. Her father's car was in front of hers. The garage doors were wide open, and the house was as dark as the midnight sky. From where I sat, all I could think was that no one was alive in there. When the hum of a car engine reached my ears, I flew out of my truck, not bothering to close my door.

My old man pulled in. I'd called him back after I'd hung up with Tyler. I jogged up to his door and opened it.

"I just got here. Things don't look good. The house is never dark." I chomped on one side of my cheek then the other, fighting like hell to keep my nerves under control, but something worse than fear darted through me. It felt as if someone had taken a knife and was carving out my soul.

Suddenly, a faint sound of someone grunting caused me to jerk my head up. "Did you hear that?" I started for the house.

"Kade, wait." My old man's voice was firm but calm. "I called the police. They said someone called not that long ago about hearing what sounded like a gunshot. They already dispatched a patrol car." He bent over, opened his glove compartment, and removed a Glock, then another. He handed me the one without the flashlight attachment as he climbed out of his car. He snatched two clips from the back pocket of his jeans then gave me one. "Let's give them two minutes. But just in case, only use the gun if necessary."

Necessary? Was he looking at the same dark house I was? Everything about the atmosphere screamed *necessary*, especially if I found Lacey... If I did, I'd go off half-cocked. Then people would die.

I took the clip and inserted it into the magazine shaft until it clicked into place. I pulled back on the slide then released it, allowing it to spring forward into position. My father did the same.

"Something isn't right. We need to go. We can't wait for the cops. Why aren't they here already?" What the fuck was taking them so long? Every beat of my heart was like a timer on a bomb. If they didn't get here in the next minute, I was going in without the law.

"Could be any number of reasons." He checked to make sure the flashlight on his Glock worked.

As I watched him, real life came into focus. Gone was my bravado. In its place, I was unnerved and moved at the same time. I was standing with my old man, loading guns, getting ready to go into battle. We'd fired guns before at the gun club and in competition. He'd taught me everything I knew about guns and gun safety. But I wasn't competing in an organized event. I wasn't the student tonight either. I was walking into an unknown situation that could get me killed. Hell, any one of us could die. I could now sympathize with my father for the times he'd fought for our country. All that aside, my old man had confidence in me, trusted that I would do the right thing and that I knew the risks and the consequences. For all that I stood up straighter. I was the man he knew me to be. I was his adult son.

He glanced at his watch.

Within seconds, a boom rent the air.

We both exchanged a what-the-fuck look and sprang into action.

"I'll lead. You follow my commands," he said.

I didn't even think to argue. He was the one in charge. He was here helping me, and for that I was his soldier.

We used the lights from the Mustang to guide us into the garage. My mind was focused. My breathing was even. My heart was anything but calm. Adrenaline pushed through my system, spiking to new heights with each step we took.

The door into the house was open. My father held up a fist. I stopped. He poked his head around the door. When he lowered his arm, we moved cautiously into the kitchen. He circled around one side of the island, and I went around the other. Broken glass was scattered on the floor. I bent down and picked up a piece. Upon close inspection, I saw that blood coated the glass. This wasn't the time for me to think the worst. I could only pray Lacey wasn't hurt. I set the glass on the island and scanned the family room—no sign of anyone. I checked the backyard through the window in the breakfast nook. A shadow moved in the distance near a cluster of trees along the perimeter.

"Out back," I said low. "There's a sunroom down the hall with an exit door and another set of doors in her father's office."

"I'll lead." Quick movements had him through the family room and into the hall.

I hurried to keep pace. With stealth and precision, he eased down the hall with his arms extended, the gun ready for any enemy who dared to cross his path.

I kept flicking a look over my shoulder just in case.

The first room we came to was the sunroom. The door leading out to the backyard was open, and the entire back wall of windows was shattered. It looked like a war zone.

My heart pounded against my chest. Or was it the faint sound of someone grunting?

Oh shit! Mr. Robinson? I pointed to the next room down the hall, which was Mr. Robinson's office. My father didn't move. He scanned the yard with a mechanical precision as though he had x-ray vision and hearing. I didn't doubt his senses were heightened and sharpened from years of fighting in the Special Forces.

"I saw a shadow out there earlier." Unless my eyes were playing tricks or a cloud had passed in front of the moon. "You check the house." We had to split up if we wanted to find Lacey. That way we could cover more ground faster.

He planted a hand on my chest. "No. Something isn't right." Matching me almost in height, he leaned in close to my ear. "You stay with me."

"We should split up," I whispered.

The muted groan sounded again from a room close by, and this time it was followed by a *thump, thump.*

"Son, you're with me." His tone left no room for argument. "Stay close." He readied his gun and headed right out of the sunroom back into the hall.

For a brief moment, I hesitated, searching the yard. The trees were as still as a rock, not a leaf moving or branch swaying. I didn't even hear the crickets. It was as though someone or something had disturbed the nighttime ecosystem. My gut told me Lacey was out there somewhere. I wasn't about to argue with my father. He was a trained soldier. So I tabled my gut feeling for now and went to join him.

When I reached the doorway to the office, my old man raised his voice. "Kade, call an ambulance. And hurry."

For a split second, my mind blanked. Mr. Robinson was sprawled on the floor, his mouth, arms, and legs bound together with duct tape. The rug beneath him was soaked with blood at his head and near his leg. My father ripped off his shirt, wadded it into a ball, and pressed the fabric onto Mr. Robinson's leg. His eyes seemed to plead with me as my father tried to stop the bleeding.

I scoured the room. The French doors behind the desk were wide open. A lamp sat askew on the floor, and a leather desk chair was toppled over in front of the couch beside Mr. Robinson.

"Son, I need you to call the ambulance." His tone hardened. "He's lost a lot of blood."

The word *blood* snapped me out of my stupor. In quick movements, I had my phone out of my jeans pocket and dialed 911. I described the scene to the calm, cool, and collected lady on the phone. Thank God someone was calm.

I gave the operator the address then asked, "Where are the cops? They should've been here by now."

"I'm sorry, sir. Busy night. The nearest car is still ten minutes out."

I growled as I hung up. I tore off my own T-shirt and gave it to my father. While he tied a tourniquet around Mr. Robinson's left thigh, I removed the tape from his mouth.

He gulped in air. Tears slipped from the corners of his eyes. "Lacey.

Where is she? I heard her arguing with that boy. Then a gun went off. Is she okay?" His voice was weak but frantic, his breathing extremely labored. "He came at me through the French doors. Before I could react, he rammed the butt of the shotgun into the back of my head. When I came to, I was tied up. He said he was waiting for Lacey. He wants revenge. He thinks she killed his father."

My old man and I shared an unspoken plea from a son to a father. I couldn't wait for the ambulance or the cops. Nor could I look at Mr. Robinson in good conscience knowing that his daughter, and the love of my fucking life, was somewhere with a guy who wanted... what? Given the gunshot to Mr. Robinson's leg, I had a bad feeling Lacey would end up like him or worse, unless she was already... I'd kill myself if I didn't do something to find my girl.

"Son, go. I'll stay with Mr. Robinson. I need to keep pressure on the wound. You be careful." Resignation infused my father's tone. "You hear me? Remember what I taught you. Use your senses, and follow your gut. Do not, I repeat, do *not* let your guard down for one second." His brown eyes held mine, steady and confident. Then a flash of worry washed over him before he banked all his emotions. "Only shoot if you have to. Understood?"

"Yes, sir." I jumped up. "Can I have your gun?" His had the one with the flashlight. I placed mine on the floor next to him.

"Gun is at my back."

I grabbed it.

"Kade, please find her," Mr. Robinson pleaded. "I can't lose her."

Neither could I. The adrenaline poured through my system as I flew through the French doors and out into the backyard, my gun out in front of me at the ready. Both sides of the yard were fenced in, but the back perimeter wasn't. A small path through the dense wooded trees led to a creek that Lacey and I had ventured down to on occasion. *Use your senses* had been my father's command.

I listened. Sirens sounded in the distance. I sniffed. Crazy. But I had a keen sense of smell, and Lacey's shampoo had a strong orange scent. The only thing my nose picked up was the faint aroma of a skunk.

As I tuned out the blaring sirens, a rustling in the trees caught my attention. I darted my gaze from right to left in a slow, methodical sweep, using the light from the gun to cut through the darkness. A tall figure ran away from me, jumping over a branch. Then a gunshot echoed, followed by a wail of a scream.

I sprinted into the dense brush. When my feet landed on the dirt path, I slowed, listening, praying like a motherfucker that the shot hadn't hit Lacey. Praying her heart was still beating. Praying I would feel her warm body in mine again. Praying we would walk down the aisle one day. Praying we would have kids together. Praying my dream of her and me together forever wasn't just a dream.

I was almost to the creek when someone roared and followed it up with, "Fuck!"

I froze.

A man began moaning. "This isn't over, Lacey. I'll get what I came here for. I'll get my revenge. I swear, if it's last thing I do," he yelled, as though he was admitting defeat. Or was it a trick?

I killed the light on the gun. I didn't want to be lit up like a target on a battlefield. I blinked, adjusting my eyes to the darkness. Then I swung to the right and went in search of the asshole. I maneuvered through brush and around trees, guided by the tiniest glow that sprayed down between the tree's branches from the moon above. His moans and a slew of swear words about his leg pulled me toward him.

As I drew close, his moans died. I edged back a step, scanned the immediate area, then listened. Ahead of me was an open area laden with rocks, small and large, and several tree stumps. The creek lay beyond. Crickets sang. Water trickled, and a shimmer of light reflected off the glassy surface of the creek.

Where was the fucker? I checked left then right then repeated the same arc before a sound split the air.

Chik, chik.

My knees locked into place. Instantly, chills blanketed my body, making me sweat. *Fuck me.*

"I never liked you," Shaun said at my back.

The air left my lungs. How the hell did he get behind me? With the Glock ready to fire, I pivoted ever so slowly, like the ballerina in my mother's jewelry box. Cautiously, I switched on the flashlight. When my gaze landed on the asshole, one side of his mouth curled into a freakishly sadistic grin. He had that shotgun pointed at me. A standoff.

"Where's Lacey?" Instinct drove me to look away, to search for Lacey, but the minute I diverted my gaze was the minute I died. *Never take your eye off the enemy*—wisdom my old man had drilled into my brothers and me.

"Floating face first down the creek," he said with a deadpan expression.

I wrestled with the mental picture of Lacey's dead body floating downstream as I locked my elbows to keep them from buckling. "Bullshit. If she were, you wouldn't be standing here." I strained every muscle to keep from either shooting him or charging the motherfucker. I couldn't risk it. I had a sinking feeling he'd pull that trigger.

I counted the rounds. Pump-action shotguns held at most five, one in the chamber and three or four in the magazine tube. He'd used one on her old man, one to blow the glass out in the sunroom, and one a few minutes ago. I had to assume he had the shotgun fully loaded. Therefore, if my assumptions were correct, he had one or maybe two rounds left.

An eerie silence sealed us into a bubble only he and I could break. We glared at one another. My mind worked to find a way out without any of the guns firing. I didn't want to shoot him. Well, I did, but certainly not to kill him. He'd made Lacey run for her life, and God knew what else. He'd shot her father, and his old man had stabbed Lacey and killed her mother and sister. It wasn't up to me to be judge and jury. I might be a dick, but I wasn't a murderer.

"I didn't count on killing anyone except Lacey and her father. Now, though, third's a charm." He held the gun steady.

"She didn't kill your old man. The cops did. I was there."

"All the more reason for me to kill you, too."

"Don't you think enough people have died?" I said as though I was talking Hunt down off a ledge.

I caught movement behind Shaun. A shadow emerged, and my heart sped up. Lacey was creeping toward us with a branch the size of a baseball bat in her hands.

Chapter 41

Lacey

I GRIPPED A TWO-INCH-THICK BRANCH IN both hands as blood dripped into my right eye. I'd cut my eyebrow when I'd sprinted past a protruding tree limb after the shotgun went off.

"Something wrong, Maxwell?" Shaun—Barry—asked.

Tingles cascaded down my arms at the sight of Kade. He was here.

"Nah, I was just thinking. What would I do in your shoes?"

Suddenly, panic clawed its way up my chest as I examined the scene. A Glock didn't hold a candle to a shotgun. Somehow I had to distract Barry. Otherwise, Kade would be the next victim on his list, and I wasn't losing another loved one.

Barry laughed cruelly. "You don't have the balls to live in my shoes."

"You're right. But I do have the balls to—" In one motion Kade tossed the Glock toward my feet as he charged Barry, knocking the shotgun out of his hands.

I traded the branch for the Glock.

"Now, let's do what real men do," Kade said, throwing a punch into Barry's jaw. "Unless you don't have the balls."

Barry growled as he turned to his left and bore his gaze into me. "Trying to be manly for your girl?"

I aimed the Glock at him, desperately wanting to wipe the smirk off his face.

As Kade went to throw another punch, Barry dove to the ground and came up with the shotgun in his hands.

"Real men use guns," Barry mocked. "Now let's see who wins this battle." The barrel was trained on Kade.

"So do girls." I shuffled closer to Barry.

"Lacey, shoot him." Kade raised his hands in a placating gesture.

Static crackled over a radio. A deep baritone voice carried on the breeze, doling out commands. The cops were headed our way.

"Eeny, meeny, miny, moe. Who will be the first to go?" Barry sang.

My knees locked. Fear comingled with anger as my heart jumped into my throat. If I didn't do something, Kade and I would be dead. The only way out of this was to shoot Barry.

I steadied my hand, inhaled, then squeezed the trigger. When I did, two shots echoed and two bodies fell to the ground.

"Kade! Kade!" *Oh, please don't be hurt or dead.* I began to tremble.

"Over here," one of the cops shouted.

Branches snapped. Radios crackled. Voices droned. A loud buzzing pierced my ears. I couldn't make heads or tails of who was talking. I labored for air as I ran to Kade.

"Oh, my God. Are you hurt?" I felt every part of his body, praying, hoping, pleading that he wasn't.

My heart slowed as he sat up.

Kade combed a hand through his hair and sighed heavily, feeling his arms and chest. "Fuck," he said. His voice was strangled. "That was close. You must've pulled the trigger a second before he did. When the bullet struck him, it must've thrown him off." He looked past me.

I was about to throw my arms around him when he took the gun out of my hands and jumped up. He marched over to Barry.

"You shot me." Barry groaned, holding his knee.

"You're lucky she didn't kill you," Kade chided.

"Hand me the gun," one of the police officers said. It was Officer Yancey. He retrieved the shotgun that lay an arm's length from Barry.

Kade hesitated.

"Go ahead," Barry taunted. "I dare you."

Kade growled. "I'm not a murderer. You need help." Kade handed the gun to Yancey. He reached out to take hold of my hand, but Barry clutched my ankle.

Barry yanked me down on top of him. I scrambled to stand, and pain zapped me in my leg where his father had stabbed me. He wrenched on my hair, keeping me fastened to him.

"Let her go," Officer Yancey said.

"Not a chance."

I looked at Kade, and his eyes went wide. Then a cold, sharp blade was at my neck. I gulped. Fear wasn't an option anymore. Pure, raw rage blinded me. My limbs hurt from running. I had cuts on my knees and over my eye. I was drenched in sweat, and I'd had enough of this asshat.

"Son," Officer Yancey warned. "You don't want to hurt her."

"Fuck you. You don't know what I want." Barry's lips grazed my ear. "We can die together."

Kade moved.

"Don't," I said to Kade. The only way to get out of this without getting hurt was to distract Barry. I clamped down on the knee I'd shot.

Barry let out a blood-curdling scream and unleashed me.

Kade rushed forward and hauled me up. Officer Yancey confiscated Barry's knife then handcuffed him as he continued to fight and swear.

Lights bobbed in the trees. More people swarmed the area.

Kade drew me into his comforting arms. "I can't believe you're alive. I thought I'd lost you again. Are you okay? Are you hurt?" He felt my hair, my face, my arms.

"I'll be fine." I peered up at him. Relief was stamped in his copper eyes.

"I'm proud of you. You didn't black out. You didn't panic. You were brave, baby."

I almost laughed. I'd been in panic mode since I'd come home. I stiffened. "Dad. Is my dad okay?"

"Your dad is dead." Barry sneered.

My pulse revved up. Kade snarled at Barry.

"Lacey, your dad is alive and on the way to the hospital," Officer Yancey said.

I silently said a prayer as the adrenaline drained from me and I sobbed into Kade's chest.

Chapter 42

Lacey

DARK ANGRY CLOUDS BLANKETED THE sky as I sat in the dugout. I was hoping the rain would hold off until we finished the last inning. We'd made it through the playoffs and were playing in the championship game against Valley High, a team with a perfect record. My nerves were all over the place. It was the bottom of the eighth inning, and the score was three to two in favor of Kensington.

Kelton came into the dugout and sat down next to me, grumbling about striking out. "Damn. That pitcher has a mean curveball."

"Shake it off," Renee said to Kelton. "We got this game. Lacey's pitching has been great. All we need to do is hold them off for three more outs."

"No pressure," I said, biting a nail.

With his forearms on his knees, Aaron angled his head to face me. "You've got it. You've proven you're tough under pressure."

Since our first game, Aaron had been nice to me, even more so after Kade's party. He was cordial, complimenting me when I threw a good pitch and explaining what I'd done wrong when I didn't. In fact, he'd started giving the team motivational speeches before each game. Coach Dean even raised an eyebrow or two. I believed the change in him had more to do with his sister, Tiffany, and how she'd been affected by a bully.

Kross stepped into the batter's box, and the entire dugout quieted.

Kross had been on a home-run streak during every game of the playoffs. The pitcher threw the ball. Kross swung and missed. The Valley High's spectators roared. I continued to nibble on my nails. I would love to go into the ninth inning with a bigger cushion. Kross took some practice swings.

"Any word from UMass?" Aaron asked.

"Not yet," I lied. I'd heard from UMass and Colby College during the last week. They both offered me a baseball scholarship. Except for my dad, I wasn't ready to share the news with anyone until I made my decision, and Kade would be the first to know anyway. Still, Aaron was curious since he'd accepted a scholarship to UMass.

The crack of the bat jarred me to focus on the game. A breeze blew, carrying the pungent smell of rain.

The entire dugout screamed for Kross to run his ass off. He'd rounded first. The centerfielder threw the ball toward second base. The shortstop intercepted the ball. Kross pumped his legs, stretched out his arms, and dove. Dirt kicked up. The shortstop tagged Kross just as he reached the base.

The umpire raised his arm, balled his hand into a fist, and shouted, "Out!"

Valley High cheered. My team gathered their gear and trotted onto the field. Three was the magic number. Three outs were all we needed. I had to pitch my absolute best to make sure no one scored.

I collected my glove and had one foot outside the dugout when Coach stopped me.

"Lacey, a second." His hands were tucked into the pockets of his jacket. His ball cap shadowed the crease between his eyebrows. Coach always had a permanent line between his eyes during games, it seemed. He inched closer to me, put his hands on my shoulders and said, "I'm so very proud of you. You've accomplished so much in the face of adversity. You've pushed past your fears to keep your head in the game. And whether we win or lose, I'm honored that you chose to play for Kensington and honored to have you on this team. Chin up. Clear your head. Get in your zone." He beamed with pride.

I stuck out my chin. "Yes, sir." The school year had been a challenging one, but one that I wouldn't have traded for anything else in the world.

Well, except to have Mom and Julie here with me. Sure, I could've done without the break-in, being held hostage, stabbing someone, running for my life, and shooting someone else, but those incidents had changed me. I'd faced my fear of the dark, thanks to Coach's advice, and for that I owed him a lot. "Thank you for your wisdom, advice, and faith in me. I don't think I would be standing here in this game if it weren't for you."

That crease between his brows became a gorge, then he relaxed, smiled once again, and tapped the bill of my ball cap. "Bring us home, Lacey Robinson. Let's win this game."

I jogged out to a screaming crowd that included all those close to me—Dad, my brother, Rob, Mary, the Pitts, Kade, Kody, Mr. Maxwell, Becca, and Tyler. Once on the mound, Mark threw me the ball. With my glove under my arm, I rubbed the ball between my palms, feeling the smoothness of the rawhide and the roughness of the raised stitches.

"Everything okay?" Kelton asked from behind me at shortstop.

"Perfect," I tossed over my shoulder.

He plastered on one of those Maxwell grins I loved, his blue eyes lighting up with excitement. "Then show these guys who the champions are."

I didn't need to be told twice. I threw several warm-up pitches before the umpire said, "Play ball!"

I circled the mound and checked the infield then the outfield. The batter stepped into position. I looked down at Mark. He gave me the signal for a curveball. I wound up and threw.

"Strike one," the umpire called.

The home crowd clapped. The stands were tightly packed with students, parents, and children.

As Mark gave me another signal for a curveball, I tuned out the voices and chatter. I concentrated on my pitching and the batter. I wanted to win this game so bad I could taste it. Mark returned the ball. I dug the heel of my cleat into the dirt, readied my stance, cocked my leg, then released the ball. The pitch barely painted the inside of the plate.

"Strike," the umpire shouted.

I released the air in my lungs.

"Okay, Lacey," Aaron said. "One more strike."

Mark flashed one finger, which meant another curveball. Valley High's third baseman swung and missed. The stands erupted in a cheer.

One out down. Batter number two, all brawn, ponied up to the batter's box.

Mark hustled out. "Their two runs came from his double. He likes the ball on the inside. So, we'll use your slider unless I give you the sign for something different."

Once everyone was in position, I tossed a look over my shoulder to Finn at first, wound up, and released. *Crack!* The ball soared into right field. The batter ran, and my heart sprinted with him. I willed Renee to catch the ball. She rushed forward then danced backward before the ball disappeared into her glove. The crowd roared, and I wiped the sweat from my brow with the back of my hand.

One more out, one more batter, three more pitches. The spectators were on their feet.

Sweat dripped down my back. If I could survive death, I could survive one more batter.

The next batter hit a line drive between Kelton and Aaron. Kross dashed forward and fielded the ball, throwing it to Kelton as the batter made it to first. The T-shirt I wore under my uniform was soaking wet.

"Shake it off," Kelton said, tossing the ball to me.

Coach came out to the mound. "Remember the next batter eats up fastballs. So stay with your curveball. And tune out the crowd." He gave a hand signal to Mark as he trotted back to the dugout.

Valley High's cleanup hitter, tall and lanky, swaggered up to the plate. The Valley High fans chanted, "Home run, home run!" The Kensington High fans chanted, "Strike out, strike out!"

As I gripped the ball, placing my fingers in position for the pitch, I remembered when Kade had first met my dad. He'd said, "Your daughter has a wicked curveball." I smiled at that thought. Suddenly, the noise around me faded into a soft drone. I glanced down at the batter, let out a breath, checked the runner at first, then wound up and pitched.

"Strike one," the ump called.

The chants from the crowd settled.

Two more strikes and we would win State. I picked up the chalk bag and massaged the white powder into my clammy hands. Then I checked the runner and my team. Satisfied, I gripped the ball and snapped my wrist. The ball traveled down to home plate, in slow motion it seemed. The batter swung. *Crack!*

As a pitcher, I hated that sound. My heart plummeted to the mound. The runner at first rounded second. Finn, at first base, dove for the ball. Renee sprinted forward. The batter from home plate rounded first. Renee fielded the ball. The runner was rounding third. I covered Mark. Mark tore off his mask and stood, waiting for Renee to throw the ball. Kelton waited at second. The easiest out was at second. Renee whipped the ball to Kelton. Just as he swung his gloved hand down, the batter slid into the base.

Complete silence on the field until the umpire shouted, "Out!"

Chaos erupted. Fans swarmed the field. Mark hugged me. Kelton, Renee, Kross, Aaron, and the rest of the team surrounded Mark and me. Before I knew what was happening, Kelton was swinging me around. "I told you we would win State with you on the team. I told you."

When he set me back down, I stumbled but was quickly lifted into the air again. I was passed around like a bowl of green beans at the dinner table. Hands were on my back, my butt, my legs as people cheered, "Kensington!" Not that I minded. But I wanted to congratulate my teammates. They were the ones who'd brought this win home for Kensington. Renee had a great batting season. Kross was a force to be reckoned with out in left field. Kelton was a gymnast at shortstop, and Aaron had an arm that could whip the ball around the bases in seconds. Finally, after I'd been hugged, carted around, and patted on the head, someone set me down in front of Coach Dean.

He removed his ball cap and peered down at me with a hint of water in his eyes. Then he wrapped his muscular arms around me. He didn't have to say anything at all. His actions were enough to make me tear up. I mean, Coach didn't hug students. I returned the gesture for many more reasons than the elation I was beginning to feel at being part of a winning team. He was more than my coach. He was like a second father to me.

When he let me go, I darted through the mosh pit of fans, parents, and teachers. I didn't have to run far. Rob was wheeling Dad down toward the dugout. Dad had the biggest smile I'd ever seen on his face.

He had spent the better part of a week in the hospital. The doctor told him he was lucky the bullet didn't do any major damage. I bent over and hugged him.

"We did it!" I gushed with so much excitement I barely recognized my own voice. "We won!"

"You were fantastic, Sweet Pea. With everything you've been through, you kept your focus. I love you."

All the emotion sprang forth, and I cried. I was over the moon that I was ending my senior year with a championship trophy, but I was happier that my dad was alive to see me play my last high school game. I was also sad that Dad was in a wheelchair and sadder that Mom and Julie couldn't be there.

"I hadn't seen you play in two years," Rob said. "I thought you were good at Crestview, but wow! Arizona doesn't know what they're missing."

At the mention of Arizona, a tiny ache spread through my chest. I wasn't sure I'd ever get over not having the opportunity to show them what I was made of. Nevertheless, I had to move on. After many sleepless nights, I'd decided not to take the chance of walking on to the ASU team. My dream was college baseball. It didn't matter where.

I dragged my gaze from Dad to Rob. Together they looked like twins with their brown hair and green eyes, only Dad had aged a great deal since the murders. Crow's feet fanned out from the corners of his eyes, and dark circles bruised the area beneath his lower lashes.

"New beginnings," I said as I spied Kade sauntering toward us. "And the Dodgers are lucky to have you." Warmth radiated through me. I was proud of my brother, and so damn excited. "I want seats behind home plate."

I was about to run to Kade when Becca bounced over with so much excitement it was almost impossible not to look at her.

"Awesome, girl! Just flipping awesome. It's time to celebrate at Wiley's," Becca said, adjusting her black hair to spill down her back. "I'm going to find Kross." As she glided off, Mary, Gloria, and Jeremy came over. Mary had flown in from California to help Dad. Her mom's hip surgery had gone well, and she was getting around.

"Your mom would be proud," Mary said as her petite frame enveloped me in a bear hug. If Mom and Julie were here, they'd be squeezing the air out of me, too.

"Mom is watching me from heaven," I said, holding back tears. Mom wouldn't want me to be sad on such a momentous occasion.

When she released me, Gloria snagged me then Jeremy. Kade waited patiently, talking to Rob as his copper eyes fixated on me.

"Amazing," Jeremy said as he pulled me in for a hug. He wore a cologne that smelled like rich leather.

Once all the congratulatory hugs were out of the way, Rob said, "I'm going to take Dad home."

"Go have fun. You deserve it." Dad grinned, and my heart swelled at how I missed the light in his eyes.

The field had thinned out with people heading for the parking lot. I spotted Chloe and Kelton walking off. I guessed I'd catch up with them later. They'd been inseparable since they started dating. Becca and Kross followed them. As soon as the Pitts, Mary, Rob, and Dad left, I ran up to Kade.

"We won! I can't believe we won," I said, throwing my arms around his neck.

"You were fantastic. I'm so horny right now. I think my dick was hard the whole game watching you throw, seeing your confidence and determination."

"Lace," Tyler called from behind me.

"Be nice," I whispered to Kade.

Tyler strode up with his hands in his pockets, the light breeze brushing his blond locks to one side. I thought back to the first day I'd met him when I'd interrupted a meeting in Coach Dean's office. Coach had yelled at me for my lack of manners, and as I'd hurried out of his office, I'd caught a glimpse of Tyler, grinning from ear to ear.

The smile he had on his face reached up to his ocean-blue eyes as he skimmed his gaze over me. "Congrats."

The tension grew as thick as the dark clouds above.

My goal wasn't to cause a fight, but I owed Tyler a hug. He'd worked tirelessly with me to perfect my pitches for tryouts. I wrapped my arms around him, and he stiffened with his hands at his side.

"It's okay. Kade isn't going to punch you. If he does, I'll help you fight him off."

Kade laughed, although I could detect a little tightness in it. "No worries, man. Lacey would probably kick my ass before yours."

Tyler softened, and he returned the hug. "I'll be following your stats at whichever college you go to. Have you decided on ASU or heard from the other colleges?"

I eased back, and looked from Kade to Tyler. I'd been leaning toward Colby College, for two reasons. I'd connected with the coach, who reminded me of Coach Dean, and I had to prove to myself that I could live without any loved ones around me. I didn't want to rely on Kade or Dad being there if I blacked out or one of my PTSD symptoms surfaced. My stomach knotted at the thought of telling Kade. I didn't know how he would take the news, but it was time to cut the cord. Besides, Colby College was in Maine, which wasn't as far away as if I'd gone to ASU.

"Not yet. I'll let you know when I do."

Kade came up and draped an arm around me. "I wish you luck at Florida State," he said to Tyler.

"Thanks, man," Tyler said. "I better go."

A fat raindrop splattered on the bill of my ball cap. The people who still remained scurried off the field with Tyler. The clouds opened up, and the rain poured down. I grabbed Kade's hand, and we sprinted into the dugout. A jagged bolt of lightning split the sky in half, and as we both gazed out at the empty field, I was reminded of my recurring dream where Kade and I were sitting on the ball field in a thunderstorm. I shivered.

"Something wrong?" he asked.

"I'm not sure. I haven't told you, but I've had the same dream over and over again where you and I are on the ball field in a thunderstorm."

His face was pinched with worry.

"And in my dream, you say to me"—I swallowed—"'Storms will roll in, the sky will grow darker, the clouds will release their tears, but through the thunder, the lightning, the rain, the sleet, and the snow, the world will right itself.' I had no idea what that meant until this very moment."

"Should I ask? Do I even want to know?" A gust of wind messed up his honey-brown hair.

Thunder boomed, followed by another lightning strike. Rain pelted the field, dinging the roof of the dugout.

"This may sound heavy. I interpret the dream to mean that my life has knitted back together, only with a new path, a new future, and a new dream that includes you and me."

"It sounds perfect. Especially the part that includes you and me."

"Have you decided what you're going to do after graduation?" He'd told me college wasn't for him, and his dad had suggested that he travel. I knew he wanted to spend time with his mom though.

"Actually, I have." He threaded his fingers through his hair.

My heart stopped for a beat. Anytime he ran his hand through his hair he was either frustrated or worried.

"Baby, I would follow you to heaven or hell. I would die for you. You know that." He closed the distance between us then tangled strong fingers through my hair. "But my dad told us last night that my mom will be home for at least the summer and maybe longer." He searched my face. "My brothers are staying in the area. Kody is taking a year off. Kross will be concentrating on boxing and taking classes at Boston College, and Kelton is going to Harvard. This is my chance to spend time with my family, with my mom. We'll all be together for the next year. I can't pass up family. Not when I haven't had my mom home in two years." He blew out a breath.

I placed my hands on his jean-clad hips. "I would never take you away from family. I know how important it is to you, Kade. That's what makes you you. That's why I love you." Tears threatened. "So, both Colby College and UMass offered me a baseball scholarship."

"That's awesome." He lifted me up and twirled me around and planted his warm lips on me. "And?" He eased me down onto two feet.

"I'm going to accept Colby College's offer." I held my breath.

"You're not taking a chance at ASU?"

"My mom always told me to follow my dreams, and baseball stands at the top of my list."

"And why not UMass's offer?" His eyes melded with mine.

"Mainly, I need to prove I can live on my own." The thought of us apart sent a sharp pain through my heart. "You and my dad won't be far. We can visit on weekends." I pressed a hand to his sculpted chest.

His arms sucked me in, his mouth crashed to mine, and he kissed me like I was his next breath. My heart beat a wild cadence as I returned the kiss. Minutes had passed. The rain slowed.

We broke away.

"You are my hero, and I love the crap out of you," he said.

"Ditto, Kade Maxwell."

Epilogue

Kade

GRADUATION CAME AND WENT. IN fact, the ceremony and the graduation party were nice, especially with my mom present. I could've done without the pomp and circumstance though. I didn't like all the hype of walking across the stage in front of tons of people. It didn't matter anymore. My senior year was behind me and the future ahead of me, and I couldn't be more stoked. Lacey had signed with Colby College. Deep down I wished she would've accepted the scholarship to UMass, but I understood her reasoning. She wanted to be on her own and prove to herself that she could take care of herself without her dad or me always around. I admired her and loved her even more for her determination and tenaciousness. My mom was living at home and had been since the beginning of July. I was still working at Rumors, helping out Mr. Robinson. My brothers were with me. My father was working from home more now. We had our family unit back together. I couldn't help but think of my sister, Karen, as I sat down by the lake on a hot, muggy August day. She would've loved it here. She loved the water, and any chance she had, she'd been swimming either in our pool at our old Texas home or in the ocean when we went out on the boat my father had owned.

My heart lit up as I watched my mom. She giggled like a schoolgirl at something my father said. He was grilling burgers while she removed paper plates from the plastic wrap at the picnic table where Lacey was helping her set up the food. Lacey's shorts rode up on her butt, exposing her pink bikini bottoms as she reached for a spoon.

My girl in a bikini was something I couldn't look at around people, not if I didn't want everyone to see my dick getting hard. Water splashed and Becca squealed, diverting my gaze away, thankfully. Kross chased her around the edge of the lake then tackled her into the water. Kody was tuning his guitar on a blanket next to Mr. Robinson, who was lounging in a chair. Mr. Robinson had offered to let Kody play one night a week at Rumors. Today, Kody had promised my mom he'd play her a song he'd written after we ate.

"Kody seems happier," Hunt said.

He and I sat on my tailgate behind everyone.

"He does." I wasn't sure if he'd come to terms with what Sullivan had said the night of the party or if his happier mood stemmed from my mom being home. Either way, a weight had lifted off my shoulders.

"So, are you going to take Pitt up on his offer?" Hunt asked.

Since Hunt had guarded Lacey, he'd found that he liked the job. So Pitt had offered him a spot at the Guardian working for Wes, and he'd extended the same position to me. "I'm going to give it a shot on a temporary basis until Mr. Robinson opens up his new club." Lacey's dad had finalized the sale of Eko Records and Zepplins in LA and had purchased another new club in Boston. I'd agreed to work there when it opened.

"I thought you hated the club scene." Hunt took a swig from his soda can.

"It's not so bad as long as I'm not cleaning up puke."

Chloe squealed. She and Kelton were playing horseshoes in a small sandy area off to our left. We'd invited Jeremy and Gloria, but they'd left town for the weekend.

"I'm surprised Pitt hasn't severed any of Kelton's limbs yet." Hunt chuckled.

"Her old man is cool with Kelton." Although I was worried that Jeremy Pitt, mob boss, would fry my brother in a vat of turkey grease if he did anything to harm or upset the blond beauty. "I don't think it will last."

"I agree. Kelton and love don't mix well," Hunt said.

He and I laughed as Lacey swayed her sexy hips toward us, her pink swim top covering her ball-squeezing breasts that bounced with each step.

"I'm going to talk to Kody." Hunt hopped off the truck.

Lacey climbed up beside me. "The last time we sat on your truck like this was at your party back in April."

"Yeah, but this is better. We're among family and friends, and I get to see you prance around in that bikini."

Her luscious green eyes lasered in on Mr. Steel. "He's awake, isn't he?"

I lifted a shoulder. "Only one way to find out." My gaze swept over the swell of her breasts, and Mr. Steel hardened. "So, when does Becca leave?" Becca had gotten accepted into the NYU Nursing Program, and Lacey and Becca had spent more time together since baseball season had ended. It was good to see them hanging and giggling. Hell, it was great to see Lacey with a smile on her face most of the time now.

"Next week. I wanted to help her move into her dorm, but I'm leaving for Maine."

At that moment, I wanted to hold her and never let go. My dreams had always been nightmares until Lacey had come into my life. I hated that I wouldn't see her every day or spend every night with her. I hated that I wouldn't be there if any of her PTSD symptoms surfaced or if she woke from a bad dream. Most of all, I hated that my heart would split in two the moment she drove away. I knew we loved the crap out of each other. I knew without a doubt I would marry her someday. I also knew that as long as we had each other, the world would right itself.

To all my fans:

This book is dedicated to you. I can't thank you enough for taking the time to read Dare to Dream and all my other books. Hugs and kisses go out to each of you!! If you have a dream follow it. One step forward is the key to unlock a world of possibilities.

When you have a moment, I'd love if you would leave a short review from the e-book/book vendor you purchased the book from. Your help in sharing your excitement and spreading the word is greatly appreciated.

I hope you enjoyed Kade and Lacey's story. You'll see them again when Dare to Love (Kelton's story) is released. I'm working on Dare to Love. However, I don't have a timeline of its release yet.

Sign up for my NEWSLETTER:
http://author.sbalexander.com/contact/

You can connect with me:

Website:
www.sbalexander.com

Facebook:
www.facebook.com/sbalexander.authorpage

Twitter:
www.twitter.com/sbalex_author

Google+:
www.google.com/+SusanAlexanderauthor

Goodreads:
www.goodreads.com/sbalexander

Friend me FB:
www.facebook.com/susan.alexander.14473

Acknowledgements

I've written several books and none have been as emotional as Dare to Dream. Not only in writing the story, but from the circle of people who have been with me every step of the way.

First and foremost, I want to thank my fans and readers. Without you guys I wouldn't be writing. You motivate me, you support me, and you encourage me. I'm humbled by all the reviews and messages I've received along the way. Hugs and kisses to each and every one of you for taking the time to take this journey with me. This book is dedicated to you.

I love, love the team at Red Adept Publishing. Without a doubt, I am a better writer because of the team of editors who have helped to bring The Maxwell Series to life.

I can't say enough about Streetlight Graphics and for my amazing covers. Love you guys.

Marketing a book is one of the hardest aspects for an author, and I'm so lucky and glad I met Marissa at JKS Communications. She had a vision for Dare to Kiss, and she has an even bigger vision for the future of my books. To Marissa and the entire team at JKS, thank you for your insight, creativity and dedication in helping me get the word out to readers around the world.

The publishing industry changes constantly, and without Katey Coffing's inspiration and coaching I wouldn't have come this far without her in the two years since my first book was published. Love you, girl.

Wendy, Kylie, Kari, Julie, Heidy and Sontae, you gals are the best. Thank you for all your love and support.

Tracy Hope, thank you for everything! You are my super fan. You've read my drafts and every line I've ever written, even when it was rewritten fifteen times. And, you've brought my books to life with your creative vision and superb producing skills of my book trailers. Love you!

Finally, to my main squeeze, Bill, for his love and support in everything I do!

Dare to Dream
Playlist

Music tells a story, defines a mood, makes you laugh, cry, dance, scream at the top of your lungs and most of all it grabs your soul. When I write, music does all that to me. It helps to define my characters and their moods.

"Lips Of An Angel" by Hinder
"Fear" by Blue October
"Broken Arrows" by Daughtry
"Love Gone Mad" by Stars Go Dim
"Hoping for Tomorrow" by Stars Go Dim
"Thinking out Loud" by Ed Sheeran
"Hanging By A Moment" by Lifehouse
"Without You" by Hinder
"Apologize" by OneRepublic
"Never Say Never" by The Fray
"One Last Breath" by Creed
"Chasing Cars" by Snow Patrol
"Kickstart My Heart" by Mötley Crüe
"Outside – Original" by Staind
"My Destiny" by Katharine McPhee
"Diamonds" by Rihanna
"Follow You Down" by Matthew Mayfield

Other books by S.B. Alexander

The 1st book in **The Maxwell Series – Dare to Kiss** is available at any of the following vendors:

Amazon:
http://amzn.com/B00MSEVKQY
iTunes:
http://bit.ly/1w9oJ4g
B&N:
http://bit.ly/1sXOkyl
Kobo:
https://store.kobobooks.com/en-US/ebook/dare-to-kiss-1

If you love paranormal and urban fantasy check out the Vampire SEAL series. It is recommended that you read the books in order.

ON THE EDGE OF HUMANITY – Book 1
FREE at the following e-book retailers.
Amazon:
http://www.amazon.com/B00ATVDEHQ
iTunes:
http://bit.ly/14ht9Kw
Kobo:
http://bit.ly/19wf9x9

ON THE EDGE OF ETERNITY – Book 2
Amazon:
http://amzn.com/B00FPA6EW8
ITunes:
http://bit.ly/18b6FvZ
B&N:
http://bit.ly/1ajt7jJ
Kobo:
http://bit.ly/1vaptFF

ON THE EDGE OF DESTINY – Book 3
Amazon:
http://amzn.com/B00OZ4BS7Q
iTunes:
http://bit.ly/1DUuiW1
B&N:
http://bit.ly/1vCHGJV

The Look of Love

by
Wendy Kupinewicz

A smile in the sunrise, a giggle in the air;

A tear that rolls down reddened cheeks, an un-averted stare.

A promise and a purpose; a wish, a dream, a feeling;

A flattering reflection, a charm that's most appealing.

A portent of the future, a memory of the past;

A sweet deliberation, expectation far surpassed.

Wendy has written and dedicated this poem to Kade and Lacey, and to anyone and everyone who dares to dream! Thank you, my friend. Your words warm my heart.

Made in the USA
Middletown, DE
28 June 2015